D1042233

Fade to Us

ALSO BY JULIA DAY

The Possibility of Somewhere

Fade to Us

✦

JULIA DAY

WEDNESDAY BOOKS
NEW YORK

FADE TO US. Copyright © 2018 by Elizabeth Langston. All rights reserved. Printed in the United States of America. For information, address St. Martin's Press, 175 Fifth Avenue, New York, N.Y. 10010.

www.stmartins.com

The Library of Congress Cataloging-in-Publication Data is available upon request.

ISBN 978-1-250-09737-8 (hardcover)
ISBN 978-1-250-09738-5 (ebook)

Our books may be purchased in bulk for promotional, educational, or business use. Please contact your local bookseller or the Macmillan Corporate and Premium Sales Department at 1-800-221-7945, extension 5442, or by email at MacmillanSpecialMarkets@macmillan.com.

First Edition: February 2018

10 9 8 7 6 5 4 3 2 1

To my beloved Amy

I am inspired and humbled by the path you've forged.

Acknowledgments

✦

It's such a joy to acknowledge everyone who helped me with this book. I'll start by thanking my fellow writers—especially the Rubies and AnMeReMa—for your support and empathy. We are in a strange business, my friends. I'm so glad that I don't have to face it alone.

I loved doing the research for this book. I'm amazed by the generosity and candor of the people who agreed to be interviewed. There are so many of you to thank: Marcia, for naming the town; Kelly, for explaining jewelry stores; my brother Jaime for his knowledge of military retirees; my dear friend Tom for sharing his love of baseball; the umpires Nick B., Chris M., and Janet Thomas, who patiently answered my questions; a special shout-out to umpire Christopher Hughes for his careful explanations of the art of calling a game and for his advice on the baseball scenes; to Tommy and Brendan for your insights into Micah; to Ann for helping me with Lisa.

I'd also like to express my gratitude to those who shared their love of the theater with me: Daniel Eckert and his passion for stage management; the drama department at Cardinal Gibbons High School, Kevin Ferguson, and the casts and production teams of *Little Women* and *Guys & Dolls* for allowing me to observe your creative process; Cary Players and the production team for *Oklahoma!* for inviting me in.

My gratitude goes to my sensitivity readers, Terri and Amy, for keeping the story authentic and respectful. To Sarah A.— you are the best beta-reader ever! I'm so lucky to have you. And to Laura Ownbey, my muse and advisor. This is the eighth book that is the better for your particular brand of magic.

Thanks to Wednesday Books, their talented team, and especially Eileen for being "the village" I needed with this book. And my admiration to Kevan Lyon, the best mentor and agent an author could have.

Finally, all of my love to my husband and daughters; your faith is the reason I can live this dream.

Fade to Us

◆ 1 ◆

Definite Opinions

I had been chasing the Thomas twins around their house for a half hour, begging them to put on their clothes, when the garage door whined up. Their mother was home.

"Guys, come here," I shouted as I flung myself onto the carpet. Five seconds later, I had two tiny bare butts bouncing on my belly. "Gotcha." I sat up, locked my arms around their squirmy bodies, and shifted them onto my lap. I'd just wiggled a pair of Pull-Ups onto both boys when Mrs. Thomas walked in the door.

She hugged them as she smiled at me. "Were my little men good today?"

"Absolutely adorable." I took the wad of cash she held out and shoved it into my pocket. "Thanks."

"Brooke?" She squinted at the calendar hanging on the kitchen wall. "Can you babysit next Saturday morning? Eight to eleven?"

"Sure. See you then." I kissed the twins on the tops of their heads and left. Once I got home, I locked up my bike in the backyard and collapsed into my hammock. A nap had just become my top priority. Eyes shut. Swaying in the breeze. Surrounded by the scent of roses.

A screen door slammed, followed by thuds across the deck and the soft swoosh of footsteps on the lawn. Maybe if I pretended not to be here, the footsteps would change direction.

"Brooke," Mom said.

Guess not. "I'm hiding."

"Not very well, since this was the first place I looked."

I smiled drowsily without opening my eyes. "Are you saying I'm predictable?"

"Completely. How were the boys?"

"Busy. And naked." I sighed. Loudly. In a way that made it obvious I would rather not be talking.

"It's time to eat."

"Now?" It couldn't be any later than five p.m. I peered at her through half-closed eyes. "What about Jeff?"

"He's home. We're having fried chicken."

Mom rarely fried chicken, even though it was one of my favorites. Too messy and unhealthy, which made today's choice highly suspicious. "Why?"

"We're holding a family meeting." Her eyes sparkled with mischief.

I rolled from the hammock, my heartbeat jumping into overdrive. "About . . . ?"

"Come and see." She jogged back to the house, her blonde ponytail bouncing behind her.

A family meeting on a Friday in the middle of June? When

nothing was going on? Mom and I had been a team long enough for me to know this meeting meant something big—and happy—for me.

Fighting off the burn of anticipation, I trailed her into the kitchen. The table looked gorgeous. Lace tablecloth. Roses in a vase. The "company" china. And not only had my only-cooks-from-scratch-under-duress mother made fried chicken, she'd added creamed potatoes and biscuits, too.

Oh, yeah. Something *big*. And there was only one thing it could be.

Jeff was holding Mom's chair for her. When he was done, I inched around him.

"Hello, Brooke." He held up his fist.

My stepfather and I had been fist-bumping for the whole time he'd been in my life. I'd hoped after their wedding that he would progress to hugging. But nine months later, I was still waiting. "Hi, Jeff." I touched my fist to his and slid onto a chair.

It quickly became apparent that the two of them had a conspiracy going to keep me in suspense during the meal. We talked about ordinary stuff, like . . . our jobs. The weather. The Chicago Cubs's chances of reaching the World Series. And after every topic, Mom and Jeff would smirk at each other and then me. Fine. I could survive on hope for a few more minutes.

As soon as they put down their forks, I pounced. "Okay, guys . . . ?"

My stepfather's phone buzzed.

Mom and I exchanged grins. Because of course. The best moments of my life were always interrupted before they happened. Like a hyper dog ruining the cookout for my ninth birthday.

Or the hurricane that canceled my first dance recital. Or the badly placed candle that torched the decorations at Mom's wedding to Jeff. At least tonight, the destruction of property wasn't involved.

He glanced at the phone and then at my mother. "It's Mei." His ex-wife. He would have to answer, although his reluctance to delay the family meeting was kind of sweet.

Mom sniffed. "Go ahead."

Jeff accepted the call. "Mei, what is it?" He narrowed his eyes, then frowned. Rocketing from his chair, he left the kitchen and disappeared into the den.

"I wonder what she wants," I said.

"Me, too." Mom covered the leftover potatoes with a piece of plastic wrap and carried them to the fridge. "Dessert?"

"Should we wait for Jeff?"

"Nope." She added the *p* with a lot of attitude.

I reached for the biscuits. Might as well clean up, too.

Jeff was gone for ten minutes. Mom and I had already finished our peach cobbler when he returned. After slipping his phone into his pocket, he stood behind his chair, gripping the seat back. He looked uncertain. Hesitant. Two words I'd never thought of for my stepfather before.

My mother rose and crossed to his side. "What's happened?"

"Mei has been having some health problems since she had her baby." He shook his head as if dazed.

"I'm sorry."

"The doctors want her to reduce her stress."

Mom and I said in unison, "Natalie."

He gave a sharp nod.

My stepsister and I chatted online often, and one of her favorite topics was her baby brother. But she'd never mentioned her mom being sick.

Jeff rubbed a hand over his nearly bald scalp. "Natalie is coming to live with us for a while."

What? I stared at him in disbelief. Natalie would be *living* here? He'd invited her without checking?

Mom recovered first. "That will be . . . an adjustment."

He wasn't looking in my direction, which bought me a few seconds to control myself. Weekends with Natalie were usually good. But when she opposed something, she became the queen of difficult. Natalie was guaranteed to oppose this. "How long is a while?" My voice cracked on the last word.

"It's undetermined. A month or two."

Emotions flashed over my mother's face in rapid succession. Concern. Sympathy. And something else that I couldn't identify. "When will you pick her up?"

"Tomorrow."

Mom and I looked at each other with widened eyes. That was too soon. There was hardly enough time to get the house ready. Or to get *us* ready.

"What else could I do, Jill? I couldn't say no."

"Of course you couldn't, sweetheart. We'll figure this out."

He switched his gaze to me. "This isn't what you expected for your summer."

It certainly wasn't. We'd been planning to have Natalie with us for two weeks in August, so I'd been mentally preparing for that. But *tomorrow*?

Jeff's daughter had Asperger's. She hadn't learned to drive, didn't cook, and couldn't be left alone for very long. She had definite opinions about how her world should be organized, and she expected her family to provide it. Our summer would be consumed with making life easy for Natalie.

I could totally understand why she had to get out of there. I also understood that she had nowhere else to go, but it stung that Jeff hadn't even asked. Mom and I would've done the right thing. Natalie was family.

Clutching my hands together in my lap, I pasted on a smile, as if everything were okay. "I'm with Mom. We'll make it work."

His answering smile was full of relief. "Thank you. That means a lot to me." He kissed Mom's forehead and took a step back. "I have a few details to puzzle through. If you need me, I'll be in the workshop."

"Wait," I said in a rush. Jeff couldn't leave yet. We had to go back to where we'd been when Mei interrupted. "We haven't finished the family meeting."

Mom and Jeff visibly flinched. They turned to each other, silent communication passing between them. He flexed his jaw. She winced. He nodded. She sighed.

When Jeff looked back at me, his gaze flickered with regret. "I'm sorry, Brooke. We'll have to delay that discussion." He strode to the back door. It clicked shut seconds later.

My mother slumped onto a chair.

Frustration twisted in my gut. They might not have used the word *car*, but it had to be the reason for the home-cooked meal and the smirks. After years of saving, I was only six thousand dollars away from my goal. I'd never asked for help, but tonight it seemed like they'd been about to offer.

I stared at my mother with enough intensity that she had to hear my thoughts begging her to look at me, but she was doing a pretty good job of resisting. "Mom?"

"Honey, I'm sorry, but we can't do it now."

She hadn't needed to hear the question. The disappointment was crushing. "You were going to help me buy a car."

"Yeah. A friend of Jeff's offered us a good deal on a used vehicle."

"A Ford Fiesta?" The perfect intersection of safe, efficient, and affordable.

"A Toyota RAV4."

I blinked with shock. I'd planned on a Fiesta because it was a realistic goal. I'd dreamed about a RAV4, but always in secret. "How did you know?"

"Jeff."

I swallowed hard. *Jeff* had noticed?

"He said you would get whiplash every time one drove by." Mom sighed. "We thought we could cover the difference, but not now. Not with Jeff starting his own business *and* Natalie living here. Until we see how much they affect our finances, we need to hold off on obligating that kind of money."

I wished I didn't know how tantalizingly close I'd been. It was easier to live with dreams when they stayed out of reach. "We'll have four people and two vehicles."

"I know. It'll be a mess."

Even though Mom and Jeff had retired to their room hours ago, their lights were on. Mom must have had some details of her own "to puzzle through" with her husband.

I was too restless to sleep. A three-mile run, a soaking bath, my happy playlist—nothing worked.

Prowling around my room, my gaze landed on the nightstand.

My scrapbook might help. I reached into the bottom drawer and lifted it out carefully, not wanting anything to spill out.

When I was younger, Mom had gone through a scrapbooking phase, where she'd memorialized everything about me through photos and bits of junk. When she lost interest, she gave me a leftover scrapbook. I'd been using it since as my secret journal. Just to be safe, I'd scrawled *Fashion Ideas* across the front. My mother wasn't interested in fashion. She would never look inside.

I set my scrapbook on the bed and flipped it open. Taped to the last page was a tattered sheet of paper, a fourth grade assignment that I'd never thrown away. During American literature month, our language arts teacher had gushed over her favorite author, Louisa May Alcott, and asked us to think about one of her most famous quotes:

Far away there in the sunshine are my highest aspirations . . .

The assignment was to list our aspirations and explain why we had chosen them. My classmates had raced to scribble item after item. Not me. I'd sat frozen at my desk, staring miserably at the blank page. Totally certain what my highest aspirations were. Equally certain there was no chance I would ever share them with a teacher or anyone else.

She'd stopped by my desk and tapped my paper with a bright red fingernail. "Can't think of anything?"

"No, ma'am."

"Try, Brooke. You don't want a zero."

I'd picked up a pencil and written in cursive:

Tap shoes—I'm tired of ballet

A corner bedroom with two windows—to see more of the world

The big red *C* at the top of the sheet was a faded reminder that the teacher hadn't been impressed. What would she have thought if she'd seen the two items I'd added later that night, in the privacy of my room?

A dad—to love me

A sister—to be my best friend

I'd received the tap shoes for my next birthday. Not long after that, Mom and I moved to this town, into this house. My corner bedroom had two windows.

But the other two? I didn't really have them yet. While the "step" part of stepdad and stepsister didn't matter to me, apparently it did to them.

I hadn't given up hope, though. It *would* change. Someday.

· 2 ·

The Awful Silence

The smell of coffee teased me awake Saturday morning. I blinked open my eyes and glanced at my desk clock. Five till eight. Jeff would be leaving for Durham soon.

I stayed where I was, not quite ready to blast myself out of bed. A single phone call had transformed my well-ordered summer into chaos. For one more minute, I would breathe in the peace of what might have been.

After a bathroom stop, I skipped down the stairs and into the kitchen. Mom stood by the coffeepot, cradling a cup. Jeff lounged beside her, sipping from a travel mug.

"Morning," I said.

He fist-bumped me. "Good morning."

"When will you be back?"

"No later than noon."

"Good luck with the state troopers on that one." I crossed to the fridge to get the cream. "We'll have everything ready."

"I appreciate how much you're pitching in." He wrapped an arm around Mom's tiny body and nuzzled her hair. She kissed his chin.

My mother and Jeff were so affectionate that it made me wistful. I was glad to see her so happy. Really. But sometimes it felt like I'd been . . . Not left behind, exactly. More like I'd become an afterthought—as if the fact that I wasn't speaking up meant that everything was going great for me. And mostly it was. But why couldn't they ask?

Mom had dated often throughout my childhood, but she'd only been serious with two guys. I'd liked both of them and thought they liked me. But they had each vanished, practically overnight and without saying good-bye. That had hurt more than I'd ever admitted to my mom.

Then Jeff appeared eighteen months ago. He seemed different from the moment she'd brought him home to meet me. I'd liked him well enough, but I'd remained wary—not wanting to be burned when this one disappeared, too.

Jeff hadn't been her "type," but I could see why he'd caught her eye. He was a retired Army engineer and matched the stereotype. Fit, strong, confident, with beautifully old-fashioned manners. He kept his clothes neat and precise and his haircut high and tight.

After Mom and Jeff married in September and he moved in, things seemed to go smoothly for them, but not so much for me. For sixteen years, it had simply been the Jill & Brooke Show. Mom had taken care of the income, and I'd taken care of everything else. It had been strange to have a man around, disrupting the way we did things and taking over my responsibilities. So, yeah, there had been a bit of a tug-of-war at first, but we'd worked things out. Jeff and I were getting along pretty well now, although not as far along as I wished.

"Enjoy your morning, Brooke," he said. After kissing Mom, he headed into the utility room. The door to the carport slammed.

Mom stared after him for a few seconds, then frowned at her coffee cup, her mood deflating. "How are you feeling about this?"

Worried. Upset. But all I said was, "Nervous."

"Me, too." She drained her cup and set it on the counter with a click. "Okay, let's get started on the chores." She pointed to a pad of paper on the counter near me.

Good. Projects were something I could handle. I skimmed the list. "You can do the shopping. I'll do the upstairs."

"Deal," she said so fast that we both laughed.

Once I was showered and dressed, I went into my stepsister's bedroom and looked around. Compared to my yellow room with its crowded shelves of cute baseball souvenirs, hers was stark. Gray walls. White furniture. No decorations except for one poster from a Broadway show she'd seen with Mei. Natalie's bedroom was soothing rather than interesting.

After opening the windows and cranking up the ceiling fan, I stripped the spare quilt off the bed and stuffed it into her closet. When I came out again, my cat blinked at me from the middle of the bare mattress.

"Leave, Tigger."

He swished his orange tail in defiance.

"Fine, but you've been warned." I plugged in the vacuum cleaner. He was gone before I turned around.

Two hours later, I'd cleaned and aired her room, made the bed with her five-zillion-thread sheets, and plumped her four hypoallergenic pillows. I'd also vacuumed or mopped the floors and switched out the soap and shampoo in the bathroom that Natalie and I shared. I'd earned a break, so I charged down the stairs and erupted into the kitchen. "I've finished my part of the list."

"We're ready for her." Mom poured two glasses of tea and handed one to me.

We sipped together quietly, waiting for time to pass. For life to change. Somehow, though, my attitude had improved. Preparing for Natalie's arrival had helped. We were as ready for her as we could be, and the rest of the summer would just have to work itself out. "What will Natalie do on weekdays?"

"Jeff and I brainstormed some ideas last night, but nothing is concrete. We'll have to wait and see how she adjusts." Mom leaned over and kissed my cheek. "All will be well."

"Is that a promise?"

"It's a prayer."

Jeff and Natalie would be getting here soon. I had to finish checking her room.

Tigger yawned disdainfully from the top of her dresser. He jumped down and strutted over, only to hiss in reproach when I scooped him up and carried him from the room. "Sorry, but you can't be in there." I shut Natalie's door behind me.

As I was going back downstairs, my phone buzzed. It was a text from my best friend Kaylynn.

Want to hang out?

I would like to, but not today, not when I had to be here for my family. I threw myself onto the couch before answering.

Can't. Natalie is moving in
 Moving? Like living there?
Yes
 Permanently?
Not sure how long

A truck rumbled into our driveway. My stepfather had estimated they'd be here by noon, and with his typical military precision, they'd arrived with three minutes to spare.

Why?
 Her mom's really sick
Sorry. Call me if you need to escape
 Thanks

Two doors ka-thunked. Before I could stand, the front door banged open. Footsteps squeaked across the hardwood floor of the foyer and up the staircase.

Next came my stepfather's heavier tread. I entered the foyer as Jeff was shutting the front door with his foot.

"How are things?" I asked.

"Hard." He plodded up the stairs.

I hovered behind him as he rapped on her door and nudged it open. She lay on her bed, curled in the fetal position, facing the wall. Her dark ponytail snaked across the quilt. Thin legs and dirty, bare feet peeked from black yoga pants.

"Natalie?" He paused. "Where should I put your bags?"

"Don't care," she said.

The hollowness of her tone filled me with compassion. I'd thought a lot about how this change affected me, and Mom, and

Jeff. Even Mei. But I hadn't spent much time wondering about how it affected Natalie. She thrived on routine and stability, and that had been ripped away from her.

Natalie's mom was her rock. Her safe place to go when the world went out of control. How had Natalie been told that she was moving? No matter what Mei had said, it would feel like *I'm well enough to be around my husband, my parents, and a baby. But I'm not well enough to be around you.* Maybe Natalie's head could understand that it was more complicated than that, but her heart wouldn't.

Well, she would be okay here. I could be her new safe place to go.

"Hi, Natalie," I said.

She rolled to her back and stared at the ceiling, hands folded across her belly, motionless as a corpse. Desolation surrounded her like a fog.

I ought to get her talking, to fill the awful silence with sound. "When did your high school let out?"

Her hazel eyes shifted toward me, dull and hopeless. "You already know the answer."

Well, okay then. Jeff said that whenever she sounded rude, she was actually "being blunt." He claimed it wasn't intentional. It was probably best to believe him. "Ten days ago?"

"Yes."

"Mine ended last Friday."

No reaction.

Jeff set the bags beside the dresser. "Here are your things."

She shut her eyes, her mouth slack.

His gaze lingered on her, full of love and yearning. "Should I bring in the other two boxes?"

"Don't care."

Seconds ticked by, with all of us frozen into place. Abruptly, he turned and brushed past me, his huge shoulders hunched.

"We'll have lunch in a half hour, Natalie. Lasagna."

There was a long pause, as if she slogged through my comment word by word, trying to absorb it. "That's my favorite."

"Which is the reason Mom made it."

"Huh." Her eyelids fluttered. "Is Jill trying to make me feel better?"

"Yeah. We're glad you're here."

"No, you're not." Her left hand reached for her right and twisted the skin on her knuckles. "But we agree, because I don't want to be here either."

My gaze swept her long, thin body and returned to those pinching fingers. Natalie was right. I wasn't *glad* that she was here, although I didn't know what the correct adjective was. "Is there anything I can do?"

"Nothing except leave."

Yeah, I could do that.

⋄ 3 ⋄

Unfiltered Honesty

Natalie appeared in the doorway to the kitchen as I was setting the table for lunch. She'd changed into a loose-fitting red sundress and taken out her ponytail. Her eyes scanned the room before finding my mother at the stove. "I like lasagna, Jill."

"I thought you'd enjoy it." My mother crossed to her and tried to give her a hug, but Natalie shrank away. Mom went back to the stove as if she hadn't noticed.

"Can I have grilled chicken tomorrow?"

"That can be arranged."

Jeff leaned against the counter, sipping a beer and searching for signs that his daughter might shatter at any moment, which, from the look on her face, was a distinct possibility.

"Will I get to decide what to eat every night?"

"Don't press your luck."

The corners of Natalie's mouth tilted up briefly in her version of a tiny smile. Then her face went blank. She crossed to her chair at the table and perched on its edge, her body trembling like a stray puppy who'd been kicked and didn't know why.

Mom brought the pan of lasagna to the table. After Natalie served herself and began to eat, the tension in the room eased.

The meal was only slightly uncomfortable. My stepsister didn't participate in the conversation, but the expressions flitting across her face showed she was paying attention. When she'd finished eating, she slid off her chair and stumbled into the den.

"Natalie?" Mom prompted.

My stepsister stopped, head bowed, brown hair slipping forward over her shoulders. "What?"

"Please load your dishes in the dishwasher."

"Oh. Right." Natalie retraced her steps, grabbed her plate and glass, banged them into the dishwasher, and walked out of the kitchen again. She'd gone a few steps into the den when she paused, her back to us. "My room doesn't have a TV."

"Nor will it."

Natalie spun around. "Another house rule?"

"Yes."

"Yours are so different from the ones at my house. How many more are there?" She sounded resigned.

I completely understood her attitude. It felt like we had house rules for everything now. Jeff said that they would make adjusting easier on Natalie, but he really liked them, too. Most of the rules had already been unspoken between Mom and me, so I didn't mind too much. It was just weird that he'd made such a big deal about writing them down.

"There are dozens," Mom said.

Natalie considered that for a couple of seconds, then gave a nod. "Don't tell me any more yet. I'd rather learn them slowly."

"Okay by me."

She took off. Muffled thumping faded up the stairs.

"Shit, Jill." Jeff's voice was harsh. "Did you have to go after her so soon?"

I gaped at him. What was he upset about? That meal had gone pretty well.

Mom's eyes narrowed. "It is *not* too soon. Might as well start the way we intend to continue."

"We agreed to cut her some slack for a few days."

"I'm not being hard on her. You're more bent out of shape than she is."

"She's *my* child."

"This is *my* house."

His lips thinned. "Throwing that in my face, are we?"

Oh, wow. Did not want to witness this. I scrambled to my feet. "I should go."

Mom glared. "Could we discuss this later? When you're ready to be reasonable?"

"Okay then," I said, "definitely leaving." I ran out the door and across the lawn to where my hammock stretched between two oaks. Flopping into it sideways, I rocked as I tried to estimate how long before it was safe to go inside again. I didn't have a whole lot of data to work with here. My mother and stepfather rarely argued, at least not in front of me. It would be difficult enough to get used to Natalie living here. It would be worse if I had to worry about them fighting.

When the weather was nice, I liked sleeping with the windows open. But not tonight. Not with my stepsister pacing beneath it, talking to herself in a voice that carried. I slipped from the bed and squinted down at the yard. "Natalie, it's three a.m.," I whispered as loudly as I dared. "Why are you outside?"

Her form stilled in the shadows. "Is that a problem?"

"Yes. Come back in the house."

"What kind of problem is it?"

"You'll disturb people."

"Like whom?"

Me. "The neighbors."

Several seconds of silence crept past. Sighing audibly, she scuffed her feet across the driveway and up the steps to the side porch. The house shook with the slamming of a door.

I'd barely collapsed into my bed again before my doorknob rattled and Natalie entered.

"Brooke. Since you're awake, we should talk."

No, we really shouldn't. "Shockingly, I'm usually asleep at this time of night."

"You can make an exception for me."

Yeah, I guess I could. I was already awake, and since it was Sunday, I could sleep in. I plumped my pillows and sat up. "Fine."

She crossed to the window and peered out. She hadn't changed into pajamas yet.

"I like your dress, Natalie."

"It's pure, soft cotton. Mama says red might make me feel better when I'm upset."

"Does it?"

"Not really, but it was worth a shot. I don't want to be here."

"Which you've already mentioned."

"It's not because I hate you or anything like that . . ."

Nice to know.

". . . although, if you went to my school, you'd be the kind of person I would avoid."

Natalie had a talent for sliding the most painful cuts into a completely casual conversation. Although she wouldn't have noticed what her unfiltered honesty had done, I averted my face so she couldn't see how much her words had affected me.

I'd learned long ago that hiding was the safest way to recover from wounds.

In the second grade, I'd stayed with my grandmother after school. One day, I was following her around, my sentences gushing out in their need to be heard. Nana's hand flew out and smacked my lips. I froze and stared at her in confusion.

"Thank God." She sniffed. "I didn't think anything would shut you up."

When Mom came to pick me up that day, she'd found me wedged between the couch and the wall. She touched her fingertip to my puffy lip and turned pale. "Did Nana pop your mouth?"

A lone tear trickled down my cheek.

Mom kissed the tear and whispered, "She will *never* do that again."

My mother had kept her promise. She started working from home after that, and I rode the bus. But even after ten years, when someone hurt me, I withdrew.

"Brooke." Natalie climbed onto the end of my bed. The moonlight spilled through the window, bathing her in a silvery glow. "Is Jill mad about having me around?"

"Does she act mad?"

"I have no idea."

This entire conversation had become too intense for the middle of the night. I would give it five more minutes before I shut it down. "Mom's not good at disguising her emotions. If she were mad, you would be able to tell."

"Can you just answer the question?"

"She's fine that you're here."

"What about you?"

Was the answer different now than it had been two minutes ago? I couldn't make up my mind. Natalie's visits generally lasted a weekend. It was hard to get used to the idea that there was no known end date this time. But . . . "I'm not mad, Mom's not mad, and Jeff's happy. It'll be okay."

"No, it won't. The three of you have jobs. I'll be alone in this house."

"Mom will be around in the mornings."

"She's always busy. It'll be boring."

I suppressed the desire to groan. Once Natalie got stuck in cranky mode, it took forever to drag her out. Although, in this case, she was right. She'd grown up in Durham, a place with an exhausting number of choices. The town of Azalea Springs would seem tame. "You can find things to do if you look for them."

"Like what?"

I reached for my laptop, brought up the county's recreation website, and went to the calendar for teens. "There are lots of camps you could sign up for."

"I'm not a camp kind of person."

Ignoring that. Natalie was the queen of exaggerations. "Horseback riding?"

"No."

"Archery?"

"No."

"Canoe trip on the Cape Fear River?"

Silence. I looked up. Her scowl was disbelieving.

Hey, a canoe trip sounded like fun to me. I scrolled down the site and stopped abruptly, excited by what I'd found. A drama camp. Natalie loved the theater, and she seemed to be equally happy in the audience or onstage. Jeff and I had driven up to Durham last fall to see her in a production at her high school. The show hadn't been all that good, but she was. A summer theater program could be the perfect solution. "How about auditioning for a play?"

"Which play?"

"*Oklahoma!*"

"That's a musical, not a play. Is it only for teens?"

Clicking on the registration link, I skimmed the details. "The cast and crew must be rising ninth through twelfth graders. The counselors and production team are adults from around here, and the arts council is bringing in a guest director from Elon University."

"Lisa Lin." Natalie slipped off the bed and came around to peer over my shoulder. "She's excellent. Very imaginative."

"So you've been to other shows she's directed?"

"Two times. Mama took me."

"Great. You might enjoy this." It was a camp, but I wouldn't be using that word. The program could hold a maximum of thirty-five campers, and there were three slots left. "It lasts five weeks, Monday through Friday, eight hours per day."

"That seems excessive."

"You start with singing auditions on the first day. On the

second, you audition for speaking parts. After that, you're either rehearsing or getting all kinds of lessons."

"I would like acting lessons. I'll give this some thought."

"Think fast. The program starts Monday, so you only have one day to decide."

"I'll let you know." She bounced from the room. There were a few thumps in the room beside mine, then silence.

I put away my laptop, wiggled into my bed, and tried to let go.

Natalie's first night had ended. Again.

· 4 ·

With Harmony at Stake

After brunch on Sunday, Mom and Jeff got in her Honda and drove away. They didn't say where they were going, but they took the tension with them.

Natalie retreated to the backyard.

I went to my room to complete a major project. Tomorrow was the first day of my summer job at the jewelry store owned by Kaylynn's family. Her dad had finally sent me an email with the dress code. Skirts or dress pants. Blouses. Understated accessories.

M'kay. That eliminated most of my clothes. I found a black maxi skirt and laid it on my bed. Next came a sleeveless purple shirt that could be buttoned to the throat.

"What are you doing?" Natalie asked from the doorway.

"Trying to find an outfit to wear for my new job."

"That outfit's ugly."

Not going to let Natalie's bluntness darken my mood. "I think my boss prefers ugly."

"Doubt it. You should pick something else."

"Thanks for the advice. You can go now." This shirt would have to do for tomorrow, but what about the rest of the week? I could borrow some tops from Mom. Even though she was two bra sizes smaller than me, she rarely wore fitted shirts. That might work—

"I watched *Oklahoma!* this morning."

Looking over my shoulder, I refocused on Natalie. "How?"

"Streamed it from PBS. The Hugh Jackman version. He's quite talented for someone famous. Not overrated at all."

"Do you have a point in there somewhere?"

"I'd like to be part of the cast."

Thank you, universe. Life would be easier on all of us if Natalie was busy. I gave her a smug smile, proud that I'd helped. "That's great. You should sign up."

"It's a camp—which I'm sure you know—and it costs five hundred dollars."

I hadn't noticed the fee. Wow. "Have you talked to your dad?

"I will."

"You need to ask him about the money."

"Won't have to. Mama gave me a debit card." Natalie leaned against the doorframe and stared at the ceiling. "What if she asks me to come home before the show's over?"

"You'll be here longer than five weeks."

"And you know that how?"

"Jeff said that it'll be a month or two."

"Will my brother be okay?"

"He'll be fine." Natalie's separation from her baby brother had to be the worst part of this move. She adored Luke, and she'd only been near him for the first month of his life. He would've grown a lot by the next time she saw him—whenever that was. "Aren't your grandparents there?"

She snorted. "Yes. They've moved into the guest suite."

I rummaged around in my walk-in closet for shoes. Sneakers were too tacky. Sandals? "I'll bet you're not sorry to miss your grandmother."

"That's the only benefit."

"There are others."

"Like what?"

"You get to be around Jeff more."

"You're right. I will like that." Natalie lowered her chin until she could see me again. Her tiny version of a smile flashed. "Will you mind if I have to live at your house for the whole summer?"

"No, I won't mind." Well, not much. I'd be too busy to spend a lot of time at home. And if we could keep her current attitude going, having her here could be fun.

"If you did mind, would you lie?"

"Probably."

"How can I tell the difference?"

"I guess you can't." I tossed a plain pair of sandals next to the bed before heading to my dresser. "Maybe you should keep asking and see whether I stay consistent. If I'm lying, I'm bound to screw up eventually."

"That might work, but it'll irritate you if I ask too often."

"It certainly will."

"You know that I prefer for you to always tell me the complete truth. Then I don't have to wonder which one it is or bug you because I'm not sure that I believe you."

"Noted." I would try, but I wouldn't promise to always be honest. Too many things could set her off. With harmony at stake, bending the truth had to remain an option.

I pawed through my jewelry and selected a necklace of twisted strands of copper wire with matching earrings. If my clothes had to be uninteresting, my jewelry could make a statement.

"Brooke, that copper stuff looks like you got it from the clearance bin at the dollar store."

"Leave, Natalie." I waved her off, closed the door, and fell backward on my bed. If the people at the store said anything to me tomorrow about how I was dressed, I would never admit it to Natalie.

Jeff grilled burgers and chicken for Sunday dinner. Since it was nice outside, we ate at the patio table on the deck.

I tried to block out what the others were saying, so I could think about my new job. I was looking forward to it, especially the money I would earn. What about my clothes, though? Natalie had me doubting them. Not that I could do anything about it now; it was all I had. I *really* wished Natalie hadn't said anything. Thankfully, Mom was talking about the ball game she'd umpired last night. I could listen to her instead of my doubts.

". . . In the top of the ninth, the away team rallied—"

"Jill," Natalie interrupted. "I don't speak baseball. Explain again in my version of English."

"The game should've ended in five minutes with the home team winning, but then the visiting team did something to make it last an hour longer."

Natalie nodded for her to go on. As Mom continued the story, my stepsister pumped her for information relentlessly. After a dozen more questions, Mom gave a delighted laugh. "Would you like to go with me to a game sometime?"

"I don't know enough about baseball to enjoy the experience."

"You don't have to know much. The food's good, and there are open spaces to pace in if you get bored."

"I'll think about it."

Jeff barged into the conversation. "Your mother called, Natalie. She wants us to find you a therapist. Your psychologist recommended someone in Lillington."

Natalie went into statue mode.

"If the new therapist can fit you in this week, I'll take the day off and drive you over."

"No, Dad. Not this week." Natalie switched from a statue to animated in an instant. "I'll be at the arts center."

"Why?"

"I'm in a musical. We're doing *Oklahoma!* Tomorrow is the first day, and you have to take me there and sign the release forms."

Everything about Jeff stilled. "Have you already signed up?"

"Of course, Dad. I asked if I could go to a summer camp, and you said that it sounded like a great idea."

"I remember." His gaze shifted to my mother. "Were you aware of this?"

Mom shook her head.

He looked back at his daughter. "How did you find out about this camp?"

"Brooke. She thinks I'll enjoy it.

His eyes narrowed on me. "Is that so?"

My neck blazed with heat. Why was he angry with me? Clearly, she'd mistaken his comment as permission, but that wasn't my fault. And it *was* a great idea. She'd needed something to do, and I found it. Now he wouldn't have to worry about her hating her summer. "The parks and rec department is sponsoring the camp. It lasts five weeks. Should be fun."

He turned to Natalie again. "What does it cost?"

"I've already paid with my debit card." Her stray-puppy trembling started up. "What's wrong, Dad? It'll be okay, won't it?"

He gave a faint nod. "Absolutely."

"Are you mad at me?"

"No, we're good." He frowned at the table, a muscle ticking in his jaw, and then pushed to his feet. "If you'll excuse me, I think I'm done." He stalked down the three steps from the deck, across the lawn, and into the workshop.

My mother grabbed his dishes and stacked them on hers as she side-eyed me.

I sent her a *What?* look. She shook her head and stood.

Natalie sprang to her feet and picked up her plate and glass. "I'm going inside."

Once the door banged behind her, I looked at Mom. "What just happened?"

"You shouldn't have gotten involved."

"Natalie asked me. She was worried about being bored, so I helped her. I didn't know that she would register without Jeff."

"Well, she did and now we have to deal with the fallout." Mom wrenched open the door.

I followed her in. Should I leave this alone? Probably. But their reaction was so extreme, I wanted to know the reason. "I get that you're surprised, but I don't see why you and Jeff are so upset."

"The camp will overstress her. You've witnessed her meltdowns."

Yes, I had, and they were scary. I couldn't see how that applied here. "She'll like being in this show."

"Anxiety attacks can be triggered by *any* kind of strong emotion, good or bad. That's why Jeff and I have to be vigilant about keeping her world calm. There is nothing calm about the theater, which is why they call it *drama*."

"Natalie's acted in plays before. Why wasn't it a problem then?"

"She was at her own school, in familiar surroundings, with Mei there to be her anchor through the tough patches." Mom leaned against the counter and sighed. "We already have enough to worry about. We did *not* need this. Jeff wants so badly for everything to go well. Having her live with him has been a dream come true."

"Then why hasn't she done it before?"

"Mei wouldn't allow it. When she filed for divorce, she asked for full custody. Jeff fought her, but the judge ruled against him because Jeff was in the Army and could've been deployed at any moment." Mom's gaze strayed out the window, toward the workshop. "He's over the moon that she's here, but he also feels guilty. With his new business, this summer was the worst possible time for her to move in. If he could, he'd be home with her *more*, not less." She looked at me. "We created a plan, but that's a wasted effort now."

I'd been so sure that the musical was the best solution. If only

I'd known all of the other stuff. "I'll talk to her, okay? I can fix this."

"*No*. Please. Leave this to us." Mom picked up a plate and bent over the dishwasher. "We'll manage, Brooke. We don't have a choice."

After a hard run and a shower, I lay on my bed in the dark and cycled through my thoughts again. I liked the direction that my relationship with Jeff was heading. Since I didn't want the night to end with bad feelings between us, I'd better take care of this now. Sliding off the bed, I went downstairs and out through the side door.

When Mom bought this house seven years ago, a big reason had been the building beyond the carport. It was too small to be an apartment and too nice to be a shed. My stepfather had claimed it as his man-cave after moving in. He'd furnished it with a ratty recliner, big TV, mini-fridge stocked with beer, and the electronics he needed for his geospatial engineering business. Even though the building served as his home office, we'd always called it *the workshop*.

I knocked on the door and pushed it open. "Jeff?"

He was sprawled in the recliner, with his laptop open and his reading glasses perched at the end of his nose. "Yes?"

The weary expression on his face killed me. "Could Natalie have one of her attacks during the camp?"

"The probability is high."

"Could you suggest that she—?" I stopped since he was already shaking his head.

"It's too late, not when she has her heart set on it." He took off his glasses and pinched the bridge of his nose. "She came out here tonight and babbled on and on about it. She's excited. I'm not taking that away from her."

"I'm sorry."

With precise movements, he set the computer aside, stood, and crossed to me, his boots scuffing on the worn floorboards. "I know you're sorry, but I won't say it's okay, because it isn't."

His resigned tone was worse than anger. "I thought I was doing a good thing."

"I know that too, and I'm glad that you're trying with Natalie, but you have to be careful with her. We can't predict what she'll fixate on. Good intentions can have bad consequences."

His words chilled me. Was this what I would have to face for the next five weeks—the constant fear of a meltdown from Natalie? The dread of Jeff's disappointment?

"We'll find a way to make this work, Brooke."

"Yes, sir." I turned to go. We reached for the doorknob at the same time, his big, scarred hand brushing mine. I jerked back, not wanting to get in his way. I'd already done that enough for one weekend.

He shook his head, pushed the door open for me, and stepped aside.

I had just escaped into the darkness, wrapped in the heat of the summer night, when he spoke again.

"Focus on being her friend, and leave the rest to me."

With a mumbled good-bye, I ran to the hammock and dove in, wishing that I could rewind the past twenty-four hours and start over.

· 5 ·

Ouch Times Three

Azalea Springs had a quaint Main Street shopping district, with brick buildings, colorful awnings, and flowering trees in wrought-iron cages. The fine jewelry store had squatted in the same proud spot for over one hundred years.

It had taken me ten minutes to walk here. I arrived by nine-thirty and peered through a window into the showroom. Even though the lights were off, I could see the outline of glass cases, antique love seats, and crystal vases full of fresh flowers. A shadowy figure moved near the back. I knocked on the door.

The person approached, a tall woman in a dark pencil skirt and a long-sleeved, mint-green silk blouse. She unlocked the door and opened it a crack. "May I help you?"

"I'm Brooke Byers, Kaylynn's friend. I have a job here this summer."

"Hello. I'm Della, the showroom manager." She stepped aside to let me in and locked the door behind us. Her gaze swept down my body, pausing on the skirt and sandals. "Did Mr. Wilson send you the dress code?"

"Yes." Really? Natalie had been right?

"I'll be honest. He must have left out the details. You're dressed too casually to wait on customers, but we have plenty of things to do in the back. Follow me."

She went first to a small break room and gestured with one of her beautifully manicured hands. "You can leave your purse in that closet. One of your responsibilities is to be in charge of the coffee. Brew a fresh pot every hour."

I glanced around at the mess in here. I'd put myself in charge of cleaning up, too.

Della crossed the hall. "Do you have any computer skills?"

"Yes." Score. Mr. Wilson had been vague about my duties. I'd hoped to spend time in the office, and the ugly outfit had worked in my favor.

"Excellent. I'll get you started on a clerical project." She entered the office and pointed at a tiny desk covered in catalogs and glossy brochures. We spent the next twenty minutes going over the phone system, email accounts, and an upcoming sales promotion. Then she glanced at the clock. "Do you understand what to do? It's time for me to open the store."

"Yes."

"Please keep an eye on the security monitor, and come out to the floor whenever you see a customer. Stay as unobtrusive as possible."

As the tap of her heels faded down the hallway, I lost myself in printing address labels and stuffing envelopes, so it startled me when a voice spoke to me about an hour later.

"Good morning, Brooke."

I looked up. "Hi, Mr. Wilson."

"Settling in?"

"Yes, sir."

"Good. Good. We're glad to have you." He put his computer case down and then perched on the desk's edge. "Della's got you started on the promotion campaign."

"Yes, sir."

"Fine. So just a few things about the business." He crossed his arms. "Your job is to help out with whatever we need, which will mostly be clerical work or serving as backup when my other staff go on vacation. You won't be on the sales floor much, but when you do have contact with customers, just be polite and respectful. If you go out for lunch, check in when you leave and when you return. And no personal calls while you're working. Wait until you're on break. Any questions?"

"No, sir."

He gestured toward the stack of envelopes. "How's the project coming?"

"Great." It wasn't exactly engaging my brain, but at ten dollars an hour, it didn't matter. "I'll have the promotional materials ready to take to the post office before I leave today."

"Excellent. Welcome aboard." He stood, grabbed his case, and headed into his office.

When I got home that afternoon, I walked into a quiet house. Mom was likely at the arts center, picking up Natalie. Yay. A moment of peace. I wouldn't be getting many of those this summer. It was strange how adding one more person to a family could make a house smaller.

I was in my room, changing into shorts, when my phone buzzed. A text from Kaylynn.

> Are you surviving Nat?
>> Fine so far
> How did you like the store?

I laid on my bed. Everything was going to be fine, especially since I wouldn't have much contact with customers.

> Good. How was lifeguarding?
>> Boring. No rescues. Some yelling. The other guard is ripped
> And?
>> Only interested in looking. So Daddy says you need help with your work clothes. Want to go shopping?

Kaylynn was an expert at finding the right clothes, but she didn't understand the value of money. I had to establish control.

> Sure, but Target
>> Coco's would be better
> No
>> K. Pick you up at 7?
> K

I set the phone aside and winced. I hadn't planned to spend money for my job, but it didn't sound like I could get out of it. Releasing a breath, I brought up the Target website to scope out prices. Time to make a budget.

Mom, Natalie, and I had already finished eating when Jeff trudged into the kitchen, his face creased with fatigue. He stopped by Natalie's chair. She held herself stiffly but didn't shrink away.

His face lit up as he laid his arm along her shoulders for a hug. "How was camp?"

"It was quite good."

He fist-bumped with me and crossed to my mom. After a whispered comment and a kiss, he pulled out a chair and groaned as he sat. His gaze rested on Natalie. "Did your camp hold auditions today?"

"The singing auditions."

"How did you do?"

"I don't know. You'd have to ask Lisa."

"Lisa who?"

"Lisa Lin Dalton, the director. She's exceptional. Her son is the stage manager. He's exceptional, too. The girls in the camp think he's hot, which is annoying and not true." Natalie's gaze flicked to her father. "My counselor is a college student named Norah. We'll have breaks every morning and afternoon, and that's when I'll go to Norah's group. I've talked to her about my diagnosis, and she understands I need to be away from people sometimes. She said as long as she could see me, that was fine."

Mom set a plate before Jeff and turned to me. "If you're willing to chauffeur Natalie tomorrow, you can take the Honda. I'll carpool to my ball game."

"Deal."

Jeff smiled at me. "How did your first day on the job go?"

"Good. It's not too hard, and the people are nice." I glanced at the wall clock, its ornate hands showing it was nearly seven. "I'll be out tonight. Kaylynn's taking me shopping."

"Why?"

"I need new clothes for my job."

Natalie bobbed her head. "I was right. They didn't like your ugly outfit."

I would *not* react. "They've given me more details about the dress code, and I don't have anything that works."

She popped to her feet. "Where are you going?"

Oh, no. This could mean trouble. "Target." I stood and cleaned off the table, avoiding her gaze. If I was lucky, she would put her plate in the dishwasher and walk away.

"Can I come?"

Too late. Choking back a groan, I wrapped the casserole dish and put it in the fridge, wondering what to say. It was no secret to anyone except Natalie that Kaylynn wasn't a fan.

When I returned to the table, Jeff was watching me, his eyebrow arched in challenge. Okay then, that decision was made. "Sure, Natalie, but you have to wear shoes."

She darted from the room.

"Brooke," Jeff said. "Thank you."

"No problem." It was a lie, which, from the curl to his lip, he knew.

As Natalie and I crawled into the car, Kaylynn muttered a greeting. I buckled up, careful not to make eye contact.

The annoyed silence lasted until we braked at the first stop sign. "You didn't mention that Natalie was coming."

"The decision was last minute."

Natalie spoke from the backseat. "Mama's sick. I'll have to live with Dad for a while."

Sympathy softened Kaylynn's face. "Sorry." She faced forward and merged onto the highway.

The reprieve lasted until we were inside the store, heading toward the juniors department. Kaylynn caught my arm and held me until my stepsister had wandered ahead. "You should've told me that Natalie was coming."

Sometimes, every available choice had guilt attached. "You would've canceled." I pulled my arm from her grasp and pushed the cart over to a rack of skirts.

"Sure would. She's obnoxious and embarrassing. And talking to her is like having a conversation with a dictionary."

"I get it, okay? Could you drop it?"

"Whatever." Kaylynn's face had already sharpened into its shopping mask. "It'll be hard to find anything here that looks expensive. And when customers spend thousands of dollars on jewelry, they want to buy from expensive-looking people."

"I can't afford—"

"I *know*. I'll do my best." She headed for the designer label section. "Pencil skirts. Blue, black, and gray." She loaded them into my cart.

"Why so many?" I snuck a peek at a price tag. Ouch—times three.

"You can't repeat an outfit in the same week. Daddy wouldn't like that." She threw in some silky pastel tops.

"Would he notice?"

"Yes." Kaylynn huffed with interest and chose a short fitted dress in a forest green print. "This one, too."

Natalie rejoined us and wrinkled her nose. "Brooke shouldn't wear anything that short. She has jiggly thighs."

Kaylynn shot me an *I told you so* look.

I sighed, but secretly, I agreed with Natalie. Trading the green dress for another pencil skirt in maroon, I dropped it into my cart. "I'm trying these on. Be right back."

Everything fit fine, but the pencil skirts would require pantyhose. Ugh. After grabbing two pairs of control-top, I was more than ready to get out of there.

Natalie continued her comments in the checkout line. "Pencil skirts aren't comfortable."

"Doesn't matter." I handed them to the cute checkout guy. He smiled. I smiled back.

"Why not?"

I hunted for the magic words that would turn her off. "They're like a uniform. I don't have a choice."

"Your butt will look big."

The checkout guy coughed.

Could this get any worse?

It didn't help that Natalie was right. Height-wise, I took after my mom. But width-wise? I must have inherited those genes from my biological father, because Mom was thin and I was not. "Kaylynn, could you and Natalie take the bags to the car? Please?"

After they left, I paid for everything, pulling more twenty-dollar bills from my purse than I'd planned. Besides the skirts and hose, I bought a pair of black pants, six tops, and silver ballet flats, which Kaylynn tried to veto but I overruled. If I was making a cringe-worthy dent in my bank account, I had to like the shoes.

When we pulled up at our house, Natalie got out and ran to

the backyard in her weird skip-hop gait. Bracing myself, I turned to Kaylynn.

She was shaking her head. "That was painful."

I didn't react. It had been more painful for me than her.

"Promise me you won't let Natalie tag along again."

"Do you mean without warning you?" My scowl should be delivering its own warning.

"You know what I mean. I can't take much more of her."

I looked through the windshield, watching as a cardinal splashed in our birdbath, carefully choosing my words. I rarely argued with Kaylynn, but I couldn't let this go. "I won't make that promise."

"Why not?"

There were too many reasons to list, so I'd go with the one Kaylynn was least likely to debate. "I want to get along with Jeff, and being horrible to his daughter won't work for him."

"Even he has to know that she's a pain in the—"

"Stop. Whether he realizes it or not, he won't forgive me for shutting her out." And I wouldn't forgive me either.

"It's impossible to have fun with her around. She ruins everything."

"No, she doesn't."

"The Memorial Day picnic?"

Not that again. "I told you she didn't like hot dogs."

"Which doesn't give her the right to explain in disgusting detail how they're made." Kaylynn sighed noisily. "The photo session before prom."

Okay, she had me there. "Sylvie's dress *was* an 'unfortunate shade of brown.'"

"I had to lie about it for the rest of the night to keep Sylvie from crying."

"Natalie won't make that mistake again. I've talked to her."

"Not good enough. I get why you want to keep Jeff happy, but you have to find a way that doesn't involve your friends."

"We're finished with this discussion." I fumbled for my bags in the backseat. "Thanks for shopping with me."

"What will you do about Natalie?"

I set the bags at my feet, surprised by how stubborn Kaylynn was being. Yes, Natalie was irritatingly "blunt," and yes, when she was in a grump, everybody suffered. But when she was in a good mood, she blended into the background. My friends could get over it. "I'll be careful about when I ask her."

"Sorry but no. I know this sounds bad—"

"Ya think?"

"—but this is our last full summer together before we graduate." Kaylynn sagged against her seat, shaking her head. "I can't do it. I just can't be around her."

"Wait." A sick feeling swamped me. Kaylynn and I had big plans. We'd both found Monday through Friday jobs so that we could spend nights and weekends with our friends—going to movies, swimming, taking a trip to her family's beach house. "Are you saying I shouldn't come if I want to bring Natalie?"

Kaylynn shrugged apologetically and nodded.

"Whoa. Guess that's clear." I slammed out of her car, closed the door with my hip, and stumbled up the sidewalk. As I marched up the veranda steps, the car of my best friend roared away. I dropped my bags beside a pillar and flopped into the glider, needing to let my frustration and . . . sadness blow away in the breeze. Why did Kaylynn make me choose?

After a four-mile run to cool my outrage, I showered, slipped on my nightshirt, and climbed into bed. Grabbing my scrapbook, I flipped to my highest aspirations.

In the ninth grade, I'd added at the bottom:

Car—to not be dependent on others

Beside that item, I'd begun the countdown to having enough money. After today's shopping trip, the amount I needed would increase again.

~~6000~~

6300

I'd have to make up the difference with babysitting, and I wouldn't try to calculate how long that would take.

There was a knock on my door. Before I could hide the scrapbook, Natalie barged in.

"Kaylynn doesn't like me."

No reason to respond. It was a statement I couldn't deny.

"She doesn't want me to be around her, does she?"

The question dredged up raw feelings that I hadn't sweated away. There was no good way to resolve this. Since Kaylynn wouldn't be backing down and neither would I, I'd be spending my evenings at home. Natalie was smart enough to figure out why, but I hated to say the words. I hated to *think* the words. "Natalie—"

"Don't make anything up. I may be socially impaired, but my senses function quite well. I can see, and I can hear. Better than you."

She overheard us? I searched my memory, trying to remember what Kaylynn and I had said to each other when my stepsister had been nearby. It had probably been bad. "What part did you hear?"

"Nothing I didn't already know." She backed into the hallway. "I'm not interested in being around people who don't want to be around me, but don't let that stop you. Do whatever you want." The door clicked shut.

I closed my eyes and leaned back, my head banging against the headboard. I wouldn't compromise about Natalie. Not now. I couldn't allow Kaylynn to dictate how I treated my stepsister. But in offering to let me off the hook, Natalie had made my decision harder, because I dreaded the thought of the empty summer stretching ahead.

⋄ 6 ⋄

Exaggerated Study

My mother's two careers had always kept her busy at nights and on the weekends. During the school year, she tutored kids in biology, physics, and earth science. In the summer, she umpired baseball games for a college league. Most games were within a one-hundred-mile radius, but some were as far away as Virginia.

The other person on her ump-team lived in Raleigh, and he was always willing to drive if she asked. I loved it when they carpooled, because I got to keep her car.

After taking Natalie to the arts center Tuesday, I backtracked across town and parked behind the jewelry store. Della was in the showroom, putting flowers in a vase. As I joined her, I saw the two of us in a mirror and blinked in surprise. I looked like a mini-Della in my dark skirt, pink blouse, pearls, and smooth knot at the nape of my neck. This was disturbing. It looked good on her. On me, it looked ridiculous.

"Very nice. I approve." Della smiled, her teeth beautifully even and white. "Do you know what Mr. Wilson has planned for you today? He said he'd given you a new project."

"Yes, merging his mailing lists."

"Excellent. Our office manager is back from vacation, so check in with her before starting. Mrs. Martin will watch the security cameras. You won't have to come to the floor today."

No argument here. I hurried to the office and introduced myself to Mrs. Martin. She nodded vaguely and continued to sort pieces of paper into stacks. I logged in to the computer and buried myself in spreadsheets and email addresses.

Late morning, my phone buzzed. I glanced at the screen. Natalie.

"Morning, ladies," Mr. Wilson boomed from the doorway. He came to my desk and squinted at the computer screen. "Can you show me what you've done so far?"

"Yes, sir." I paged through the spreadsheet, explaining as I went.

When he'd run out of questions, he patted me on the shoulder. "Good job. You're further along than I expected."

"Thank you." I tried not to fidget. He wore nice cologne but too much of it.

Buzz.

Mr. Wilson sucked in a breath that made an annoying whistle sound. "Do you know how to create graphs in Excel?"

"Yes, sir."

"Excellent. I'll send you my data and instructions in email."

My phone buzzed for the third time. Something was up. I was dying to answer it. Ignoring Natalie was never a good idea.

My boss frowned. "Everything okay?"

"Yes, sir." I smiled apologetically.

"Remember what I said about personal calls." He disappeared into his private office and shut the door.

"Taking a break, Mrs. Martin." I dived for the phone and hurried into the break room. There were three texts from Natalie.

I forgot my lunch. Can you bring it?

That was ten minutes ago. A couple of minutes later . . .

Where is Jill?

Three minutes after that.

A guy is taking me home

Her last text jolted me. She shouldn't get into a car with someone she didn't know. What was she thinking?

Well, that was the problem. She didn't always think things through. She acted.

I texted her back.

Have you left the arts center yet?
    Yes
Where are you now?

A minute ticked by and no response. My fear heightened. If the guy took her directly to our house, they'd be halfway there. If my mom hadn't left for the game yet, she would be home. But when I tried calling her, it rolled to voice mail.

"Mrs. Martin? I'm taking my lunch break."

She frowned. "This early?"

"Yes, ma'am. Sorry." I grabbed my purse and ran for the parking lot. Another text had come in from Natalie.

In Micah's car

Who is Micah?

The guy driving me home

I slid into the car, closed the windows, and cranked up the AC. Before I pulled away, I texted her again.

How do you know Micah?

From the arts center

Is he a camper?

No

A counselor?

No. Stop texting me

I got home in record time, nerves twitching. A shiny new Subaru had parked in front of our house. I pulled into the driveway and threw the car into park. Natalie was pacing on the veranda. She seemed fine, but my fear wasn't ready to trickle away. I turned my attention to the guy with her. He leaned against a pillar, hands jammed in his pockets, shades hiding his eyes, a hint of a smile on his lips. His head shifted in my direction as I marched up the sidewalk.

Stopping at the bottom of the steps, I crossed my arms and glared. "Are you Micah?"

He straightened, his expression flattening. "Yes."

"How do you know my sister?"

Natalie halted her pacing. "Stepsister."

"We met at camp." His chin lifted.

"She says you aren't a camper or a counselor."

"All true."

"Then why did you drive her home?"

"It was a better plan than letting her starve."

"Chill, Brooke," Natalie said. "Dad gave the camp staff permission to drive me if necessary. Can you let me in the house? I need my lunch."

As I hurried up the steps, I located the key and unlocked the door. After she disappeared inside, I whirled around and faced Micah. He looked too young to be a college student. "So you're camp *staff*? How old are you?"

"Seventeen. How old are you?"

"Seventeen."

He made an exaggerated study of me from head to toe. "I would've guessed *much* older."

Heat rose in my cheeks at how skillfully he'd found my weak spot. My hand crept self-consciously to the fake pearls around my neck. "I thought camp staff were adults."

"That would make me the exception." His upper lip curled into a sneer. "You must have a low opinion of your parks and rec department if you think they would've let a stranger drive your stepsister anywhere."

There was no good comeback to that, since he was right. My worry about having something bad happen to Natalie had left me looking for problems, and I'd found one that wasn't really there.

She banged out of the house, a lunch pack in her hand. "I'm ready. We can go," she said as she ran by.

"Right behind you, Natalie." Micah came down the steps, saying softly as he passed, "You're welcome."

Around midnight, a car whined to a halt at the curb before our house. Footsteps crunched on the driveway. The front door opened and closed. I listened, expecting to hear my mom climb the stairs, but she didn't. Minutes passed. The front door opened and closed again.

Why had she gone back outside?

Bolting from my bed, I ran downstairs and out to the veranda. Mom was sitting on the glider, holding a glass of wine.

"How was the game?"

"Draining." She grimaced. "The Sandhill Egrets were the visiting team."

"Did Jerkface mess with you?"

"Yes. He ran off his mouth, too quietly for the fans to hear, but I did and so did the second baseman."

Mom usually had good rapport with the players, but the Egrets' shortstop liked to harass her, and not in a nice way. "What did he do tonight?"

"Finley thought he'd tagged someone out. I called the runner safe, and he just couldn't let it go."

I eased onto the glider beside her. "What did you do?"

"Mostly I didn't pay attention, but when the comments bled over into another inning, I let him know I'd had enough." She sighed. "He's talented, but he's also hotheaded and undisciplined. Catchers can trash-talk him into trying for bad pitches, and he gets pissed at everyone but himself. It won't be too much longer before he crosses the line and then . . ."

"And then what?"

"I'll do what I have to. I don't care what he thinks about me, but I won't let him disrespect the game." She set the glass on a side table and dropped her head to the back of the glider.

We rocked in silence. The breeze whispered around us, teasing us with the scent of mown grass and gardenias. This felt nice. Familiar. A glimpse into the way life used to be.

"How are things going between you and Natalie?" Mom asked.

"Good."

"It's likely that she'll live with us until school starts."

Somehow, I wasn't surprised. "When are you going to tell her?"

"Soon. Jeff wants her to believe that we like having her around first."

"Do you?"

"Like having her around? Yes, I do. I have to put up with so much testosterone-fueled drama on the ball field that it's nice to come home to her. She lets you know exactly how she feels. No crap. No dissembling. Just truth."

"She's a slob." Probably even worse than Mom realized, because I cleaned up after Natalie in the mornings. I couldn't take a shower in a nasty bathroom.

"I don't like that part either, and I intend to work on it."

"How?"

"I'm toying with options, but it's tricky. Jeff is resistant to pushing her."

I agreed with him. It would be best for everybody if we left her alone until she reached her happy place and stayed there for a while. "She's not ready. She'd fail."

"Failure isn't all bad." Mom lifted her glass. "Even the best ballplayers fail seventy percent of the time at bat."

"No, please." I groaned at her favorite way to tease me into a good mood. "No baseball metaphors."

She kissed my cheek. "Sorry. I was trying to cover all the bases."

"Mom." I tried to control a smile.

"Just hoping to strike out swinging."

"I'm officially leaving now." It was good to hear her laughing as I ran inside.

· 7 ·

A Strong Possibility

Natalie ran out to the car on Wednesday afternoon, bouncing with excitement. "I got a part in *Oklahoma!*" she shouted as she buckled in.

Mom and I exchanged relieved glances.

"That's great," I said. "Which part?"

"Friend-of-Laurey number three. I have a solo. Want to hear?"

"Sure."

She sang ten words. Just ten. But the joy on her face was so complete that I had to smile. "You have a nice voice."

"I know. Jill, there's a meeting tonight, and a family member needs to attend. Then you won't be invited back because they don't want adults hanging around to disrupt the synergy. Can you come?"

"No, I'm sorry." Mom's voice was clouded with regret. "I have a baseball game tonight. I'll have to leave as soon as I've changed into my uniform."

"Can Dad?"

"He's at a town council meeting to answer questions about his new project."

Natalie went into statue mode.

"What about me?" I asked. "I'm a family member."

Her gaze flicked in my general direction. "Jill will have the car."

I looked at my mother. "Is the game close enough that I can drive you?"

"It's only forty minutes away. If you get me there, I can car-pool with Steven coming home."

Natalie stared out the window. "That would work."

The plan went smoothly. After dropping Mom off at the ball-field, we drove the half hour to the arts center. Natalie must have been nervous, because she talked nonstop about her coun-selor, her small group, and Micah. I grunted encouragement and only half-listened, my focus on the truck ahead of me with its load of unsecured furniture sitting in the bed.

"What if people don't like my voice?"

That question caught my attention. "They'll like it."

"What if I don't do a good enough job singing my one line?"

I kept the smile on my face and hoped I could sidetrack her anxiety. "You'll be fine. The director wouldn't have given you the role if she wasn't confident about you."

"What if I'm teased?"

"Ignore it."

"I'll try, but I don't know if I can."

We rode in silence until we took the turnoff to the arts center.

"I'll ask Norah, too," Natalie said, as if we hadn't ended the conversation ten minutes ago. "She says we can always talk to her unless she's teaching acting lessons."

I pulled into a parking spot. "Do all of the camp staff have duties like that?"

"They each have a job on the production team. Only five are counselors leading small groups. Since that doesn't involve much time, the counselors are busy doing other tasks when they're not with the campers."

I wondered what Micah's job was, but it was too late to ask. Natalie was already out of the car and running for the entrance. I walked more slowly, feeling hopeful. She was acting like her version of happy. She'd been assigned a solo that was big enough to count and small enough not to be too stressful. Maybe Mom and Jeff were overestimating the issue.

When I entered the auditorium, I hesitated at the back and took in the scene. Most of the seats in the center section were filled. The lights had been dimmed except at the front, where a college-age girl stood.

"That's it for me," she was saying, "so I'll turn this over to our director, Lisa Lin."

An older Asian woman gave a slight wave from where she sat on the edge of the stage, legs dangling, wearing jeans, tunic, and several braided bracelets. "Hello, family members. Thank you for coming on such short notice. As Elena said, I'm Lisa Lin. During the school year, I'm an associate professor of musical theater at Elon University. This summer, I'll be directing *Oklahoma!*" She gestured toward the side wall, where a mix of adults and college-age people were lined up. "Let me introduce our production team."

Micah stood at the end of the line, his feet apart, hands in pockets, staring at me. He held my gaze for a few seconds before looking at the director.

One by one, we learned the names of the technical director, the music director, the camp counselors who were also handling sets, choreography, makeup, costumes, props . . .

I searched the auditorium for Natalie and found her fidgeting in the shadows.

". . . And finally, let me introduce you to the stage manager and my son, Micah Dalton."

My gaze snapped back to Micah. The director's son? Since I wasn't sure what a stage manager did, I'd have to ask Natalie, but it sounded important.

Ms. Lin nodded toward him. "When it comes to the show, I'm in charge of providing the artistic vision. Micah is in charge of everything else."

He waved.

"If you have questions about your camper, Elena's the camp manager. Call her. All other questions go to Micah. There is no reason to ask for me, because I'll just send you to one of them. Alright, I'm done."

The girl, Elena, stepped forward again. "If the number of calls I've been receiving is any clue, you're *really* interested in what's happening at the camp. We'll do our best to keep you informed, and I'm not trying to be rude here, but family members? We don't need you around during the day. This is a teen production. Adult involvement needs to stay to a minimum, so please don't show up. Not during rehearsals. Not during breaks. Any questions?"

A bald man sitting in the front row raised his hand. "What about discipline problems?"

"There won't be any." She smiled the kind of smile that would've intimidated me if I were a cast member.

A flood of hands shot up.

When I looked back at Micah, he was staring at me, unsmiling. Seconds passed and neither of us blinked. Okay, I could accept a challenge. Besides, I owed him an apology. I walked around the perimeter of the auditorium to join him. His eyes tracked me the whole way.

"Hi, I'm Brooke Byers."

"Micah Dalton."

Yesterday, he'd worn shades. Today, he wore glasses with edgy black frames that were adorable on him. He would've looked ordinary without them. "I apologize for the way I spoke to you."

He inclined his head.

Hmm. Being difficult. Why? "Are you going to say anything?"

His expression hovered near arrogant. "My reaction isn't good enough for you?"

"No, it isn't."

"What did you expect?"

"An 'okay' or 'sure' would've been nice."

"Okay. Sure."

I would *not* take offense. At least, not for now. That choice could always be changed later. "I'm protective of her."

"Is that what you call it?"

Really? A guy who was practically a stranger to us thought

he had the right to question how I took care of my stepsister? Clamping my lips together, I started to back away when his gaze slid to someone behind me.

He smiled warmly. "Hey."

Natalie galloped past me as if I weren't there. "When do we learn movement?"

"Next week."

"I'm not much of a dancer."

"You don't have to be. We'll teach you . . ."

I studied him as they talked. He was only a few inches taller than my stepsister, maybe five-ten. He had short, dark hair. Some acne on his forehead. A black watch on his right wrist and a dark gold silicone bracelet on his left. His body looked lean— but good—in his jeans and T-shirt. Although nobody would think of him as gorgeous, cute was a strong possibility.

". . . Don't worry, Natalie. The choreography won't be too hard . . ."

She relaxed as he spoke, and I relaxed, too. While I didn't like his attitude toward me, he was earning points with the way he treated Natalie.

"Thank you, everyone," Elena was saying loudly. "We're done. If you have more questions, the team will stick around for a few minutes."

The room filled with noise. Immediately, the director was mobbed.

"You're about to get swarmed, Micah." Natalie hurried away from him and out through the rear doors of the auditorium.

I watched long enough to see him engulfed by campers and parents. He noticed my grin and gave an impatient shake of his head before turning to two girls vying for his attention. I ran after my stepsister, determined to get out of the parking lot before the rest of the crowd.

My bedroom door creaked open at midnight. There was a rustle as Natalie settled onto a chair. She didn't say anything or switch on the lamp.

This was the third time she'd come in for a late-night conversation since she moved here. It was becoming a pattern, and I didn't mind as long as I was awake. In fact, I found myself looking forward to our chats.

When the silence lengthened, I realized that was my signal to initiate things. "Do you want to talk about the musical?"

"I want to know what the problem is with Dad. He stays upset."

Sure, that was a good topic, too.

Was she concerned it was all about her? That accounted for some of it, but her father had been through a lot of change this year. We all had.

After Jeff retired from the military two years ago, he'd been hired by a contracting firm that mapped the terrain of new housing developments. This spring, he'd gone into business for himself and signed his first major client in May. He would be working long hours to keep up. "Jeff just got a big contract, and he's trying hard to do it right."

"Is there some reason why he wouldn't do it right?"

"It's natural to worry even when you're confident that everything is fine."

"Not me. I don't bother to try things if I think I'll fail."

"So you don't worry about your part in the show?"

"Okay, you got me there." She stood and went to her favorite spot by the window, looking out at who-knows-what. "Does it bother you that you don't have a father?"

It was surprising how long she'd waited to ask me that. She'd known for months. "Most of the time, no. I don't know what I'm missing." The lights would remain off for this discussion, since I couldn't trust my face to look calm. Plumping the pillows behind me, I wiggled into a comfortable position. "I've always been curious about dads, but it wasn't until Jeff that I got to spend any real time near one."

"When did Jill tell you about the circumstances surrounding your conception?"

"I always knew that she'd chosen to have me on my own, but it was close to middle school before I understood the biology of the process." Mom had made a big deal about choosing to have me. She'd lived with a guy for eight years who was completely opposed to having kids. She kept hoping he would change his mind. When she finally believed him, she moved out and "practically drove straight to the fertility center."

"How did Jill pick the sperm donor?"

I was glad Natalie was asking me instead of my mother. That could have gotten weird, because Mom-the-scientist would have supplied too many graphic details. It was just better for everyone if I controlled the volume of information. "At the sperm bank, she was allowed to search through a list of potential donors. Each candidate had background info and a photo. She picked someone who seemed smart, fit, and looked different from her." It had succeeded, because I hadn't inherited her blue eyes and blonde hair.

"Do you know his name?"

"No. We have a copy of his medical profile, and that's about it."

"What do your grandparents think?"

This time, it was Natalie who'd found my weak spot. "They believe my mom 'cheated' to get a kid."

"How do you know?"

"I overheard them tell her." It was one of those moments in life where I'd been taught a truth that would've been better left unlearned.

"So they think you don't count unless sex was involved?"

I choked on a laugh. Tonight, Natalie's honesty was refreshing. "Something like that. They moved to Idaho, to be near their other grandchildren. I see them occasionally, but I can never shake the feeling that I'm not a real grandkid since I wasn't the result of an actual relationship."

"That sucks. I've heard enough about this topic. I'm going to bed."

"Can I ask a question first?"

She shrugged.

"What's so interesting about Micah?"

"A lot of things, really. The biggest is how much power he has for someone who's still in high school. The stage manager runs everything in the show except the director. Realistically, Micah is more essential than Lisa is. I already knew who he was."

"You did?"

"Yes. If you're a high school kid in this state who's serious about theater, you've heard of Micah Dalton."

"Because of his mom?"

"It doesn't hurt that he's Lisa Lin's son, but he'd be known without her. His high school's theater department gets all kinds of awards, and he's the reason." Natalie turned her back on the window and stared vaguely in my direction. "I walked into the auditorium on the first morning of camp, knowing that Lisa would be there. But when they introduced Micah as the stage manager, you could hear the whispers. It was like winning the lottery twice."

I thought back to the team members lined up beside them. They'd all been college-age or older. Except Micah. "The others aren't bothered that he's so young?"

"No. Being a teen is the best part. Since Lisa's an adult, we have to revere her from a distance. But we can revere Micah up close. He's one of us." Natalie bobbed her head for emphasis. "Especially for me."

"Why?"

"We both have Chinese mothers and white fathers, and neither one of us wanted to go to Chinese school. Those are major commonalities." She looked at the ceiling, scrunching her forehead in concentration. "He never acts like I'm wasting his time. Even though he's super busy, he still answers all of my questions." Her smile flashed for an instant, then disappeared.

"He probably does that with everyone."

"Actually, no. Just with me."

Okay, I would leave that comment alone for now. "Would you call Micah a friend?"

"No." She crossed to the door and paused. "He's epically awesome, and he doesn't make mistakes. I like that in a person."

"I'm sure that Micah makes mistakes."

"If you knew him better, you'd know you were wrong."

· 8 ·

Loose and Untethered

My hours at the jewelry store had fallen into a boring routine. By Thursday, I was spending most of my time on
computer projects and a tiny amount standing around in the
showroom, backing up Della if Mrs. Martin was busy.

I had finished my morning to-do list and was cleaning the
break room when my phone rang with the default ringtone. I
pulled it from my pants pocket and glanced at the screen. Even
though I didn't recognize the number, I answered. "Hello?"

"Is this Brooke?"

"Yes."

"It's Micah Dalton."

My heartbeat rocketed at the strain in his voice. "What's
wrong?"

"We need your help with Natalie."

I could hear her in the background, mumbling "stop" over

and over again in rapid bursts. Unmistakably a meltdown. No use asking what happened. He probably didn't know. "Have you checked with my mom?"

"I've called all of Natalie's emergency contacts. Trust me, you were the last one I tried. Hey, wait a sec." The sound muffled while he murmured to Natalie. "Okay, back again. I couldn't reach your mom. Mr. Kane is on his way, but he said it would take him an hour."

Oh, damn, Jeff was leaving the construction site in the middle of the day. Would Natalie be completely out of control by the time he got there? Possibly.

It was only eleven, too early for lunch, but that didn't matter. Natalie couldn't wait. "I'm leaving now. It'll take me fifteen minutes to get there. Bye."

I ran to the office. "Mrs. Martin. I'm taking my lunch break."

"Already?"

"Yes, ma'am."

"When will you be back?"

I smiled with more confidence than I felt. "By noon." Not. It would take me thirty minutes of driving time alone—more if I had to take Natalie home. An hour would be a stretch.

If I was lucky, they wouldn't notice.

I screeched into the arts center lot in record time, parked in the drop-off lane, and was out of the car seconds later. Jeff's truck wasn't there.

I saw a garden to the right of the building with a small brick patio at its center. Crepe myrtles provided shade and color.

Natalie was stomping back and forth on the lawn just beyond them. She muttered fractured phrases, her hands clenched at her sides.

The wide-eyed camp manager sat on a concrete bench. Micah was standing nearer to my stepsister, arms crossed, his back to me.

I detoured to his side. "How long has Natalie been like this?"

"About thirty minutes." He didn't look my way. Just kept monitoring her movements.

"Slow buildup or fast?"

"Fast. Seemed to come from nowhere."

"Have you been able to get the reason out of her?"

"No."

"Okay. Thanks." Fear pricked my skin, clawing for attention. *I don't want to do this.*

But I had to. She needed my confidence. She needed *me.*

I took a deep breath to gather my courage and don a detached mask, then circled past Micah to stand in her path. She halted, head bowed, fists thumping violently against her thighs.

"Natalie," I said, low and controlled.

No response. Just *thump, thump, thump.*

"Natalie. Will you look at me?"

She raised her gaze enough to stare at my chin. Although she remained silent, I had her attention.

"I'm here to listen. What do you want to say?"

She shook her head rapidly. Anxiety churned inside her, I knew, like a beast threatening to spew through her skin. I hated to see her hurting like this—

Stop. Focus. "Whenever you're ready, I'll be over by Micah." I backed out of her way.

She continued her pacing, although it had lost some speed. Marginally. Probably. At least I thought so.

The muttering resumed. She was reliving the moment. Or maybe debating within herself. Whichever it was, the dialogue was consistent. "Give me a break" and "How do you know?" drifted to us repeatedly in the humid heat of the morning.

Micah leaned closer to me. "How long does it take for her to . . . ?"

"Chill?" I exhaled an optimistic breath. For Natalie, her family was her best drug. "Now that I'm here, it shouldn't be much longer."

She was passing us for the dozenth time when she paused. Seconds passed as her fists opened and closed, then she executed a crisp ninety-degree turn and halted before our shoes bumped. "Ignoring jealous people doesn't work."

Outrage spasmed through me at her words. She flinched, as if she'd been blasted by the strength of my emotion.

Not helpful. I willed myself to let go of the anger. "What was the last thing she did before this happened?" I murmured to Micah.

"They were in their small groups."

"And before that?"

"The girls' ensemble was rehearsing 'Out of My Dreams.'"

Uh-huh. "Is that when you have your solo, Natalie?"

She gave a sharp nod and one last fist-thump against her thighs before her hands went still.

I wrestled with my emotions, trying not to scare her. I'd known it was possible for a cast member to set her off, but I hadn't expected it this soon, as if inside these walls, with the camp staff around, Natalie would be vaccinated against the petty crap. I glared at Micah, upset that he hadn't protected her, surprised that I'd thought it was even likely. He answered with a puzzled frown.

At some point, I'd have to find out exactly what had been said, but not now. I had to get her mind off the trigger, whatever it had been. "If you want, you can join me, Natalie." I walked to a shady spot near the low brick wall edging the patio and sat gingerly on the lawn.

She followed me and executed a figure-eight pattern of rapid steps, like a dog chasing its tail. It made me dizzy to watch her, but I wouldn't intervene.

The speed slowed to a crawl until finally she stopped. I didn't meet her eyes and simply remained where I was, allowing an eerie calm to steal over me. She plopped cross-legged onto the lawn before me, her knuckles covered in scratches.

I counted down from one hundred and scooted forward until our knees almost touched. "Better?"

"I'm sitting here. I'd say that's better than jabbering."

"Got it." She might get mad about the next question, but it had to be asked. "Do you need a pill?"

She shook her head, although her fists unfolded on her knees. "It's good that you're here."

"You knew one of us would come."

"Yes. Is it okay if we don't speak?"

"Sure." I sent an *I got this* look to Micah. He nodded his understanding, pointed at his watch, and jogged to the theater. The camp manager ran after him.

We'd been sitting quietly for several minutes when Jeff's truck rumbled into the lot and halted behind the Honda in the drop-off lane. His boots thudded in our direction.

He glanced at me before looking at Natalie. "How are things?"

"Okay," I said.

"Natalie?" he prompted.

She leapt up and slammed into his torso, her hands twisting in his shirt. His arms swooped around her, sheltering his little girl in a protective bubble. Her shoulders wobbled, as if her father's touch had left them loose and untethered.

"Would you like me to take you home?"

"Yes, Dad."

This was the closest thing to a normal reaction that he would ever see from her. It was heartbreaking that she embraced him only when she was at her worst.

"We'll leave now."

"Rehearsal isn't over." She trembled.

His face softened into an expression so loving it made tears well in my eyes. Jeff still looked like a battle-ready soldier— big, muscled, and tough, but he'd always been tender with his daughter.

Micah appeared out of nowhere. "Natalie, your part's done for today. Mom will work with the principals this afternoon. Everybody else will be rehearsing the choruses or playing games in their small groups. You can skip that if you want."

"Let's go, Dad."

My stepfather watched her take off at a run, stress evident in the rigid posture of his body. He shot an accusatory glance at me before following.

That look made me die a little inside. Not that he needed to make me feel bad. I was already drenched in guilt.

As I struggled to rise, a hand cupped my elbow. Once I was on my feet, I gave Micah a grateful smile. "Thanks."

His eyes met mine briefly before he turned and called to my stepfather. "Mr. Kane, can Brooke sign out Natalie?"

"Yes," Jeff tossed over his shoulder and hurried to join Natalie at the truck.

I waited until they'd pulled away to look at Micah. "Where do I sign her out?"

"Mom and I would like to talk to you first."

Dread clogged my throat. "Sure."

I walked beside him on unsteady legs, each new step harder than the last. Now that the storm had passed, reaction was beginning to set in. He held the door for me, and I entered the wonderful cool of the theater lobby. Within seconds, though, the shakes had taken over.

"Just a sec," I choked out as I wobbled over to a bench. Today's meltdown was only the sixth I'd witnessed, and the first I'd handled completely on my own. I braced my arms against my knees and fought the shudders that were threatening to take over my body.

"Hey, Brooke." Micah crouched before me. "You okay?"

"I will be." *Please let me hold it together in front of this guy.*

"You were great out there with her."

I tried to smile, but my mouth refused to cooperate.

"Do you want to be alone?"

"*No.*" Actually, I liked having him here. He didn't seem to be judging me. Just waited patiently. A solid presence whose composure I could absorb. "I'll be fine, if you'll give me a moment."

I concentrated on bringing myself under control. Calming my breathing. Willing the tremors to end. It took a couple of minutes before I reached the point where I could trust my legs again. "I'm ready."

He rose and offered me his hand. "You sure?"

"Yeah." I took his hand and let him pull me to my feet.

"Hey, if it helps, once Natalie knew you were on the way, her . . . anxiety leveled off."

"Thanks." It did help.

He matched his stride to mine, held the auditorium door for me, and led the way down the aisle to where Lisa sat, chewing on a pen. The stage was empty.

"Mom, this is Brooke. Natalie's stepsister."

With a sigh, Lisa stood and met my gaze full-on. "How is she?"

"My stepdad is taking her home. She was almost back to normal before they left."

"Elena says you had her settled down in under fifteen minutes."

The dread spread to my stomach. Where was this going? "I've done this before."

"We enjoy having your stepsister in the show, but today was a problem." She looked at Micah.

"Natalie usually does well with her counselor," he said, "but when the problem hit, she only responded to me. That was fine for once. Since we were near lunchtime, it was no trouble to adjust a few things in the schedule. But we might not be as lucky next time."

Lisa gestured dismissively with her hand. "Micah is being too nice. He was out of commission until you got here. We can't allow him to be monopolized."

I had to reassure them. "Natalie would've been okay by herself. She likes solitude."

Micah was shaking his head. "Not safe."

Lisa spoke over him. "The consequences of being wrong

about that are too serious to rely on. We have to create better alternatives. How often does Natalie have these meltdowns?"

"It's unpredictable. There has to be a trigger."

"Do you know what triggered this one?"

"Not for sure." How much could I say without breaking Natalie's confidence? "Another kid may have said something that hurt her feelings."

Micah crossed his arms. "Do you know who?"

I shook my head.

"If another cast member caused this, *I* can fix that." Micah's lips thinned into a grim line. "Is it always a person saying the wrong thing?"

"No." I wished that I didn't have to ask the next question. "What do you plan to do?"

Lisa glanced at her watch. "I'd rather not be the one to make that decision. We'll have to talk with Natalie's father. This afternoon, if possible." She strode away and disappeared through a door at the side of the stage.

I looked at Micah. "Should I have Jeff call you to schedule something?"

"Sure."

Okay, I had to know. "You won't make her quit, will you?"

"We don't want to, and I don't mind doing what I can for her, but . . ."

"You can't be monopolized."

"Yeah. I'm sorry."

Sorry about what? That Natalie had a meltdown? That he wouldn't be allowed to stay with her again? Or was his meaning more ominous?

· 9 ·

Intensely Personal

Mom, Jeff, and Natalie returned from the meeting with Lisa. No one was smiling.

Whatever they'd discussed, we had to make this okay. Natalie couldn't take any more trauma.

I sat silently at the table, hoping to figure out what had happened without asking questions. Natalie pressed against the window and stared into the yard. Jeff watched her, agitation evident in his jerky movements. Only Mom seemed relaxed as she set out cartons of Chinese food.

"We're ready to eat, Natalie."

"Not hungry."

"Why don't you come over and sit with us anyway? The camp staff needs a plan for the meltdowns in the morning, and I have to leave for a game soon."

Jeff shot Mom a hard look. Her chin lifted. She wasn't backing down.

Natalie crossed to the table. "I'm here now. What?"

Mom continued in a matter-of-fact tone, "Since the rehearsals can't pause and the staff can't suspend what they're doing,
your family needs to be available to show up."

"You mean Dad?" Natalie slid onto her chair.

"And me and Brooke." Mom's mouth tightened with hurt.
When she spoke again, her voice had grown husky. "It might
help you to recover if you knew we could be there quickly."

Natalie scrunched her face as she served herself rice and vegetables. "I agree. That could work."

"Maybe it would make you less likely to have one."

"No, it wouldn't do that." Natalie deftly scooped food with
her chopsticks and ate. At least she wasn't making idle promises.

"How many minutes is 'quickly'?" I asked.

"Ten," my stepsister barked out. She looked up to see our reaction.

Jeff glared at Mom again. "The construction site is thirty
miles away. I can't get here any sooner than forty-five minutes."

"We don't have to worry about the mornings," Mom said. "I
can cover most of them."

"What about after lunch?"

There was silence. We were all busy in the afternoons.

"Dad?" Natalie sounded panicky.

"I'll stay home tomorrow. I have some computer work to finish." He rubbed his head. "I could get the week of July fourth
off, but I don't know if I can manage more than that. It's a bad
time for me."

Natalie cast her eyes down and sucked her lips into her mouth
until they disappeared.

I touched my mother's arm. "You're usually at home until five."

Mom shook her head. "If my games are more than a hundred miles away, I leave midafternoon. I also have several overnight games coming up."

Natalie trembled. She knew it wasn't enough. Not for the show. Not for *her.* "Lisa will make me drop out."

"No, she won't," Jeff said. "Your director seems like a nice person. She won't make you quit."

"I can't disrupt anybody, I can't have Micah or Norah take care of me, and I can't be alone. So I'll have to stay where I'm visible, and I can't stand thinking the other campers might see me like that."

"Lisa says that theater kids think 'weird' is normal. They won't care."

"I will."

"Her son said you can use the staff lounge if you need solitude, and the camp manager would be across the hall. That would give you privacy."

"Elena got really distressed during my meltdown. That would make me worse. I do best when I'm around soothing people." Natalie stabbed a piece of chicken. "Maybe an empty room can work until one of you gets there."

I'd been sitting there like a lump, more of a spectator than a participant. It was my turn to try. "I'll talk to my boss. He might let me arrange my schedule so I can leave if there's an emergency."

"Raymond Wilson?" Jeff's lip curled. "He's not known for his flexibility."

I wouldn't let Jeff's skepticism bother me. "I'll ask. In the meantime, we have tomorrow handled, and we can decide the rest this weekend."

Natalie lurched away from the table. Seconds later, she exploded into the backyard, where she started an immediate conversation with herself in loud, forceful bursts.

Mom and Jeff stared at their plates. They weren't looking at me, but I knew what they were thinking.

The whole mess was my fault. If I hadn't told Natalie about *Oklahoma!* If I'd checked with Mom and Jeff first. If I'd simply thought it through instead of rushing in to "save" Natalie's summer. She would've been better off not knowing about the show, because now it was on the verge of being ruined.

I took a long shower, as hot as I could stand, and hoped it would rinse away how badly this day had gone. It didn't succeed.

After wrapping my hair in a towel and pulling on a robe, I returned to my room and stopped abruptly. Natalie was sitting cross-legged on the top of my bed, flipping through my scrapbook.

"Excuse me, what are you doing?" I ran over to yank it from her hands, but she held it out of my reach.

"Who is this man, and why do you have a drawing of him?"

I knew exactly who she meant, and I was *not* answering. "That's private. You don't have any right to look through my scrapbook."

She handed it to me. "Then you shouldn't have left it lying around."

"You had to walk in here to find it." Under my quilt. Out of view.

"The door was open."

"That doesn't matter." I crossed to my nightstand and shoved the scrapbook into the bottom drawer. Then I seethed at the wall. I couldn't face her, not when I was this furious. I'd never told anyone about my scrapbook. Not my mom. Not Kaylynn. Natalie had not only come in here and found it, she'd pawed through my most private thoughts. It was a . . . violation. "You can't walk into someone's bedroom and touch their things without permission."

"That's not the rule at my house. Closed doors denote *stay out*. Open doors are fair game."

I'd bet Mei kept all of the doors closed all of the time. "There are different rules here, and going into private places is definitely on the list."

"What counts as private in your house?"

If it were anyone but Natalie, I'd think she was being a jerk, but she didn't make up stuff like that. She really wasn't sure. Clutching my fists to my gut, I turned around. "All computers are private. All bedrooms are private, and Mom's home office and Jeff's workshop. Stay out unless you're invited in."

Her forehead creased, as if she was trying to concentrate. "Do phones count?"

"Um, yeah."

She dug into her pocket and tossed an object onto the bed. "There you are."

"Wait," I said, snatching it up. "That's my phone."

"If you look in your contacts, I've added two. Norah and Elena. You already had Micah." She snorted in exasperation. "Your birthday is not a good password."

Oh, no, she did not. I held in a scream, but it was a struggle. "Phones are off-limits to everyone except their owner."

"More rules. Do you want me to delete those phone numbers?"

"No, it makes sense to have them."

"I thought so, too." She went to the window and looked out.

What should I do next? Order her to leave and lock the door behind her? Change into shorts and go run for two miles? Kick something?

She'd taken over my house. Trashed my bathroom. Driven away my friends. Disrupted the relationships building in my family. And now . . . invaded my privacy. How much more could I take?

"Natalie, you can go," I said through gritted teeth.

She didn't respond. Not a muscle twitched. Something about the way she hunched against the window frame made me pause. I shifted until I could see her face. She was staring blankly ahead, her mouth slack. It had been a horrible day for her.

My anger faded. I'd have to bring this up again, but I would let it go tonight. "I'm listening if there's anything you want to say."

She shrugged and picked at a scab on her knuckle.

Since she hadn't refused, I'd keep pushing. Gently. "What was the trigger today? Is it how the other campers treat you?"

"They're tolerable," she said in a flat voice. "Nicer than people are at my school."

"Are the kids at school mean?"

"Not mean, exactly. I'd say that the way they treat me is peculiar. More like I'm a zoo animal than a person." A fist bounced against her leg. "I figured it out when I was visiting a primates exhibit once. People were staring at the gorilla, wondering what he would do next, hoping to be fascinated or creeped out. When he did something gross, they gasped and leaned closer. But when nothing more happened, they got bored and walked off." The fist-thumping ended. "All the gorilla wanted was to be left alone. Instead, he was caged and made to entertain people against his will. I felt sorry for him until I realized the cage protected *him*. Then I was jealous."

She was more aware of how people viewed her than I'd realized. "I'm sorry, Natalie."

"It's okay. If the gorilla has to be caged, at least he's in a beautiful habitat all his own. The masses come to see him. I think it's better to be alone and interesting than to be one more dreary person in a crowd." She faced me. "Who is the man in the drawing?"

I'd never told anyone this before, but she'd shared something intensely personal with me, and I wanted to take my turn. Strangely, though, I trusted her with my secret. "It's an artist's rendering of my biological father."

"The sperm donor?"

"Yeah."

"I thought you didn't know who he was."

"I don't. I handed over the information I'd collected to one of those police sketch artists, and she created that drawing for me."

"Very clever. Does Jill know?"

"No, and please don't tell her."

"I don't plan to." She wrinkled her nose. "Why did you care enough to go to the trouble?"

"I don't know."

"You probably do, but I can understand why you wouldn't want to analyze it." She shuffled across the room and dropped into the desk chair. "I'm ready. What else would you like to know about my meltdown?"

"You're okay talking about it?" She'd never been willing before. This was unexpected—and good.

"I offered, didn't I?"

I crawled onto my bed as I mentally organized my questions. I would start with an easy one. "How bad was it?"

"On a scale of one to five, I'd say a three."

"It seemed worse than that."

"You're my stepsister. You're destined to overestimate things about me."

My lips twitched. "That almost sounds like you're teasing."

Her tiny smile flashed so quickly that I nearly missed it. "Humor was the intention."

"Okay, next. Can you tell me how a meltdown feels?"

She tilted her head to stare at the ceiling. "Itchy. And *bad*. You get so mad at yourself, because you know the thing that set you off isn't worth the reaction you're having, but you can't control it. It's like . . . knocking over a cup of tea. It goes everywhere, staining as it spreads, but you can't take it back. You just have to get over yourself and mop up the mess."

Life felt the same way to me sometimes. "You haven't told me what exactly caused today's meltdown."

"Must we go into that?" Her tone said that she knew we did.

"We must."

"I can't overlook what people say about my voice."

"What about it?"

"The girl next to me in the chorus said that I sing my line too loud, and it doesn't sound good."

Frustration tickled in my throat. The whole miserable day had been triggered by a cast member butting herself into some-

thing that wasn't her business. "If it bothered the music director, she would've told you."

"I said the same thing. The girl didn't mention it again, but
I couldn't stop worrying about whether she was right."

"Who was it?"

"Why do you want to know?"

"If I know who it was, I can decide how to handle it."

"Involving adults rarely helps and usually makes things
worse."

I couldn't argue with that. "If I promise not to involve an
adult, will you give me a name?"

"Tesla."

Uh-huh. Tesla had played a role in the high school's spring
musical. She must be upset that an unknown had gotten a solo
line while she was stuck in the chorus. But she wasn't someone
I thought of as being mean. Maybe she'd been having a bad day,
too.

Maybe what she'd said about Natalie's voice had been true.
I hoped not. "I'll think of something."

"If she retaliates . . ."

"She won't. She's usually a nice person."

Natalie's chin lowered until she could see me. "You realize,
of course, it'll be something else that sets me off next time."

"Is there anything you can do to prevent your feelings from
getting out of control?"

"The *Hamilton* soundtrack can sometimes neutralize a slow-
building attack. The lyrics are engrossing and take me outside
myself. My psychologist wants me to think about waves wash-
ing up on the beach, but that doesn't work as well as she hoped.

And my meds always solve it, but I don't like the idea of getting addicted."

Her voice shook on the word *addicted*. Like it was major fear of hers. Maybe I should ask Jeff why that worried her so much. For now, preventing a meltdown from ever happening seemed like the best option. "Lisa said that you didn't want anyone to help you except Micah."

"He's the only one I completely trust."

"What about Norah?"

"She's nice, too. But . . ." Natalie shrugged. "I just get along better with males. They don't judge as much. And Micah says there are kids on the autism spectrum in the theater department at his high school, so he understands." She pinched her knuckles. "Do you think I should quit?"

"*No.*" I shook my head firmly. "Lisa told me that she enjoys having you in the show. She wouldn't have said so unless it was true."

"But we don't have a solution for emergencies yet."

"Your family will figure something out. Like we said. Everything will be fine."

"Do you think your boss will let you help me?"

I flicked off my bedside lamp. Some truths were best told in the dark. "I'm afraid he'll say no."

· 10 ·

Expected and Dreaded

My first project Friday morning was to tackle my boss. I went to his office and stood in the doorway, ignoring the flutter of nerves. "Mr. Wilson?"

"Hmm?" He sat behind his chrome desk, frowning at his iPad.

"May I ask a favor about my schedule?"

His gaze remained on the screen. "Go ahead."

"I have to be on call in the afternoons. To check on my stepsister."

He looked up. "I didn't know she was here."

Interesting. Kaylynn hadn't told him. What else hadn't she mentioned? "Natalie's living with us for the summer."

He folded his hands on the desk, his complete attention on me now. "What's the problem?"

"Natalie has a health issue. It would be best if she has someone who can check in with her in the afternoons."

"Not the mornings?"

"My mom's available in the mornings."

"Will your stepsister require help every day?"

"It won't be that often." The expression on his face didn't look promising. "Probably not every week."

"But it's possible."

"Yes, sir."

He picked up a pen and tapped it against the desk. "Could you fit one of these checks into your afternoon break?"

"I would need closer to an hour." Only in the most optimistic of circumstances would that be true.

"One of your main duties is to replace other staff who aren't available, which requires that you be in the store."

"If Natalie needed me, I could call that my lunch break."

"Is it predictable when you'd go?"

"No, sir."

"We can't plan our whole schedule around the possibility that you have to leave for an hour at a moment's notice. It's not fair to the other staff. I'm sorry, but the answer is no." He bent over his computer.

I went to my desk and perched on the edge of my chair, hands in my lap, staring at the bouquet of fresh flowers that Della had left there. They were pretty and, most days, they would've made me smile. But not today. When Natalie got home this afternoon, she'd ask for the verdict, and she would hear the answer that she expected and dreaded.

I put my hands on the keyboard and logged in to the computer. There was an email from Mr. Wilson. I clicked on the attachment and began to read, but thoughts of my stepsister wouldn't let me go. I could just imagine her reaction. There would be a flash of alarm in her eyes, and her face would go blank. She'd obsess over how it would feel to be alone in a staff lounge, trying not to explode, unsure if it would be ten minutes or an hour before her family rescued her.

Natalie would use the word *quit* again and mean it.

I refocused on the computer screen and the attachment. Mr. Wilson had downloaded website data from Google Analytics, and he wanted me to play around with it to look for patterns. I would enjoy this project.

My hands slipped back to my lap as anguish shivered through me. We'd have our trembling puppy back, and it would be my fault. I couldn't let that happen to Natalie. Not this summer. Definitely not today.

I would beg my boss again—this time with a schedule he could count on. I stood, smoothed my skirt, and returned to his office. "I'm sorry to disturb you, Mr. Wilson."

"What is it now?"

"Could I work part-time? Mornings only?"

He sighed. "My staff have their vacations planned. I need you to cover for them, which means you have to be in the store nine to five."

"I know, but—"

"Brooke." He frowned. "Do you want this job? Yes or no?"

I did want the job, but I wanted to help Natalie, too.

Two thousand dollars. That's the income I could be giving up if I quit. Maybe I should take the weekend to brainstorm other ideas.

Wait, no. I didn't have to think through this any further. Natalie needed to count on her family more than I needed this job. I was a hard worker. I would find something else.

I'd barely earned enough this week to cover the clothes I'd bought, but that was the way it would have to be. "The answer is no. I'll resign."

"Pardon?"

"I want to help my stepsister, even if it means I quit."

His lips thinned. "I'm disappointed in you, Brooke. I gave you the job because Kaylynn said you were the most responsible teenager she knew. I would've expected you to show more professionalism." He dismissed me with a wave of his hand. "There's no need to stay any longer. Go ahead and pack your things. I'll have a check ready before you leave."

I walked home from the store and climbed the steps to the veranda. When Mom bought this house, it had been an eighty-year-old fixer-upper on a big, overgrown yard. The veranda had sold us.

Sagging onto the glider, I closed my eyes. I'd had a tough morning. A few moments out here might make it better.

A barking dog nudged me from my stupor. Okay, not better. I rose and entered the house. Hearing voices drift from the kitchen, I walked back there and stuck my head in.

Jeff had his tablet propped on the counter and his phone against his ear. "I understand," he was saying. "I'll check on it and let you know. Certainly. Good-bye." He set his phone down and eyed me curiously. "Did you come home for an early lunch?"

I shook my head.

Mom glanced over from the stove, then set down her spoon. "Is anything wrong?"

"I quit my job."

"What?" They spoke in unison.

"I asked Mr. Wilson if I could work part-time or be on call in the afternoons. He said no to both. So I resigned." I turned around, not wanting to see their reactions. "I'll be in my room, if you need anything."

Running footsteps caught up with me in the foyer. Mom's arms wrapped around me and so did her scent. "Are you sure?"

"Yes."

"You're giving up your—"

"I *know*." I couldn't talk about it yet. Or ever.

"Oh, honey. You make me proud." She kissed my cheek and ran back to the kitchen.

Upstairs, I went into my closet and stripped off the mini-Della outfit that I would never wear again. I would put a trip to Target on the schedule this weekend and try to return the stuff I hadn't worn yet. After changing into shorts and a T-shirt, I stretched out on my bed. It felt unreal, what I'd done. The kind of thing a badass heroine might do in a movie. I didn't feel bad-ass, though. More like something numb that was awakening painfully. I stared hot-eyed at the wall, hating that I'd been forced into this choice.

What did I do next?

It was odd to have a summer with nothing planned. I wasn't sure what to do. I'd never been much on hobbies. I liked working. No, what I really liked was earning a paycheck.

I had to think about the money.

Scooting to the edge of my bed, I opened the bottom drawer in the nightstand, pulled out my scrapbook, and flipped to the page with the amount I still needed to earn to buy a car. Mr. Wilson had given me a check for three hundred and thirty dollars.

~~6300~~
5970

I'd never been so discouraged about my chances for buying a car.

There was a knock at the door. I closed the scrapbook and slipped it behind my pillows. "Come in."

Jeff opened the door. "What you did today means a lot to me."

"It's fine." *My fault. My solution.*

"It's huge. You gave up your job for Natalie. I can't . . ." He pressed his lips together and looked at the floor.

Okay, I was really uncomfortable with where this conversation was headed. I had to get him out of here before we both got emotional. "She deserves a good summer."

"You do, too." He looked up. "Would you let us pay you?"

"For what?"

"Babysitting."

Blinking against the sting in my eyes, I bowed my head. "She's my family. It's not babysitting."

He came into the room and paused at the foot of the bed, close enough that I got the faintest whiff of his aftershave. "Thank you, Brooke."

I didn't look up. "Sure."

He shifted awkwardly, as if he had more to say. I should let him. But when I raised my eyes, he was already walking away. He shut the door behind him with a soft click.

I hadn't wanted thanks, but it was nice that he'd tried.

Hesitating in the Shadows

Mom made me and Jeff grilled cheese sandwiches. The best kind of comfort food. If it was supposed to make me feel better, it succeeded.

After lunch, things got quiet fast. Mom grabbed an overnight bag and ran out to her carpool. Now that I was around to cover for Natalie, Jeff left for the construction site.

There was nothing on TV that interested me. I was too restless to stream anything from Netflix. And it was too hot to go for a run.

The silence drove me from the house. I flopped into the hammock, but it was too hot for that, too. I ended up in the Honda and found myself driving to the arts center.

When I walked in the rear of the auditorium, six cast members were sitting on the edge of the stage. Lisa perched against a small table in front of the first row, talking in a quiet, insistent voice. Micah sat behind the table, writing in a big black binder.

I stepped into the back row and dropped onto the thickly cushioned seat. As if he felt my presence, Micah whipped around, met my gaze, and faced forward again. Touching his mother's shoulder, he spoke in her ear, then walked this way. I was his destination.

"Are you here for Natalie?"

"Yes."

"She's doing great today."

"Is it okay if I wait here for her?"

His brow creased. "There are three more hours until she's done."

"I don't mind."

"Then—"

"Micah?" Someone spoke from behind me.

"Yes, Elena?"

"The seamstress wants to know if she can measure for costumes on Wednesday afternoon instead of Tuesday morning."

"That works. After two."

The camp manager hurried past us down the aisle and disappeared through a door at the side of the stage. I looked back at Micah, intrigued. He hadn't checked a schedule or hesitated. Just agreed and moved on. That kind of confidence was hot.

He frowned at my expression. "What?"

"Do you really run everything?"

"I don't direct the actors."

"But everything else?"

He nodded grudgingly.

"What are you doing at the table with your mom?"

"Taking dictation mostly, and I need to get back. You can stay."

I smiled with relief. "Thanks."

Micah called the afternoon break at three. As everyone on the stage scattered, he rose and went through a side door. Lisa slumped in her seat, her sigh audible from a dozen rows away.

Would it be okay to disturb her? She should be told that we had a solution for Natalie, only it didn't seem fair to intrude on her thoughts. How often did she get to do nothing?

I was wasting my chance, though. It was quiet, with no one around to distract or overhear. I walked down the aisle and waited until she glanced my way. "I'm Brooke. Natalie's stepsister."

"I remember. How can I help you?"

"Her problem is solved. I'm available now."

Micah reappeared and set two water bottles on the table. "What did I miss?"

Lisa gestured toward me. "It sounds as if she's the backup plan for Natalie."

His eyes widened. "You're free? All the time?"

I nodded.

"Your boss is okay with that?"

"I don't have a boss anymore."

"Did you quit?"

"Yes." I flinched at the question. I ought to be used to that word already, but wasn't there yet. "Would I be allowed to come down here occasionally? I'm not an adult." *At least, not for another five months.*

"Sure, it's okay." Micah opened his water bottle and took a swig.

Lisa's face had taken on a calculating look. "Do you have anything else lined up for the summer?"

"Not really."

"*Mom.*" His tone held a warning.

"You're the one who suggested getting an assistant. It wasn't my idea. Well, asking Brooke is." Her head tilted as she considered me. "Natalie says you've been working in an office."

Four days' worth. That counted. "Yes."

"How would you like to be our assistant for the show? It's mostly clerical stuff . . ."

He hissed in frustration.

". . . and it would eliminate some of the noise for Micah and me."

Lisa was offering me a job. Excitement flared at the thought of being involved, but I needed details. "Would I be paid?"

"No, it's a volunteer position."

Disappointing, but not a deal breaker. Yet. "What are the hours?"

"We can be flexible, although I prefer the same hours as the campers."

Flexibility was great. But nine to five? That would make my job search harder. "What are the duties?"

"Anything we ask." She ticked items off her fingers. "Sit behind me and take notes. Keep me supplied with water. Deliver messages that we can't say over the headset. Run errands for both of us."

"It would include a few more things than that," Micah said.

My excitement dimmed at his attitude. "I'm trainable."

"I'm sure you are." He flipped through the binder to a section marked SCHEDULE. "Actually, I agree that this makes sense. I can focus more on the blocking, and Brooke will have a valid excuse to be in the arts center. None of the other campers would question it, if Natalie would worry about that."

His agreement wasn't exactly enthusiastic, but he was right. Being a volunteer assistant could work well—for all of us. It wasn't the same thing as earning money, but I could still claim the experience on my résumé. Probably I should think harder about this, but I wouldn't because I wanted to do it. I nodded at Lisa. "I accept."

"Wonderful. Can you stay till five-thirty today? There's a production team meeting every afternoon after the campers leave. We could introduce you to the others. Then plan to be here each morning by eight, or earlier if Micah asks."

Wow. Five seconds after accepting and the demands had already started. "I'll be there."

"Oh, and Brooke? We don't have time for *please* and *thank you* around here. We simply work hard. A spectacular show is the only reward you get."

After my first production team meeting, I couldn't find Natalie inside the building. When I walked out to the parking lot, she was waiting by the Honda. After I told her my news, she stared from the car window, saying nothing as we drove home. But as I ran up the stairs and into my bedroom, she was right behind me, nearly kicking my heels.

"Did you quit your job because of me?"

I should've prepared for an inquisition, but I hadn't. "It was mostly because Mr. Wilson couldn't give me any flexibility."

Her face tightened. "Am I the reason you volunteered for the show?"

"I'm the director's assistant because Lisa asked me."

"We've already discussed this, Brooke. I like the truth. I like facts. When you tell me something but word it to mislead me so that I won't completely get it? I hate that."

"Got it. No misleading words."

"Am I the reason you quit?"

"Yes."

"Are you in the show to be near me?"

I sat on the bed beside Tigger and scratched his chin. "I'm actually looking forward to the job but, yes, you're the reason."

"Am I a burden?"

It was more complicated than a yes/no kind of answer. "Some."

"You mean yes."

"Being a burden doesn't have to be a bad thing."

"Tell that to Nai Nai."

Oh, wow. Natalie's grandmother wasn't a nice woman. I had experience with that, too. Fortunately, I could say with all honesty that Natalie's grandmother was wrong. I scooped my cat into my arms. "Tigger is amazing and irritating. He hides from me when I want him and curls up around me when I don't. He has fish breath, and his trips to the vet are expensive. Tigger's a burden, and I don't care. I love him anyway. If he were easy, he wouldn't be as much fun."

Natalie rolled her eyes, but her shoulders weren't hunched anymore. "As an analogy, that wasn't so great, especially the part about fish breath."

"I irritate you, too."

"True."

"Am I a burden to you?"

"Okay, you can stop now. I get your point." She darted from the room, then returned immediately, hesitating in the shadows of the hallway. "I won't mind having you there."

· 12 ·

The Simple Answer

I babysat for the Thomas twins on Saturday morning, then drove over to Target to take back the clothes I hadn't worn. When I returned, I followed a delicious smell to the kitchen. Natalie was frowning at the oven.

"Has Mom come home yet?" I asked.

"An hour ago. She said last night's game continued until midnight, and they didn't get to the hotel until one. She's taking a nap now."

I crossed to stand next to Natalie and peered through the window of the oven. There was a glass dish covered in aluminum foil. "Do you know what that is?"

"Yes, since I made it."

"*You* did?"

"I watched this *Five Ingredients or Less* show on the Food Network yesterday. When I said I'd like to try this one, Dad bought what I needed. Chicken, cream of mushroom soup, a bag of mixed vegetables, and crescent-roll dough. Except I added salt and pepper, so really six ingredients."

"Sounds good."

"It will be. It's ready to come out." She gestured at me. "Can you get it?"

I found two pot holders and lifted the dish from the oven. "I thought you didn't cook."

"I don't, but I like to bake. Ovens only. No stove tops."

"Nice to know." As I was setting the pan on the table, the side door opened and Jeff walked in. His clothes were saturated with grime and sweat.

Natalie pointed at the casserole dish. "I made chicken pot pie, Dad."

His smile held pride. "Great. I'll wash up." He backtracked into the utility room.

"Here's another house rule," I said as I set the table. "The cook or baker never has to clean the dishes."

"Why?"

"You did your share of the chores by preparing the food."

"I like that rule a lot."

Jeff laughed as we both slid into our seats and filled our plates.

Lunch was quiet. My stepfather made a few halfhearted attempts at conversation but gave it up to focus on the pot pie, which was so good that it rated complete attention. When we were done, Natalie disappeared down the hallway. Jeff collected the dishes and crossed to the dishwasher. I carried the pot pie to the stove and covered it with foil.

"Brooke?"

I looked over my shoulder. "Yes, sir?"

"Your mom and I . . ." He swallowed. "This week has been hard, and you've been great. We've noticed, and we're grateful."

I nodded, warmed by the praise, not sure how to respond.

"Go on. I've got this." He bent over the dishwasher.

When I went up to my room, Natalie was thumping and singing next door, practicing her role and everybody else's. I gave her an hour, then knocked on her door. "Interested in going to a ball game today?"

"Jill has another one?"

"Mom has games most nights. This one starts at four."

"Is today's game special?"

"It's Mom's turn to be the plate umpire." The Sandhill Egrets were the home team. I was hoping that didn't add to the specialness. "She's in control of the game."

"People have to do whatever Jill says?"

"They do."

"Okay. I'll go."

Mom drove. Natalie rode shotgun, talking nonstop the whole way to the field, with Mom chuckling often. I sat in the back and watched the farmland and forest change over to housing developments and strip shopping centers.

We arrived forty-five minutes before game time. As we were walking in, the home team was heading toward their dugout. Several of them stopped and watched us pass. It was hard to know who they were staring at. Me, because they knew who I was. Or my stepsister, because she was beautiful.

While Mom disappeared into the press box, Natalie and I went to the snack bar. Armed with junk food, we searched for seats in the half-filled stands. I found a great spot near the top, directly behind home plate. As we wiggled into place, the two umpires were walking to the field. Mom spoke, and Steven listened.

Natalie's hand stilled in her bag of popcorn. "Does that man have to do what Jill says?"

"He's responsible for making most of the calls on the field. Since Mom's behind the plate tonight, she's the final authority on any disputes. But that's rarely necessary. Mom and Steven call games together all the time, and they're both really good."

It was the bottom of the first inning when I noticed a ballplayer from the home team on deck, waiting his turn to bat, smirking at me. I knew who he was. I called him Jerkface. Everyone else called him Finley.

When the current batter struck out, Finley took his place and got into his stance.

The first pitch screamed past. Mom called a strike.

Finley stepped out of the batter's box and gave her a disgusted look.

"Why's he acting that way?" Natalie asked.

"He thinks she's calling them inside."

"Which means . . . ?"

"When the pitcher throws the ball, the batter is supposed to hit it if he can. But to give him a fair shot, the ball has to be over the plate and between the player's chest and knees. Mom's calling them right over the inner edge of the plate."

"So that's correct?"

"They look like strikes to me, but this guy doesn't agree."

"Will he say anything to her?"

"He'd better not. It never ends well for a player when he voices an opinion to the ump."

Finley struck out. Inning over. He shrugged angrily and strutted to the dugout.

Natalie demanded to know every detail and nuance for the first half hour. Then she lost interest until the visiting team got a two-run homer in the fifth inning. That perked her up.

The home team got their turn. When Finley stepped into the batter's box, the bases were loaded, and the tension was high. He grinned at the crowd, ready to hit his teammates in and be the hero.

Here came the first pitch.

"Strike."

The batter stepped back and muttered. His words weren't audible, but the tone was. The fans behind home plate grumbled. I shook my head uneasily.

"Get back in the box, Finley," Mom said.

He did as she asked, took a practice swing, and got ready.

"Strike."

The catcher laughed and said something. The batter responded with manly attitude.

Mom said, "Enough."

Natalie nudged me hard in the side. "What's happening?"

"Apparently, Finley is upset about her strike zone. The catcher is probably trash-talking him and making him madder." I blew out an anxious breath. "I don't like the way this is going."

The batter stepped to the plate. The next pitch screamed past, over the inside edge.

"Strike."

Jerkface used his bat to draw a line in the dirt, about an inch from the plate.

"Ohmigod," I said as the crowd fell into a shocked silence.

"Finley," his coach roared.

Natalie smacked my thigh. "What?"

Mom pointed at the batter and flung her hand in an arc toward the parking lot.

All sorts of things happened at once. Noise exploded from the stands. Laughter, applause, and gasps. The catcher jogged to the pitcher's mound. Finley's coach raced for home plate.

With an apparent lack of concern, Mom reached into her pocket and drew out her lineup card to jot down her decision.

"What did that mean?" Natalie asked.

"Drawing a line in the dirt is Finley's immature way of telling Mom she's a bad umpire. It's disrespectful, both to her and to baseball. So she's ejected him."

"He can't play anymore?"

"Not in this game."

Finley's face flushed to a shade of red so dark that it nearly glowed. He thumped his bat against the ground.

The other umpire trotted toward Mom.

"Come on, Finley," the coach shouted as he skidded to a stop beside his player. "Now."

But the idiot wasn't listening. Instead, he spoke too softly to hear in the stands but Mom could.

Shifting her body enough to lock her gaze on the coach, she said in a low, lethal voice, "Coach, you have one minute to get him out of this park, or you'll forfeit the game." Turning her back on the player, she sauntered over to Steven and began a conversation.

The coach practically pushed Finley off the field.

Finley's team won without him.

Mom disappeared into the ump's locker room, emerging five minutes later in a fresh T-shirt, the same sweaty uniform pants, and her gear gripped in one hand. She gestured for us to head to the parking lot. "You can drive home, Brooke." She tossed her things into the backseat, got in, and buckled up.

The ejection must've upset her more than she was letting on. She rarely allowed me to drive if she was in the car.

Natalie immediately blasted into obsessive questions about this new interest. "How did that feel, Jill? To throw a guy out?"

"Not good." Mom sounded tired.

"You had the power."

"Having power isn't always fun."

I checked on her from the rearview mirror. She had her head thrown back and eyes closed.

"Did it scare you?" Natalie asked.

"A little, but Steven and the coach were right there. The player would've had a hard time getting near me."

"What if he had? What if he'd touched you?"

"That would be assault. He could've spent the rest of the season in jail."

Natalie opened her mouth to say more, but I waved for her to stop. She shrugged and stared out the window, into the darkness. Not another word was said for the rest of the drive.

Jeff was waiting on the veranda when we pulled into the driveway. He stood as we walked up the steps, his smile dying when he read Mom's face.

His gaze shifted to Natalie. "What did you think about the game?"

"It was interesting. For one time."

He nodded at me as he extended a hand to my mom. She clutched him like a lifeline. When he pulled her to his side, she seemed to melt against his body. Without saying a word, they entered the house, wrapped around each other.

"What's that about?" Natalie frowned after them.

This was the way I loved to see the two of them. Communicating without words. Comfort given and received. "Jeff's very good at knowing when Mom's worn out."

"If she's tired, does she want him around?"

"Oh, yeah. She does." After the tension of the past week, it was wonderful to see them in sync.

I got up Sunday with one major goal for the day. Since I'd quit the job that should've paid for my car, I would have to find another source of income. Before launching another job search, though, I ought to reassess my available skills. I already claimed that I could do website updates, spreadsheets, and image editing on my résumé. From the jewelry store, I could add official experience with WordPress and a database, although a week wasn't much. But still . . . more than nothing.

Now, a reality check. Without reliable transportation, I couldn't get a job outside of biking distance. With the heat picking up, biking to a job would get increasingly less manageable. Smells were an issue.

Schedule could be a problem, too. For the next month, I had

to be at the theater every weekday until five p.m. or later. There weren't many paying jobs for teens in this area anyway, and my available hours weren't great. Any decent after-five job options had been snapped up long ago.

Food service would be an exception. I could do that, but standing on my feet all evening after nine hours in the theater wouldn't be pleasant. I would put it down as a last resort.

Babysitting was still an option. I'd let my regular families know that I was free again in the evenings.

With my limitations, the prospects didn't look good. I would have to widen the list of possibilities. The ideal job would allow me to work from home, on a schedule I set, without anyone caring how I dressed or smelled. I needed to explore internet options. While I'd never considered crowd-sourcing jobs before, I would now with an open mind and my creep-radar turned on full blast.

I'd been scouring the internet for an hour when my stepfather's tread went past my door. I called, "Jeff, I need your opinion."

His presence filled my room. "What can I do for you?"

"Look at this." I pointed at my laptop.

He dragged a chair closer and peered at the screen. "Catch me up."

I loved when he spoke like that. Businesslike. Treating my concerns seriously. "I'm looking for a job."

"To do what?"

"Whatever I can get. Office work. Maintaining websites. Data entry in Excel." I pointed to some online ads that I might respond to. "Like these."

His gaze went to the screen, lingered for a few seconds, and returned to me. "Why are you doing this?"

"For the money."

"Is this about the car?"

"Yes, sir." No reason to lie. I hadn't given up.

He eyed me thoughtfully. "I'm in a bind with my business. What would you think about working for me?"

Interest spiked. Work for Jeff *and* actually earn money? Sounded about perfect. "Sure, if I can. What do you need?"

"I've just bid on a pair of terrain mapping projects. If I win them, it'll be more than I can handle alone, so I'm hiring a retired Army buddy of mine. I've started on the paperwork, and it's taking too much of my time. I didn't realize how many forms there would be."

"Do we file online or in person?"

"Some of both. The process has ten steps. I shut down after two."

"I would definitely consider working for you." *As in*, yes. *No further thinking necessary.* Could he hear how happy I was?

"Good. Tomorrow night, I could show you, and you can make your decision then. The Small Business Administration site has a checklist that we can review." His smile was hesitant. "I'd have to pay minimum wage."

"But I could count on extreme flexibility in my schedule. Right?"

"Whatever you want, as long as we meet our deadlines." He rubbed the back of his head. "If I could, I would give you the car, but I can't do it right now."

He would? That was unexpected. And sweet. And a bit overwhelming. I looked away from him, my gaze landing on the computer screen. "I'd like to earn it anyway."

"Fair enough. Give my offer some thought, and we'll talk tomorrow." He left.

I had managed Mom's tutoring business for years, so I had decent familiarity with the legalities of being self-employed. But it had just been her. No staff. I started searching for information about hiring new employees. Jeff would show me again, but it couldn't hurt to already understand what I was facing. If I worked fast and did this project well, maybe he'd find other things for me to do.

After my shower, I was returning to my bedroom when I heard Kaylynn's ringtone. I raced for the nightstand and picked up the phone. "Hi." I flopped onto my bed, so glad that she'd called.

"Hi. How are things?" Her voice didn't have its usual happy bounce.

"Good." Did she miss me? I missed her. We had to find a way to fix this. "Everything okay?"

"We went to the beach house this weekend."

The trip that she and I had planned together. I tried to think of something to say, but my mind was feeling kind of thick and sloppy. "That sounds like fun."

"Um, Daddy says you quit."

"I did." Here was the real point of the call. Weirdly, I'd forgotten. Even though I'd resigned only two days ago, I'd put it behind me, and that's where I wanted it to stay.

"Is Natalie the reason?"

"Yes."

"Because?"

"Mom and Jeff are gone a lot. It's better to have someone available for her."

"She's had another meltdown, and you're afraid she'll have more."

I didn't say anything, although my silence confirmed it.

"Thought so. You're sacrificing for her again, and she won't even notice." Kaylynn sighed. "I knew it was something like this, so I talked to Daddy. He said you were doing great work on the computer, and he's willing to reconsider. If you'd prefer the mornings only, he'll find someone else for the afternoons."

"Wow, that's nice." Mr. Wilson could be pretty stubborn, so this was generous of him, although it was too late to accept. "I have to turn him down, but tell your dad thanks."

"What? Why?"

"I have a new job." Two, actually, but I wasn't ready to go into the details.

"Already?"

"Yeah. It starts tomorrow."

She snorted. "Doing what?"

No need for her to get like that. I couldn't have predicted her father would take me back. "I'm volunteering at the theater camp."

"For no pay." Her voice was tight. "I asked Daddy to hire you. Twice."

"I appreciate that, but you should've checked with me first."

"I didn't want to raise your hopes if it didn't work out."

A solid decision, but she wasn't going to make me feel guilty for not reading her mind. She didn't speak, and neither did I. Instead, we sat there, listening to each other fume. Somebody had to break through the standoff. Guess that should be me. "Can we hang out this week? I'll be free after five."

"I switched some shifts with another lifeguard, so I'm on in the evenings."

"Every night?"

She hesitated. "I have one night off, but I've got a date."

I waited for more information, but none came. "How about next weekend?"

"Sylvie and I were thinking about hitting a spa on Sunday."

Natalie hated spas. This outing avoided issues all around. "A mani-pedi sounds good. I don't have any plans."

"Okay, I'll text you after I get the reservation. Bye."

I ended the call, then tossed my phone onto the nightstand.

A sound from the hall caught my attention. "Were you talking to Kaylynn?"

"Yes." What had Natalie heard this time? My side of the conversation couldn't have been that bad.

"Would her dad have given your job back?"

The simple answer was yes, but the truth was that I was happy with the change in plans. I was looking forward to volunteering at the theater, and I loved the idea of working for Jeff and earning income again. "It's no big deal, Natalie."

She shook her head and went into her room. The lock snapped into place.

Wow. I didn't know Natalie's reason for being upset, and I didn't care about Kaylynn's. But I was getting tired of having everything I did right turn out wrong.

· 13 ·

Mysterious but Essential

Choosing clothes to wear to the arts center was harder than finding an outfit for the jewelry store. Nearly everything in my closet met the camp's dress code, which made my decision worse. Did I want to look good? Be comfortable? Would anyone even notice? I glanced at the clock. It was almost time to leave the house, and I was running late. On the first day of my new, unpaid job.

Denim shorts, my favorite sandals, and a Durham Bulls T-shirt. Cute and casual. The only thing left to do was face and hair. I adjourned to the bathroom and pondered the possibilities.

There was a knock at the door as it opened. "Ready?" Natalie asked.

"No, and you shouldn't walk into an occupied bathroom unless the person inside says it's okay."

"Whatever. I think makeup is a waste of your time."

I scowled. "Sometimes, you should just say nothing."

"I said that wrong. You weren't supposed to take offense."

My hands stilled on my makeup bag. "Go on."

Her face joined mine in the mirror. "When you're already pretty enough and you put on makeup anyway, it's like you're trying too hard."

"Thanks. I guess." Okay then. No makeup today, since I didn't need it.

While I was whipping my hair into a high ponytail, Mom called up the stairs, "Girls, let's go."

I posed for Natalie. "How am I?"

"Fine, except you have to lose the shoes."

"Why?"

"No open-toe shoes in the theater. Not safe. Micah's particular about safety."

I ran to my closet, rummaged around for a pair of running shoes, tossed them into my backpack, and trailed Natalie down the stairs.

We'd just been dropped off when Micah and his mom pulled into a parking spot. Lisa hurried past us, so deeply lost in her thoughts that I doubted she saw us. He detoured in our direction.

"Hey, Natalie."

"What's on today's schedule?"

He reached into his backpack and pulled out a sheet of paper. "Here's the plan."

She snatched it from him, frowning as she read.

"Can you post it for me in the campers' lounge?" he asked.

"Yes." She took off for the building.

His gaze swept me from head to toe and lingered on my sandals. "You can't wear those backstage."

And good morning to you, too. "I have a pair of running shoes in my backpack. I'll change inside."

"That works."

We entered the building together, not saying anything, which was okay with me. I was strangely nervous. I expected to do well at this job, so why was I worried? Anything I did for them would be a bonus.

"I'll show you around first, starting back here."

Micah unlocked a door at the rear of the auditorium and ushered me into a small, raised room. It held all kinds of electronic equipment and had a huge window that gave us a clear view of the stage.

"We call this the booth. It's where we control sound and lights. During the performances, this is where I'll spend most of my time, running the show."

"Where will I be spending most of my time?"

"For now, with my mom. If she runs out of things for you to do, find me." He preceded me from the booth, locked the door behind me, and led the way past some curtains at the front. "I only have twenty minutes before I have to set up the stage. We'll tour backstage while I explain the rules."

"Sure."

"Rule number one. Safety first." He pointed at my feet. "You have to put the other shoes on before we go any farther."

I lowered myself onto a long, low black box, only to have him grasp my arm and haul me up again. I glanced at him, startled. "What?"

"Rule number two. If you don't know what it is, don't touch it."

"Okay." I shifted to a stool behind a stack of ropes and changed shoes.

The tour roared past in a blaze of information. Micah guided me through a maze of hallways, explaining what the different rooms were used for. Happily, they had their purpose painted on the doors. He reintroduced the other members of the production team as we came across them and filled in the details of what they did. Every chance he got, he threw in more safety rules.

He gestured at a ladder. "I'm big on safety."

"I've already noticed."

"It's best not to climb ladders at all, but if you must, have a spotter around. Always."

I hid a smile. Would he tell me not to run with scissors next? "Yes, sir."

"Never lift anything without work gloves on."

"You don't have to worry about me lifting anything heavier than a pencil."

His lips twitched. "Never move stuff around without the tech director's instructions."

"Got it."

"No running backstage, no playing with power tools, no painting without ventilation."

I exhaled loudly. "Are we done yet?"

"Almost. We'll make a stop by the camp office. You can leave your backpack in there, if you want."

He walked over to a closed door, knocked once, and entered. It was a tiny room, with little more than a desk, filing cabinet, computer, and printer. The camp manager spun around in her chair and gave Micah a big smile.

"Elena, do you remember Brooke?"

She directed her big smile at me. "Natalie's stepsister."

Micah nodded. "Since you missed the production meeting Friday, you might not have heard that Brooke's volunteered to be the director's assistant."

While she and I were saying hi to each other, Micah crossed to the cabinet and dragged open a drawer. When he turned back to me, he held a headset.

"You can monitor what's going on in the theater with this. May I?" At my nod, he slid the headset onto my head and adjusted it over my ear, his fingers brushing softly against my neck. "It's off for now, but to turn it on, there's a switch on the side."

"Got it."

"We'll end the tour on the stage." He left the office and strode down the hall.

I hurried to catch up. "What are we going to do?"

"Set up for today's first scene. Laurey and Curly will be rehearsing 'The Surrey with the Fringe on Top.'"

"Are those their real names?"

"No, Mom prefers to call the principals by their character's name. She thinks it helps the actors grow into their roles faster. Laurey and Curly are the two leads. We're about to make them a pretend bench."

"And we do that how?"

"Imagination." He led me through the wings onto the stage. "See those two wooden boxes at the back? They're a bench. Put them downstage."

"Which is where?"

He laughed. "Near the audience, but not so close to the edge that they fall off."

"I think I can handle that." My career as a director's assistant had begun.

As the campers trickled into the auditorium over the next half hour, the noise built. Promptly at nine, Micah shooed me off the stage and joined his mother in front as they gave speeches that vaguely resembled pep talks. At the end, the campers rose and split up, with the two leads coming onstage, and the rest of the cast heading off to lessons or singing.

Lisa walked over to the actors and talked, hands gesturing gracefully. Micah crossed to the table in front of the first row and sat on an empty chair. He waved me over and indicated the chair next to him.

I eased onto it and waited.

"Here." He handed me a thin green binder and a mechanical pencil. "This is yours."

"What is it?"

"You have an abridged version of my binder. It has space for notes, a schedule, and a script." He studied me through his cute glasses. "Mom will join us in a minute to block the scene. Write down whatever she says on the script. We'll compare later."

I settled the binder on my lap and flipped it open. There were color-coded tabs. Pockets containing CONTACT LISTS, DAILY SCHEDULE, REHEARSAL CALENDAR. And the script. This binder held everything I could think of and more. I averted my head to hide my smile of delight.

On Friday, Micah had resisted offering me the job. Today, he'd included me in his process—had made me a member of his team. It was probably a small thing to him. Practical, even. But to me? It was huge. I'd only been here an hour and already felt like part of the production. All because of this ugly green binder.

Looking up, I started to say thanks.

He was bent over the table, scratching notes. I'd been forgotten.

Yeah. A member of the team.

For my first hour as the director's assistant, I shadowed Micah. When he sat, I sat. When he talked, I listened. If he scribbled something down, I duplicated it in my binder.

During a lull between two scenes, he snatched up his binder and went backstage, with me trailing behind. We went to the workshop, where the technical director was sawing lumber. Chip turned off the saw when he spotted Micah. They chatted, speaking a kind of English that communicated nothing to me. I wrote down their conversation verbatim.

Micah spun around and blinked, as if surprised I was there. He glanced at my notes. "Did you record everything we said?"

"Yes."

"Good thinking."

Then he was off again, striding down the hall, with me hurrying to keep up. We ended in the auditorium, sitting at the table with Lisa, writing down everything she said.

Midmorning, Micah called a break.

Lisa rose. "I'll be in the office."

I watched her go. "Should we follow?"

"No, she's on her own during breaks."

"What do we do now?"

"I'm taking Sam's small group while he makes a phone call. You can hang out in the staff lounge, if you like."

"I'll come with you." I was eager to see what the small groups did, especially the one run by Norah. As we exited the auditorium, I asked, "Why aren't you a counselor?"

"I'm not at the moment, but I will be. Sort of." He held the exterior door to the patio for me. "Right now, the camp only has actors. In another week, a new set of campers will show up to be our backstage crew. I'll fill in as a counselor for the ninjas."

"The what?"

"The people who dress in black and creep around backstage doing mysterious but essential things." He laughed—and for once, he sounded like a kid who was still in high school. "When we're not creeping around, we get to whine about the cast and play with the cool technology your county crammed into this arts center."

We reached the lawn. Most of the groups were already standing in noisy circles, playing games that were incomprehensible to me but enormously funny to them.

"Why are the campers outside?"

"That's what the counselors want. While the weather's mild enough in the mornings, we'll use the outdoors as much as possible." He traded his glasses for shades. "What're you going to do?"

"Observe."

"Would you mind switching on your headset and monitoring what's happening inside? It should be quiet, and I'd like to turn mine off and get involved with the activity."

"Okay."

"Thanks."

I found a bench and watched Natalie's group. She stood next to her counselor, aloof from the other teens, not participating but interested. Shifting my attention to the others in her group, I searched for signs of irritation but didn't see any. It was surprising to think that they'd accepted her so easily, but maybe what Lisa had told Jeff was right. Differences were okay here.

Thirty minutes later, Micah ended the break, and campers drifted toward the building. I stayed where I was, avoiding Natalie, knowing she wouldn't want to make a big deal about my presence. But I shouldn't have worried. She didn't even look my way. Instead, she ran over to Micah and hovered behind him as he finished listening, arms crossed, to two giggling, hair-flipping girls. When they left and Natalie stepped up for her turn, Micah's lips curved into a genuine smile of welcome. They walked inside together as she spoke in a firehose of words and he laughed. It was wonderful that she'd found someone she felt so comfortable with.

By the time I caught up with Micah in the lobby, Natalie was gone. "Hey," I said. "Where next?"

"The auditorium. Mom will continue with the same scene."

"I'd like to take the lead on writing down the blocking."

He halted. "Already?"

"Yeah."

He eyed me curiously. "Sure, let's see how you do. You stay at the director's table. I'll watch from the booth. We can compare notes at the next break." He grinned. "Good luck with Mom."

Lisa was onstage with the actors playing Laurey and Curly, speaking softly. Remaining at the director's table wouldn't work. I grabbed my binder and pencil, then climbed onto the stage and concentrated on what she was saying. Phrase after phrase appeared on my script.

"I need Aunt Eller."

After scribbling the sentence down, I read it again and looked up. Lisa and the two leads were watching me. I glanced over at the booth. Micah gave me a *go ahead* gesture.

"Be right back." I hurried into the wings and paused to check the schedule to see who was where. And . . . music room.

Five minutes later, Aunt Eller joined the other two actors and Lisa.

A small victory, yet I felt childishly pleased.

Someone slid onto the makeshift bench beside me. "Hey," Micah said, speaking in a near-whisper. "You okay?"

"Fine."

"May I?" He reached over and skimmed my notes. "Not too bad. You can compare them to mine later. Do you have a watch?"

"I have a phone."

"It's best to have a cheap watch." He stood. "We'll be breaking for lunch soon. If you want, you can go on. I'll take over here."

"Thanks."

I left through the wings. But instead of heading straight to the staff lounge, I paused for a moment and closed my eyes. The energy of this place swirled around me. It was thrilling and unique and . . . absorbing. I was loving this job.

The day ended. Finally. I worked dismissal, making sure each camper had been signed out. Once I'd seen that Natalie was safely occupied, I joined the team meeting, the last one in.

Micah crossed to me and said, for my ears only, "You look worn out."

"A little."

"Go on. You can miss this."

"I'd rather stick around. I need this meeting if I want to learn."

His smile was wide with approval. "Awesome job today."

"Thanks."

He spun around and said at a normal volume, "Okay, everyone. Let's get this over with. Who has notes?"

As I made my way to an empty chair, Chip, the technical director, described a potential problem. I didn't understand everything he said, but I understood more than I would have last Friday. The thought made me relax. I could do this.

After supper, Jeff and I drafted our official agreement. He gave me a checklist of tasks to complete, and I estimated ten hours at minimum wage. Once he'd gone, I drew up a plan, enough to pencil in deadlines and determine priorities. Then I set the checklist aside. It could wait until tomorrow, because I had other homework tonight. I was volunteering on a musical I didn't know. It was time to change that. I went to pbs.org and clicked on the Hugh Jackman version of *Oklahoma!*

Natalie appeared in my doorway after I'd been streaming the show for a half hour.

I paused the movie. "Hi. What's up?"

"I've been texting with Micah."

"Why?"

"I wanted to know what he thought about you today."

"And?"

"He says you don't suck."

Was that actually what he'd said, or had she paraphrased? "Did he think there was a chance that I would?"

"Not really. You have a dream job."

"I do?"

"Yes. There are people in the chorus who are jealous. They would've given anything to be Lisa and Micah's assistant, but they didn't know the job was even available until you got it."

"Lucky me."

"Are you being sarcastic?"

I opened my mouth to say yes, then closed it again. Today had been fun. Tomorrow, after I'd actually watched the musical, should be even more fun. So, yeah, I was lucky. It was too bad that some cast members were upset, but I wasn't sorry. Nope. "I'm not being sarcastic."

"I thought so." Natalie pointed at my laptop screen. "Can I watch with you?"

I coughed against the surprise tickling my throat. She'd never asked to do anything with me requiring physical closeness. "That's fine." Somehow, this moment made an amazing day even better. I scooted over.

She climbed gingerly into the bed beside me, not quite touching. Once she'd squirmed into a comfortable position, she asked, "Do you know anything about *Oklahoma!*?"

"Only a little."

"It takes place in 1906. In Oklahoma. Duh. The people have split into two groups—the farmers and the ranchers. And even though they're annoyed with each other, they do a lot of singing and dancing together. Then a farm girl falls in love with a cowboy, her stalker tries to mess things up, he dies, everything turns out fine, and it ends." Natalie wrinkled her nose. "It's not as bad as it sounds."

"Okay, then. Thanks for the synopsis." I clicked play. It didn't take long to become engrossed by the movie.

Natalie kept a running commentary throughout, which helped a lot. We watched the whole movie, staying up later than we should have, but it was completely worth it.

· 14 ·

Guilt-Free Fun

By my second afternoon as a volunteer, I'd realized three things.

Realization number one: Lisa was a brilliant director.

Everybody—the counselors, cast, and crew—worshiped her, which was surprising on the surface since she wasn't particularly nice. Not that she was mean either. Her voice was gruff. Her words clipped and careful. But she had this look that came over her face when she was pleased. Once I'd had it directed at me—I got the devotion.

Realization number two: Being a director's assistant was a major amount of work.

Lisa tossed so many chores my way that I couldn't imagine how she'd functioned without a full-time assistant before me. Either that or Micah was a magician.

He was sitting next to her today, binder open, pencil scratching, his attention on a dozen things at the same time. Camp staff would show up, whisper to him, and take off again. Those visits often resulted in another errand for me.

I'd never been so stretched by a job. Most of the time, I lounged behind Lisa and Micah, writing, writing, writing. But then, one of them would send me off to research questions on the internet, deliver messages to Elena, or sort through junk in the prop room.

Maybe this was typical for a drama camp, but everything just seemed to flow. The production team did their stuff with little direction. The counselors maximized the fun, whether it was chatting in their small groups about serious issues, playing games, or giving lessons. The campers seemed really happy.

And so was I.

On this afternoon's schedule, the lead actors were rehearsing a scene from Act One. While Laurey was awkwardly flirting with Curly, Lisa was squirming in front of me. I'd already figured out that a squirmy Lisa was waiting for an opportunity to—

She erupted from her chair. "Let's do the lead-up to 'People Will Say We're in Love' again."

The two actors nodded and shifted to a different spot on the stage.

She clutched her son's wrist and whispered, "Delay at will. Break is imminent."

He stood, offered me a hand, and pulled me to my feet. "Let's go." He grabbed his binder and headed backstage.

Once we were clear of the wings, I asked him something that I was dying to know. "How long have you been doing theater with your mother?"

"Since I was seven."

"Is that why you understand the strange things she says?"

"Like what?"

"'Delay at will'?"

He grinned. "Delay *Ado and Will*. They're the other couple in the musical. Ado Annie and Will Parker should be rehearsing next, but Mom's decided to continue with this scene. Curly and Laurey must have hit a snag she wants to fix immediately."

"Micah!"

We looked toward the rear hallway where two counselors stood. One of them called, "There's a problem."

He faced me, walking backward a couple of steps as he talked. "Tell Mom we'll break in ten minutes, after I've checked on this."

Micah huddled with the counselors, listening as one of them spoke and gestured with choppy hands. I headed back to the stage.

And there came realization number three: Micah in action fascinated me.

Although he was the youngest person on the production team, they treated him with respect. He made backstage decisions without hesitation. He managed people, things, and his mother—and did it with scary efficiency.

Natalie hadn't exaggerated about him being epically awesome. He didn't make mistakes. It was no wonder that some of the girls in the cast had a crush on Micah Dalton. Competence was sexy.

I attended Tuesday's staff meeting feeling tired but satisfied. Every seat in the staff lounge was taken except a spot on the couch next to Micah. I hesitated. He kept these meetings so short, it wouldn't be a problem to stand the whole time.

He caught my eye and pointed at the empty spot. It was sit or be rude. I sat.

Micah called on each counselor and listened as they shared any concerns while I jotted down notes. Finally, there was no one left to speak except Lisa.

"Brooke?" Micah said.

I looked up. Everyone was staring at me. "Yes?"

"Do you have anything to report?"

My cheeks heated at the unexpected attention. Was I supposed to do that? "About what?"

"Whatever you want," Micah said. "Status. Impressions. You came a week late, so you might have seen things the rest of us missed."

His expression encouraged me. Good, then. I had noticed something that might be worth sharing. "I think the principals are trying too hard to be perfect."

Lisa narrowed her eyes at me. "Explain."

"Audra and Channing and the other leads are my classmates. In high school productions, they seem more natural. It could be because I'm used to seeing the final production, but I wonder if they're holding back because of you. Your reputation could be intimidating them. No one's willing to be the first person to try something bold and fail."

"Interesting thought. I'll observe tomorrow and see if I agree. Thanks."

Micah wrapped up the meeting, but I hardly heard a word he said, too focused on that "thanks." She'd warned me she didn't use it often, and she'd been right. This was my first one, and it felt amazing.

Natalie hardly waited for the Honda to stop in our driveway before flinging herself from the car and running for the backyard. My mother and I got out more slowly and went inside.

"She seems to be doing well," Mom said.

"Agreed." If I hadn't been so impulsive about pointing out the camp to Natalie, I might have remembered her intense need for solitude. Maybe it was good, though, that I'd messed up in this instance because Natalie was really enjoying the show. She didn't fully participate with the other kids, she sat by herself in the auditorium, but she had loosened up with her group.

"How are you doing?"

"Great. There is so much to do, and I like working with Micah and Lisa."

"I'm glad." Mom nodded absently. "I'll leave soon for the game. Can you make sandwiches for dinner?"

"Sure, but Natalie won't like that."

"She'll get over it." Mom started for the doorway and paused, shooting me a meaningful look over her shoulder. "She has to eat what you make or prepare her own."

"Go on. I'll take care of it." As Mom blended into the gloom of the hallway, I asked, "Where's Jeff?"

"Working until dark."

Swallowing a sigh, I arranged a buffet of sandwich fixings on the counter. After a tiring day, I wasn't in the mood for taking any crap from Natalie either. Better give her a warning. I raised the window over the sink and paused. She was pacing in the shade, singing a chorus from the musical. She really did have a good voice. I hated to interrupt but she needed to know about dinner. "Natalie?"

She stopped. "What?"

"We're having sandwiches."

She ran inside. "Already had that today."

"And it's what we'll have again tonight." I gestured at the buffet.

"Is this one of those things where Jill will get mad if I resist?"

"Yes."

"Fine, but no bread." Natalie grabbed a plate and laid a slice of ham on one side and a slice of cheese on the other.

"Any veggies?"

"No." She reached into the fruit bowl for a banana before crossing to the table. "Move, Tigger."

My cat jumped disdainfully off Natalie's chair, swished his tail to emphasize that moving had been his choice, and strutted into the den.

Natalie dropped onto her chair. "I prefer dogs."

"As you've mentioned before."

"But Tigger is tolerable for a cat."

I hid my grin.

When Mom returned to the kitchen, wearing her uniform minus padding, I had her sandwich done. "Do you want yours to go?"

"Please."

Natalie set her empty plate in the sink, then raced up the stairs. Seconds later, the door to her bedroom banged shut.

I wrapped three roast beef sandwiches in plastic, handed the first to Mom, and stuck the other two in the fridge. After leaving a note for Jeff about his dinner, I went upstairs to my room.

It didn't take long before I heard singing. I crossed to my closet and pressed my ear to the wall. Natalie was practicing her solo over and over—the same ten words—even though she already had them flawless. Then she started speaking. This time, though, she was reciting all of the lines for the members of the girls' ensemble, changing to use different voices for the different parts. Natalie already had the entire scene memorized.

I picked up my laptop and carried it downstairs and out to the veranda. There had been a storm earlier this afternoon, but the skies were clear now. The world had that wonderful, rain-fresh scent.

Okay, time to make progress for Jeff.

My first task required the internet. Fortunately, the State of North Carolina had a decent checklist on their website. There were so many reports and forms to file that it was a wonder anyone ever bothered with setting up a legal business. Not that I'd ever say that to my stepfather. He was ethical to the point of absurdity.

Two hours later, I'd finished handling insurance, taxes, reports, and ID numbers. I'd downloaded the government posters that would have to be displayed in Jeff's workshop. I was caught up with nearly everything he'd asked for except setting up direct deposit for his new employee, but I wouldn't have any trouble with that. I'd managed Mom's banking before she married.

As a bonus task, I'd studied his website. It was . . . not good. Fortunately, he'd created it in WordPress. I would make a list of recommended updates and send him a proposal.

Before I shut down for the night, I checked my email. There

was spam, an awkwardly done newsletter from Elena to parents, cast, and crew, and one email from Sylvie. Apparently, the guy she'd been crushing on for months had finally asked her out for Sunday. No spa this weekend for us.

She and Kaylynn had tried, though, which made it my turn to ask. The weird thing was—now that Natalie had the musical to fixate on and didn't need to hang out with my friends, I could have guilt-free fun. So why was I reluctant to tell them?

The front door creaked, and Natalie joined me on the veranda. She was yawning.

"What have you been doing tonight?" I asked.

"Talking to people."

"Such as?"

"Dad when he got home. I texted Micah earlier."

"How often do you text with him?"

"Whenever I have a question."

That was curious. How much longer before it got too annoying for him? Maybe I should I say something. "What do you talk about?"

"Mostly the theater. It's an unending source of topics. Problems, especially. Actors forgetting to turn off their mics when they go to the bathroom. Thunderstorms knocking out the power. Wardrobe malfunctions. Since I've seen two of Elon's productions, we can even talk about the same performances."

Okay, where was her . . . interest in him going? Was it possible that she was hoping for more? I hated to ask the next question, but I had to. "Do you have a crush on Micah?"

"*Crush* is not the right word."

"Then what is?"

"*Entranced.*"

Entranced? Hmm. What did that word mean to her? She was very literal. I'd look it up in dictionary.com before I got too concerned.

Natalie turned to face me. Full eye contact. "Mama called."

"Good. Does she call often?"

"She promised to speak with me every Tuesday, Thursday, and Saturday. So far, she has. If Luke's awake, he's with her, and I talk to him." Natalie flopped onto a rocking chair. "She recorded me narrating a picture book before I left, and she says Luke always smiles while he listens."

That was a great idea. Mei wasn't one of my favorite people, but she was trying to minimize the bad effects of the separation. "How's your mom?"

"They're trying a new antidepressant."

I gave my stepsister a careful look. I hadn't known that Mei was depressed. "Maybe it will help."

"It could. The color of her voice was different."

"Which means?"

"Her words have been coming out brown lately, and today they were more pink."

"That's an improvement?"

"Duh. Who wants to sound brown?"

"Sorry. Of course." I would *not* laugh. "How do my words sound?"

"Always vivid." She tilted her head and considered me. "Orange this week."

"Is orange good?"

"Well, yeah." She yawned again.

"Do people ever call you Nat?"

"Not if they want me to acknowledge their existence."

I couldn't control my laughter any longer. She shrugged and looked toward the street.

Closing the lid to my laptop, I debated whether to ask something uncomfortable. The night inspired confidence, though. "Natalie, do you often talk about words having color?"

She shook her head. "Most people already think I'm strange enough. No reason to give them more ammunition."

Before knowing Natalie, I would've thought that people with Asperger's were completely tuned out socially, but it wasn't true of her. She fumbled what most people our age could do easily and aced the harder stuff. "What do you miss most about living with your mom?"

"The way she smells."

"Which is?"

Natalie studied the night sky as if it held the answer. "She smells like love."

Wow. Yeah. I understood exactly. "Does my mom have a smell?"

"Jill smells like determination." My stepsister looked at me and gave a little laugh.

"I cannot argue with that."

Natalie rose and crossed to the front door, then hesitated with her hand on the knob. "Did you get in trouble for telling me about the musical?"

"Not really." At her scowl, I huffed a sigh. "Maybe a little, but it passed soon."

"They were right to be worried. I was, too. I'm still glad you found it."

· 15 ·

A Hot Combination

On the drive to the arts center on Wednesday, the sky had been dark and threatening. By midmorning, rain was pouring in steady sheets. The weather must've been stirring up the cast, because today's rehearsal was the worst I'd seen.

Lisa growled with exasperation. "Laurey is reluctant to kiss Curly." She twisted in her seat to face me. "Is she scared of him? Or is this not being bold?"

"Neither." The actor playing Laurey had been dating the same guy since middle school. She wasn't scared of Curly; she was *worried*. "Audra has a long-term boyfriend. I think she's feeling guilty."

"She's been in several productions. This can't be her first stage kiss."

"It might be the first time she's been attracted to the actor she's kissing."

"Ah-ha. This could get interesting. Micah, I'm giving a private lesson in the makeup room. Thirty minutes." She jumped to her feet and said loudly, "Laurey, Curly, follow me."

"Okay, change in plans." Micah flipped to his schedule. "We'll work on 'The Farmer and the Cowman' next. Brooke, can you ask Claire if she has the fight scene choreography ready yet? I'll tell the counselors to stretch whatever classes they're teaching for now."

I talked to Claire, who said she was ready. After I relayed the message to Micah, I found myself, for the first time this week, with nothing immediate to do. I wandered backstage and out to the scene shop. The tech director was alone, bent over something blueprint-y that lay flat on a table. The space smelled of sawdust and paint.

"Hi, Chip," I said.

He shifted until I came into view. "Hello . . . Brooke."

"Anything I can help with?"

"How much time do you have?"

"Thirty minutes."

He chuckled. "Can't get too much done in a half hour, but I'll take you up on it another time. Check again when the crew campers arrive next Wednesday. We'll stick a paintbrush in your hand then."

"Okay." I left and headed next to the office.

Elena was on the phone, but she waved me in. "We can do that tomorrow. Thanks. Bye." Grabbing her mug, she spun the chair around. "What's up?" She sucked down a mouthful of spicy orange tea.

"Could I ask a favor?"

"Shoot."

I closed the door behind me. "If you have any office work that you'd like to pass along, I could take some off your hands."

"How is that a favor to you?"

"I could put it on my résumé as experience."

"Did you have a project in mind?" She swiveled back to the desk and logged in to her computer.

"The newsletter."

She giggled. "You could tell how much I hate doing that."

There was no polite way to respond.

"Yeah, you can take over the newsletter, but I'll have to be the person to actually send it. Privacy reasons."

"Great. You have my email address?"

"Yeah. I'll get the information to you by tomorrow."

We were nearing the end of the afternoon break. The cast members were either having quiet time in the campers' lounge or being measured for costumes. Lisa was on a phone call with the head of the board of directors for the arts center. Micah was nowhere to be found.

When I stumbled across him in the staff lounge, I was almost sorry that I had. He looked tired and peaceful, slumped on the couch, eyes closed, an empty water bottle in his hand.

As I backed away, he said, "It's okay. You can come in."

"Sure?"

His eyes opened. "Yeah. What can I do for you?"

"Nothing. There is absolutely nothing happening that requires your attention."

"Now that, I refuse to believe." He rose and came over to me, so close his arm brushed mine. "You doing okay?"

"Yeah. This job is a lot of fun."

His lips curved into a gorgeous smile. "And addictive."

"I love the problems."

"The talent."

"The excitement."

"The surprises." He tossed his bottle into the recycling bin. "Having you here steadies Natalie."

"I think so, too."

He scooped up his binder and lifted his hand in a wave as he left.

I stayed where I was, watching him go, hugging that hint of a compliment to myself. Unlike his mother, it was something he did often, sliding out praise to people in that offhand way.

There came realization number four: I loved working with Micah.

It had taken us less than a day to put our early hostility behind us. Awkward moments had changed to teamwork. He could murmur a couple of words or flash a smile or make a tiny gesture—and I was already anticipating his wishes. His attitude gave me the freedom to leave behind my insecurities and allow myself to be good.

I was helping with afternoon pickup when my stepfather's truck pulled into the carpool lane. "Natalie, why is Jeff here so early?"

She slung her backpack over her shoulder. "To take me to the movie. I told you."

Not the part about it being the five-thirty show. "I can't leave yet."

"That's your problem."

"I can take Brooke home," Micah said from beside me.

"Thanks." I struggled to keep my expression light, pleased with this change in plans.

Natalie was already shuffling down the sidewalk to her father's truck.

Sweet anticipation filled me. Driving me home would mean nothing to Micah. He was too focused on the show to notice me as a person. But I was thrilled with the idea of spending fifteen minutes alone with him, just the two of us, talking like regular people.

Yeah, it didn't take much to make me happy.

Once the team meeting had ended, Lisa leaned wearily against her son. "I think takeout tonight."

"Sure, but I have to take Brooke home first." He looped his arms around his mom with affectionate ease and rested his chin on the top of her head. "Want to come with us? Or should I return for you?"

"The latter. I have a few things to finish here."

"Okay."

"Stop for burgers at that place."

His eyes lit up. "Sounds good." He stepped away from her and looked at me. "Ready?"

"Yeah."

Once we were on the highway, I asked, "Which burger place is she talking about?"

"Winston's."

"I'm impressed you know about them. They're the best."

"Yeah." His fingers drummed on the steering wheel. "Mom doesn't enjoy cooking, so getting recommendations for good food is high on our list of questions when she's a visiting director."

"Does she do this often?"

"Our third summer. It's fun, and tons of work."

"Where are you staying?"

"We've rented a house."

"Do you stay on the weekends?"

"It depends. Last weekend, it was date night, so we went home. I doubt we'll do that again until the show's done." He braked for a stop sign. "Which way?"

Wow, the phrase *date night* had distracted me so much that I'd forgotten about directions. "Go straight ahead, then left at the next light." I stared out the side window. Micah had a girlfriend. Of course he did. He was cute and smart and wielded power with confidence. A hot combination. This news disappointed me. A lot. Which was wrong on many levels.

He continued through the intersection. "Do you regret agreeing to be an assistant?"

"No."

I must've sounded odd, because his fingers stopped drumming. "Do you miss the other job?"

"Not really. Mostly, I miss the paycheck."

"Did you have plans for it?"

"I was hoping to buy a car." I turned to catch him smirking. "Yes, a conventional goal. Do you get paid?"

"All production team members are paid."

"Except me."

He laughed. "True."

"Natalie texts with you."

"That's an interesting transition." His hands clenched the wheel. "Yes, she does."

"Do you mind?"

"No, I enjoy it."

"Do you do that with other campers?"

"None have asked." His voice had cooled into icy disapproval. "I'm trying to be a mentor for Natalie. If you have a problem with that, you don't need to. It's completely innocent."

"Oh, sorry. It's not a problem. I was worried she might be taking up too much of your time."

He relaxed as he made the left turn onto our street. "I don't mind at all. When Natalie asks a question, she's only after an answer. I don't have to examine every word, wondering what she wants from me, or worry about her hidden agenda. She's not bothering me."

"Good, because she enjoys it, too." I pointed. "Do you remember where we live? It's the white house with the big veranda."

He pulled to the curb.

Wow, that had sped by. "Thanks for the ride."

"Anytime. Brooke?" He twisted in his seat to face me, his shades dangling from one hand. "You're really doing a good job. My mom's not easy to work for, and you're managing her well."

"Thanks." I released my seat belt and glanced over at him, gripped by a sudden shyness. This close, I could see his eyes. Too brown for gold. Too gold for brown. His own uniquely gorgeous color. It had been a long time since I'd been this aware of a guy. As in *never.* "So . . . see ya tomorrow."

"I'm glad you've joined the show."

His statement shivered through me. I repeated the words in my head. Memorized them. Would spend the rest of the evening pretending they meant more than they did. "For Natalie's sake."

He held my gaze for a few seconds, then looked away. "And ours."

Natalie had been home for two hours before she came to my room. She sat cross-legged at the end of my bed and picked at a scab on her ankle.

I would have to kick off tonight's chat. "Was it a good movie?"

"I'd give it a B plus."

"Romance?"

She looked up, her eyes wide with horror. "You know the answer to that."

I swallowed my laugh. "Yeah, I do."

Her gaze returned to the ankle. "It was sci-fi. Interesting story, although I'm skeptical of their research. Not believable. It would've been better to call it a futuristic fantasy. But if you forget the credibility issues, fine."

"So you liked it."

"Yes." Her lips twitched up at the corners. "Micah drove you home."

"Yeah, it was nice of him." Could she hear the warmth in my voice when I mentioned him? Probably not. "He said he went home last weekend."

"His mom misses his dad."

"And he wanted to see his girlfriend."

She scowled. "Why would you think that? Micah doesn't have a girlfriend."

Could she be right? "He said it was date night."

"For his parents. Micah doesn't have time to date . . ."

The news left me dizzy with relief, which meant something it really shouldn't. I was foolish to be happy that he was single. It put me in danger of crushing on a guy who was technically my boss, a guy who didn't notice me that way.

". . . He can't fit anything else into his schedule. He's either working on a production or trying to relax."

Okay, still stuck at the *Micah is single* news. "I can't believe he just answers such personal questions."

"Clearly, he does, since I know. I've found asking is the best way to get the data I want."

"What if people don't want to answer?"

"Then they don't. I can handle no's. Well, those kinds of no's." She hopped from the bed and left, leaving behind welcome information and the silence needed to indulge in the possibilities.

· 16 ·

Two Kinds of Like

The principals were pushing the limit today, and Lisa was letting it slide. Sometimes she smiled. Sometimes she sighed in frustration. But she let them do whatever they wanted, rarely giving feedback.

I leaned over. "Are you going to say anything?"

"Not much, at least not today." She chuckled. "During this morning's pep talk, I told them not to hold back. They need to believe that I meant what I said."

I lowered my chin to hide my smile. She'd listened to my suggestion and acted on it. I'd become a real part of this creation, no longer just the stepsister who'd been given a role to disguise her primary purpose. I belonged.

"Laurey, can we try that again? I like the way you're expressing frustration, but you won't be able to throw the props so hard." Lisa spoke to me without looking my way, "Go to the prop room and see if it has a basket and fake food."

After unlocking the prop room and flicking on the light, I checked in the closest cupboard. A bowl of fake fruit. Yay. And there was a basket on top of a tall cabinet. Except it was three feet out of my reach. Ladder?

A scan of the room revealed a stepladder in the corner. Dragging it over, I frowned as I tried to decide if that would be high enough. Probably. I climbed to the third rung and stretched for the basket. Not quite there. I went up to the top rung.

"Dammit, Brooke," Micah growled from behind me.

I gasped and clawed at the cabinet as the stepladder wobbled.

He braced the ladder with his body, his hand locking around my knee. "Safety . . ."

". . . first," we said together.

"Yeah, yeah, yeah." I wouldn't have wobbled if he hadn't yelled. "The lecture will have to wait. I'm close to success."

"Get down." It was a command, a highly pissed command.

Somebody was overreacting. "Not until I have the basket." I stretched forward, my fingers brushing it, pushing it farther away.

"Now."

Alright, time to admit defeat. I went carefully down each rung until I hit the floor, aware of his body behind me, his hands firm on my waist.

I hung my head, ready for the lecture.

"If you ever do that again, you're gone."

I stiffened. Whoa. "That's extreme."

"What is the rule?"

"No climbing ladders without a spotter. Got it." His behavior was beginning to tick me off. I hadn't come here by choice. I turned to face him. "Is your presence a coincidence, or were you stalking me?"

"I knew where the baskets were. I was trying to prevent you from killing yourself."

"Oh. Solid reason." How incredibly . . . nice. Was there anything he did wrong? "Thanks."

He gave a curt nod, his hands dropping away.

Neither of us moved. Just stood there in an awkward silence. His anger hung around him like a shield.

"Your mom sent me down here for props. I have to get—"

"Leave it." He lifted the stepladder and carried it back to its corner.

Had I really been in any danger? I studied the cupboard I would've fallen into. It held an odd assortment of props. A butter churn. Two fake guns. A fake knife. A glass perfume bottle. Yeah, crashing into the props would've been bad for them—and me.

"Hey," he said, his voice marginally less tense. "We ought to get back."

I crossed to the doorway in front of him, then stopped. He deserved an apology. "I'm sorry—"

Micah tried to avoid me, but it was too late. Full body slam, the momentum knocking me into the hall. I fumbled for the doorframe, but all I came up with was air.

His arms locked around my waist and hauled me against him. "Hey. Did I hurt you?"

"No." *You have your arms around me. Please don't talk.* I pressed my cheek to his chest. Any moment now, he would realize where we were and release me. Until then, I would indulge in how amazing it felt to be so close to him.

"Brooke," he whispered against my hair, and instead of letting me go, his arms tightened.

I breathed in his scent—citrusy, clean, and thoroughly

delicious. He had kept me from falling, and now he held me. While I had the chance, I would try to smooth things between us. "I'm sorry, Micah. I'll be more careful."

"Promise?" His voice sounded gruff.

I looked up at him. "Yes, I promise."

From deep within the arts center, a piano pounded out the introduction to a song. Sanity returned, not that I wanted it to. "Micah? What are we doing?"

"We're, um . . ." He shook his head.

"What?"

Abruptly, his arms dropped. "I have to . . ." He took a step back and ran his fingers through his hair, ruffling it into a never-before-seen mess. "I've gotta go." He went around me and took off down the hall.

"Micah, wait."

He paused but didn't face me. Just stood there, head bowed.

"Are we okay?"

"I don't know what we are." He adjusted his headset over his ears as he disappeared into the wings.

I flicked off the light in the prop room, closed its door, then leaned against the wall. That moment had been unexpected and sweet, but what did it mean?

When I returned to the auditorium—without the basket—Micah was sitting in the booth, writing in his binder. There were extra people onstage, including my stepsister. I sent Lisa a questioning frown.

"We're blocking 'Out of My Dreams.'"

So much for the errand. I slipped onto my seat, my attention focused on the ensemble. I'd never had the opportunity to watch this scene all the way through.

Laurey stayed where she was while a group of girls clustered around.

When Lisa clapped her hands, there was instant silence. "Let's try the song." She said to me, "Find a rocking chair for next time."

"Sure." *Please shut up long enough for me to hear my step-sister sing.*

The soundtrack started and the soloists began their lines, one by one. Natalie was a hair late on her entrance. She knew it too, because her face turned red.

Laurey had barely started singing when Lisa said, "Stop. And again."

This time, Natalie nailed it, her gaze never leaving Laurey's ponytail.

Pride wrapped me in a bubble—muffling everything except the sight and sound of my stepsister. I'd known Natalie's voice was clear and lovely, but I hadn't thought about how stunning she was onstage. When she was up there, it was hard to take my eyes off her. Not that I was biased or anything.

"Brooke?" Lisa rapped on the table in front of me.

I dragged my attention away from the singers. "What?"

"Did you hear what I said?"

"When?"

Lisa smiled. "Forgotten your job?"

"Oh. Sorry."

"You're fine." She half-sat on the table and crossed her arms. "We'll sit here and listen. I promise not to interrupt until they're done."

"Thanks." I relaxed in my seat and enjoyed watching my stepsister own her part.

When Natalie and I got home from the center, something in the Crock-Pot was filling the air with the scent of garlic and herbs.

She sniffed. "Roasted chicken. Another of my favorites. I guess Jill doesn't mind me being here."

"She doesn't mind." I would say that as often as it took, but it was annoying. "You did well today."

"Yes, I did, except not the first time."

"The first time doesn't matter anymore."

She shrugged. "Do you like working at the arts center?"

"A lot."

"Does it make you nervous when I'm singing my line?"

"Yes."

"Because you're afraid I'll make mistakes?"

"No. I get nervous when something important is going on with my family. Like when I go to Mom's games. She's a great umpire, and I still get the shakes."

"Don't let me see you. It might rub off." She charged into the den and turned on the TV.

I went to my room to update Jeff's website. Currently, it was nothing more than white text on a black background, with a description of the services he provided. I would love to make his website more visually appealing, add a contact form, and design a logo. But not tonight. He'd been specific about the parts of my proposal that he would permit. "Nothing fancy. Just plain information, plainly given," he'd said.

Probably it was too early for him to trust me with more than the simple things, but I wasn't ready to give up. Tonight, I would limit myself to making the home page more mobile friendly.

After completing the changes, I logged off the computer, picked up a paperback mystery, and went outside to the hammock.

The book was an excuse. I wanted to think about Micah.

It surprised me how much I liked him. My feelings had bypassed the *will he? won't he?* torment of a new crush and gone straight to *this could be very good.* Maybe that's because I liked him the friendly way, too.

Two kinds of like.

Which kind did he feel for me?

Until today, I would've said Micah was purely professional toward me. He seemed to pay more attention to me than the girls in the cast, but that could be explained as his general attitude toward anyone on the production team.

Then he showed up in the prop room. That mesmerizing intensity had been focused on me, a taste of how incredible it would feel to be the person Micah wanted. Afterward, though, his professional self had reappeared, as if that burst of emotion had never occurred.

But he'd left behind a glimmer of hope.

If I'd met Micah at school, I would've watched him for another month, remembering every word he said or every touch he made, giving myself plenty of time to decide if we were simply friends—or if the potential existed for more.

This wasn't school. It was a summer camp, and he would be gone in three more weeks.

If I asked Mom's opinion, she'd tell me to go for it. To be "cautiously bold." When I was in eighth grade, she'd had *The Talk* with me. She told me to make my own choices and hold out for healthy relationships. As long as I was protecting myself physically and emotionally, I should trust my instincts.

Mom's attitude both freed me and made me wary. I'd dated around in high school, although nothing serious until last year. Until Jonas. He and I had hinted around for months, neither of us willing to be embarrassed if we were reading each other wrong. Finally, I'd made the move. Jonas and I dated for seven months. In April, he decided he was "bored." I hadn't argued at all.

To have a chance with Micah, I didn't have time to hint around or agonize over signals. I would have to act soon.

There were two things about him that worried me. First, he was in charge of too much and ought to be delegating more. There were people who could help him—like me—but he didn't share control. Why? It would make me crazy to go out with someone who had power issues.

Secondly—and even bigger—there was Natalie. She was entranced with Micah. An innocent but deep emotion. He had been her discovery, and anything more personal from me would be trespassing on her territory.

Would she be upset enough to trigger another meltdown?

Would I damage the relationship Natalie and I were slowly building?

A yes to either question would be awful.

I stretched full length into the hammock and let it rock. As the sounds of the evening lulled me, I tried to convince myself that three weeks with Micah wasn't worth the cost.

· 17 ·

Without Brainpower Attached

Micah came into the office Friday morning while I was putting away my backpack.

"Hey, Brooke, did you get an updated schedule?" He held out a sheet.

I searched his face and detected nothing but polite detachment. Our sweet moment in the prop room hadn't changed anything. "Thanks. I have one."

He nodded and left. I trailed him to the auditorium, aware of my mood clouding with each step.

Lisa waved me over. "I'm about to watch the dream ballet onstage for the first time. I need you in the booth. Monitor entrances and exits. Make notes of anything that seems strange or out of place. Keep your headset on."

"Okay." I knew most of the show now, so it shouldn't be too hard.

I carried my binder to the booth. The choreography was really good, but it didn't take long to decide that I disliked this task more than anything else Lisa had given me. Not because it was boring. I had to stay vigilant about everything happening on-stage. No, the worst part was that I was isolated.

"Brooke." Micah's voice came through the headset. "Can you meet me during lunch break?"

Gladly. Any reason to leave the booth. "Where?"

"Staff lounge."

I spent my whole lunch in the lounge, waiting. He jogged in at the end, a big backpack slung over one shoulder.

"Hey. Sorry." He set the backpack on a table and waved me closer. "This won't take long. I'm introducing you to the emergency kit." He unzipped pockets. "It has all kinds of stuff. Pencils. Duct tape. Scissors. Rope. Safety pins. First-aid kit—"

"Wait." I put my hand over his.

He tensed, looked down at our hands, then up at me.

"Why are you telling me this, Micah?"

"I need you to know what's in here. You'll use it, too."

"Use it how?"

He slipped his hand away from mine. "People forget things, or they get hurt. Or Mom will ask for an object that seems obscure, but you realize it's obviously needed. This backpack has everything you can think of. It's where we go for any emergency."

"Why me?"

"If you understand it too, you can be the person who fixes things, and I can be your backup."

"Really? You're sharing power?"

His gaze locked with mine. An electric awareness sizzled between us.

"I'm not sharing power." He smiled lazily. "I'm trusting you."

He went through every pocket, explaining the items and the various uses that each could have. It made so much sense that I didn't even worry about remembering or writing anything down. If a situation came up, this backpack would have a solution.

"You've thought of everything. This is wonderful."

He zipped it again and hauled it onto one shoulder. "It'll be next to the filing cabinet in the office."

"Thanks. For trusting me."

"Sure." His eyes narrowed, as if he was about to say more. Instead, he shook his head.

"What?"

"Gotta go. Lunch break is over."

Micah joined the production team meeting late and leaned against the doorframe. "Okay, everyone, let's get this done." He nodded at Elena. "Any camper news to share?"

"Not today."

"Who wants to go next?"

Lisa did a brain dump, which took a long time. The rest of the team passed on their turns, eager to go home.

As the meeting broke up, I remained seated on the couch until everyone had left. Scrubbing my clammy hands against my shorts, I took a deep breath. This was a little crazy, but I had to ask him about us. Maybe I could've believed that our first intense moment meant nothing, but not the second. This sense of connection to him was getting stronger. I just had to know whether he felt it too, even if I regretted the truth.

Micah looked up from his phone and blinked when he saw me. "Do you need me?"

Yes. I might be about to flame out here, but I would plunge ahead. "What happened to us yesterday in the prop room?"

"I don't know." He straightened smoothly and turned to walk out the door.

"It happened again while you were explaining the kit. Was it nothing?"

He stopped, his back to me, and ran his fingers through his hair. Seconds passed before he responded. "No, it was *something*."

"Do you plan to ignore it?"

"I'm . . ." He paused. "What to do about the *something* is complicated."

He'd acknowledged the awareness and dismissed it at the same time. I shivered against the doubts creeping in. "Am I crazy to think that there could be more?"

"You're not crazy."

Yes.

Maybe he hadn't given me much hope, but I was clinging to it with greedy hands anyway. "Micah, please. One of us has to be brave."

He turned to look at me, his lips twisting into a half-smile. "I vote for you."

Tiny or not, that smile sent my confidence soaring. "Can I call you tonight, so we can talk about what the *something* is?"

"Brooke." With a quick shake of his head, he crossed the room, offered me his hand, and hauled me to my feet. He let go but didn't step away. We were so close that I had to beg myself not to grab him.

He sighed. "Okay, but we should talk in person. Can I come over to your house instead?"

"Definitely."

"I'll be there by eight-thirty." He gestured toward the door. "Did you drive today?"

I nodded. "Natalie's waiting on me in the lobby."

"Come on. I'll walk you out."

Micah's text came at exactly eight-thirty. I knew that because I'd been staring at my phone for the past fifteen minutes.

I'm here

I was down the stairs and out the door before he could ring the doorbell. Since I wasn't sure what Micah and I might become, I'd rather Natalie didn't know about this yet.

As I skipped down the front steps, he was walking up the driveway but halted halfway.

I stopped on the sidewalk, a careful distance between us. "Hi."

"Hey." He wore his neutral expression, the one where his not-quite-a-smile hid his feelings behind a polite mask.

I gestured behind me at the porch swing. "Do you want to sit down?"

"No, this won't take long." He crossed his arms, his attitude confident. Tonight, professional Micah had shown up. "I'm the stage manager, and you're an assistant. That's all we can be."

His words punched me in the gut. How could I have been so wrong? "You felt something."

"Yes, but I don't know what it is and . . ." He glanced toward the street, waiting for a car blasting music to pass. When his head swung back to me, his eyes mirrored regret. "I'm sorry, Brooke, but I can't get too . . . personal with a member of the production team."

"Why?"

"I can't afford for anything to go wrong. It would have a bad effect on the crew."

Oh, no. We were both too mature to let anything go wrong. "Actors get too personal all the time."

"And when it blows up, they keep pretending, because that's what actors do." His voice deepened. "I can't pretend."

I widened my eyes and hoped the suspicious moisture would behave. I really hadn't expected the conversation to go this way. We'd both felt a connection. He'd admitted that. The next step ought to be for us to see where it led. Right?

Around us, the neighborhood went through its nightly settling-down routine. A couple jogged by with their dogs and stroller. A lady paced in her front yard, talking on a phone. Then there was me, with a guy I liked, a guy who was rejecting me for reasons that made complete sense. I didn't want to be sensible. "It's only three more weeks. That's not enough time for things to blow up."

"It's a theater camp. Things can blow up in a day." He shook his head. "The show comes first. I just can't risk it. I'm sorry." He held my gaze for a moment longer, then dug keys from his pocket and headed back down the driveway.

Panic fluttered in my throat. He'd reduced us to guy-in-charge and member-of-the-crew, and that wasn't enough for me. "Micah."

He turned to face me again. "Yeah?"

"Can we be friends?"

He tilted his head, as if surprised. "I hope so."

Friends, then. If all I got was the other kind of like, I'd take it. I might get good at pretending.

Wait. The other kind of like?

Yes. That could work. Time to be cautiously bold. "Could we hang out sometimes—as friends?"

"What do you mean?"

Words tumbled from my mouth, eager and out of control, hoping to convince him while I still had his attention. "You've probably been too busy to check out this part of North Carolina. I could show you around. Friendly. Not too personal." Wow, that had ended up fairly coherent.

"Friendly hanging out." His gaze lingered on me. The world seemed to hush, as if it knew his answer mattered at some cosmic level. "Okay."

Had I imagined that? "Okay?"

"Yeah." He grinned—a real, genuine Micah grin. "I think I can do friendly."

Could a person explode from happiness? Maybe we were about to find out.

He walked back up the driveway toward me, stopping a foot away. "When?"

Oh, right. We needed a plan. Fast. Since this idea had popped up impulsively, I'd have to wing it. Fortunately, letting words pour from my mouth without brainpower attached was working for me tonight. "Tomorrow?"

"Not wasting time, I see."

"Not a single day."

"I have some things to do at the arts center in the morning, and I have a few errands to run for Mom, but I'll be done by noon."

"All those words mean you're free."

"Yeah. After lunch."

"I'll have to ask my folks if I can have the car."

"We can take mine. So, what'll we do?"

"Does it matter?"

"I'm going with yes."

He was so cute like this, all relieved and charming and . . . normal teen instead of epically awesome god. "Miniature golf?"

"I'm not much into miniature golf."

"Movie?"

"All drama-ed out."

"Are you being intentionally difficult?"

He laughed. "No."

I'd only seen him act like this in small groups, and I loved having it directed at me. Playful Micah was irresistible. How could I get him to show up again tomorrow?

I had to pick something fun and light, and I knew the perfect place. "Have you ever been to Pullen Park in Raleigh? It has a carousel, paddleboats, and beautiful gardens to stroll through. As an added bonus—amazing food."

"Sounds good. One o'clock?"

I nodded.

"I'm going now. See you in a few hours."

· 18 ·

Safe Topics

Natalie stomped into the den Saturday morning with her backpack slung over both shoulders.

I muted the TV and tried not to wince when Tigger kneaded my thigh. "Going somewhere?"

"Norah invited our group to go swimming with her."

Wow. Norah was a saint. "Where?"

"Laurel Lake."

"That can be good if it's not crowded. So you're going?"

"Clearly, since you basically asked the same question twelve words ago and I confirmed that I was. In case you're wondering, I asked Dad."

Keep the smile in place. She's leaving soon. "I didn't know you liked to swim."

"I don't. I'll take my bathing suit anyway."

"You could wear it under a T-shirt."

"I don't like the sensation of bathing suit fabric against my skin." She opened her backpack. It held a towel, suit, sunscreen, bug spray, bottled water, and snack pack of crackers.

"You look ready. Do you need money?"

"I have my card."

"The concession stand at Laurel Lake takes cash only." I crawled down to the end of the couch, dislodging my cat, and rummaged in a drawer. "Here's a ten."

She stuffed it into her pocket and left the den. The front door banged behind her. Another twenty minutes passed before a car crunched to a stop in front of the house. Seconds later, it was speeding away.

Lucky for me. Natalie wouldn't be home to ask questions when my friend got here.

Micah arrived promptly at one. I was at the curb before he had a chance to make it around the front of the car.

"You look nice," he said.

"You do, too." I gave him an exaggerated inspection. "I've never seen you in shorts before."

"Not wise for the theater." He opened my door for me, then ran back to the driver's side and slipped inside.

"Do you need directions?"

"I have it in GPS."

On the drive north to Raleigh, he steered the conversation to safe topics. The show, the backstage crew, the sound equipment. That was fine with me. I liked hearing him talk. Less than an hour later, we were pulling into the spillover lot at the park. Apparently, hundreds of other people had had the same idea as me.

Micah went to the ticket booth and bought a strip of ride tickets. "What would you like to do first?"

"The carousel."

"Lead on."

We did it all, at least everything that made sense for people our ages. We rode the carousel three times. The mini-train and the paddleboats once each. We listened to a country band in the amphitheater before hitting the snack bar. I loaded a tray and paid, while Micah found us an empty picnic table.

"What do we have?" he asked when I slid onto the bench across from him.

"Nachos, iced tea, and snickerdoodles."

"I approve of your choices."

"Thank you." I let him tackle the nachos first because, hey, dessert. Initially, we focused on our personal food priorities in silence. But half a cookie later, I was ready to talk. "Are you game for an inquisition?"

"Sure," he mumbled around a chip.

"What will you do after the show's over?"

He sipped his drink before responding. "I have a week off, then I'm heading to New York for a pre-college theater intensive."

"What's that?"

"Two weeks of high-intensity classes on different aspects of technical design, taught by Broadway professionals. My focus will be on sound."

"Wow. Did you have to audition?"

He blushed. "Something like that."

"How many will be there with you?"

"Twelve in this intensive. All rising seniors in high school."

Twelve? I wondered how many applied, but it would likely embarrass him if I asked. "Think of all the things you will have learned this summer."

"Not the least of which is how to power a paddleboat on my own." He grinned.

"Hey." I tossed a cookie crumb at him. "I was pedaling."

"Sorry. Couldn't tell. So how about you? What's left of your summer?"

"I've been working for my stepfather's business. I'm hoping he'll give me more hours when my current project runs out."

"No plans with your friends?"

I developed a sudden interest in the nachos. "Nothing specific."

"Sounds like there's more to the story."

"Not something I want to discuss."

"Okay." He methodically began to collect his trash, his expression blank.

What was wrong with me? He was being curious, and I'd just shut down the conversation. Maybe I wasn't as ready to be friends as I thought.

Around us, the crowds had begun to thin. Cranky little kids were strapped into strollers and pushed toward the parking lot. The park quieted. Couples had it to themselves.

"Ready to go?" he asked after we'd finished cleaning up.

"Can I show you one of my favorite spots first?"

"Of course."

"There's a garden on the far side of the lake and, above it, a hill with a great view. Come on."

I played tour-guide/botanist along the way. The gardeners had created a unique presentation of plants and flowers that shouldn't have gone together but did. Different colors, heights, scents, and textures. Once we'd chosen a shady patch of lawn, Micah waited for me to sit and lowered himself beside me. A friendly distance away. We sat there in silence. It wasn't awkward either. Just . . . comfortable. Like we'd agreed not to fill our time with empty words. Instead, we just took in the park.

It was lovely at this hour, with the sun descending behind the huge oak trees and a light breeze swirling about us. Someone on the opposite side of the lake had brought a guitar and was strumming a mournful tune. I peeked at Micah, to see if he was enjoying it, too. He was leaning on his hands, head thrown back, eyes closed. It must be rare for him to have nothing to do. No responsibilities. No one asking him for anything. It felt good that he could be quiet with me.

He must've felt my gaze, because his eyes opened. When he turned his head toward me, I caught something lonely in his expression.

"Is everything okay, Micah?"

"Sure."

"I'm glad we did this. I like being here with you."

He closed his eyes briefly. "Thanks." He stood and then helped me up. "We should be getting back."

We retraced our path down the slope and onto the boardwalk around the lake, not saying anything until we reached the car. I checked my phone and found two missed texts from Kaylynn. The first had come in at two-thirty.

Trying to plan something. Want to go?

Of course, she had to ask today. When I was busy. Not that I would've canceled my time with Micah for any reason.

The second text had arrived a few minutes later.

Heading to Laurel Lake. You should come

Too late now, but I liked that she'd tried.

After Micah had merged onto the highway toward Azalea Springs, I made an attempt to talk. He answered in a quietly disinterested tone and flipped on the satellite radio. I gave up, looked out the window, and listened to his music.

We'd barely left Raleigh behind when my phone buzzed. Another text from Kaylynn.

We saw Natalie at the lake. Were you there?

Of course they would cross paths.

No. She went with friends
  We're at Winston's. Join us?

I was curious about who was with her. If I'd been home, I would've gone to meet them. But I couldn't make it today.

Can't. I'm in Raleigh
  K. Bye

I tossed my phone into my purse.

"Anything important?" Micah asked.

"No, it was my friend Kaylynn. She asked me to hang out tonight, but we'll have to do it another time."

When we got to my house, Micah parked at the curb and

walked with me as far as the veranda. He wouldn't look at me, though. Instead, he slipped his hands into his pockets. Pulled them out again. Crossed his arms.

Were things about to get awkward? I would make it easy on him to say good-bye. Rocking back on my heels, I put some space between us. "Thanks for going with me today."

"Yeah. I had fun."

Was it the kind of fun that he'd want to repeat? Or a polite way to put me off without either of us being embarrassed? I wished I knew. As much as I wanted to schedule another event, I didn't want to be shot down.

We stood there, neither moving, each waiting for the other to speak up.

Say something already.

Guess I'd have to be the brave one again. I clasped my hands behind my back to hide their shaking. Not that he would see anyway. He was studying the veranda floor with ridiculous concentration. "Um, so maybe we could hang out another time."

"Okay." He looked up, his expression more thoughtful than worried. "How about tomorrow?"

"*Yes*," I said before he finished the question.

He grinned. "Sure you won't take a minute to think about it?"

"I'm good." I grinned back. "What should we do?"

"Hiking?"

Hmm, he'd come prepared. Which was amazingly hopeful. Dirty, sweaty tramping through the woods would be a purely friendly thing to do, but if it meant I got to be with him, I would take it. "Yes. Can I choose where?"

"This *is* your part of North Carolina."

"Raven Rock State Park. It's not far."

"Good. Should I pick you up after breakfast?"

"Afternoon would be better. The trails will be crammed with families in the morning. We won't have to fight crowds in the afternoon. Want me to pack food?"

"I'll take care of everything."

"Okay." I ran up the steps and hesitated by the door. "Good night."

"Later." He jogged to his car and waved.

Behind me, the front door opened. "What are you doing out there?" Natalie asked.

I whipped around. Had she seen Micah? "Just got back."

"From where?"

The sound of his car faded down the street. "I went to a park with a friend."

She shrugged and stomped up the stairs. I watched her go uneasily. It was doubtful she would be happy about any after-hours contact I had with Micah. Now wasn't the right time to tell her.

⋅ 19 ⋅

The Friendly Line

It was hard to know what the trigger could've been, but my stepsister was in a hideous mood Sunday morning. When my mother and I got home from church, Natalie had her door closed and locked. The three of us tried to coax her out, but had to give up after she snapped "Leave me alone" to every question.

Jeff was tied up in knots. He'd had an outing planned for her, and it was in danger of being canceled. "Do you know what caused this?" he asked me as we were eating brunch.

"No, sir."

"You can't think of anything?"

Mom sighed. "Brooke doesn't know, and neither do I. As we've said."

His face tightened. He picked up his knife and fork and meticulously cut a slice of ham into squares.

I tried to intervene before an argument escalated between

them. "Maybe something happened at Laurel Lake. That's out of her routine."

"How can we know for sure?"

"I could call Norah."

Jeff considered that. "Maybe—"

"That's too much trouble," Mom interrupted. "Natalie will calm down on her own."

Jeff exhaled loudly, placed his silverware on the table with extreme care, pushed to his feet, and left the house.

"Mom, really. Do you have to speak to him like that?"

"Leave it alone, Brooke. This isn't your fight."

Yes, it was, if they made me a witness.

The person I was really mad at was Natalie. I didn't care if she wanted to sit in her room and sulk like a baby, but Jeff finally had some free time. He was disappointed that he wasn't spending it with her, and I was going to make sure she understood, even if it meant getting into it with her. I raced upstairs and pounded on her door. "Natalie?"

"Leave me alone."

"I'm not going anywhere. Tell me what the problem is."

"I will not."

"Your dad is worried."

"He'll get over it."

She was being an ungrateful brat. What could I do to blast her from her room? "If you don't come out and tell me what your problem is, I will go in my room and turn One Direction on so loud you can't avoid them."

"I hate One Direction."

"That would be the reason I chose them."

The door was wrenched open. "Don't do it."

"Okay, then. Why are you pissed off?"

"I'm not pissed off. I'm recovering."

"From what?"

"Swimming."

"If it does this to you, don't go again."

"I won't." She slammed the door shut, and the lock clicked.

"Natalie, go and talk to your dad."

"That wasn't part of the deal. You asked for a reason. I gave one. Now leave me alone."

Wow. She was right. She'd done exactly what I'd asked and no more. I had to change tactics. "It would be nice if you would explain things to Jeff," I said in a quieter tone. "This is his day off, and he can't enjoy it if he's worried about you." I added the magic phrase for her. "It isn't fair."

Crickets. She wasn't budging. Dragging my feet with noisy attitude, I went into my room and stood uncertainly in the middle. Micah wouldn't be here for another three hours. That was enough time for something productive, but what?

Natalie's door opened. She ran past my room and down the stairs. A minute later, the shutting of the side door reverberated throughout the house.

I flung myself belly-down across the bed and squealed into the quilt. Dealing with Natalie could be hard, but I'd won this round.

Fifteen minutes before Micah was due, I flung my backpack onto my bed and tossed in a water bottle and sunscreen. After zipping my phone into another pocket, I started out the bedroom door just as Natalie erupted from the bathroom.

"Where are you going?"

I hesitated. There was nothing to feel guilty about, and this might be a good moment to ease into an explanation. "Hiking."

"Alone?"

"With Micah."

Her eyes narrowed at me. "Why?"

I smiled as guilelessly as possible. "Raven Rock State Park is nearby, and he's never been there. I said I'd hike with him. Do you like to hike?"

"No." Her gaze flitted away and bounced restlessly about the landing as she processed what I'd said. She gave a soft snort, then rushed to her room, the door banging shut behind her.

I'd told the truth—well, mostly—and she'd tolerated it. Since Micah only wanted to be friends, we'd be sticking to hanging out. Maybe everything would be okay after all.

A car was pulling into the driveway, so I skipped down the stairs and out the front.

"Hi," I said as I got in.

"Hey." He smiled. "Ready?"

"Yeah."

"Let's do it." He backed out, and we were on our way.

It wouldn't take long to get there, but I planned to fill every second with conversation. "Tell me about your family."

"You know Mom. She was born in the U.S., but her parents are from Taiwan. My dad is white. Born and raised in North Carolina. They met in college."

"What does he do?"

"He's a farmer."

"A farmer?" Did not expect that.

"Yeah. CSA. Community-supported agriculture."

"Which is?"

"He grows organic produce. A cooperative of families and restaurants buy from him."

"Do you help?"

"As little as possible." He laughed. "I have two older brothers, Peter and Jude. Both in college. Your turn."

"I suspect you know everything about me."

"From Natalie's perspective. Not yours."

"Okay. I was born in Wilmington. Mom and I moved here when I was ten . . ."

The words flowed. Back and forth, we asked and answered. I hardly noticed our surroundings until he turned onto the lane leading to the park. After we'd found a shady parking place, we got out, slipped on our backpacks, and checked our water bottles. Then we made a detour to use the bathroom and study the park map.

The trailhead was clearly marked. We walked, side by side, on the wide dirt trail toward the Cape Fear River, descending a sharp incline into a thick tunnel of trees. The only sounds were the call of birds and the bubbling of a nearby but unseen creek.

"Do you hike often?" I asked.

"Not as much as I would like." His lips twisted. "I stay busy."

"With what?"

He scanned the canopy of trees overhead. "School. Theater. More theater." There was a weird edge to his voice.

As we picked our way over a crumbling slide of rock, I over-balanced and wobbled. He caught my hand and steadied me.

"Thanks." I smiled my gratitude.

"Sure." He released my hand and looked down the trail. Another couple approached from the opposite direction. We shifted to one side and mumbled a greeting as they passed.

My stumble seemed to lighten things between us. We continued along the trail, chatting occasionally, soaking up the sunlight drifting through the trees. The hidden creek finally made its appearance, paralleling the trail. Micah's head shifted from side to side as he took in the serenity of the forest.

We paused at the top of a ridge. There were a lot of people out today, but most of the crowd seemed to be leaving. Little kids hurried to keep up with their parents, voices piping loudly. Younger couples walked by, holding hands, some with a sweaty, sleeping baby in a carrier, its legs flopping with each step the parent took.

I pointed to a set of wooden steps that disappeared over a bluff. "That's the easiest way down."

"Let's go."

Once we reached the riverbank and the rock—as if it made sense to call a mile-wide formation "a rock"—nature had worked its charm. Micah had relaxed and told me about the school he attended, the classes he would take this fall, and his nerdy group of friends.

I spread a blanket on a clear spot with a great view of the Cape Fear River. He set our backpacks on a corner of the blanket and sat beside me.

After a minute, I'd had enough of watching the water flow. I laid down and wiggled for comfort.

"What are you doing?" he asked.

"Looking at the clouds. Join me."

He held out for a minute before lying down on his side of the blanket.

"Micah, do you ever get tired of the theater?"

His head turned toward me. "You noticed that earlier, huh?"

I nodded.

He looked back at the sky. "Yeah, I do get tired, especially at my high school. The drama teacher counts on me to be the stage manager for every production. I don't mind occasionally, but it would be nice to have a semester free."

"So do it. Take the fall semester off."

"I don't have a good excuse."

"Yes, you do. You'd like a semester free. That ought to be good enough. But if you'd rather give her an excuse that sounds more important, remind her that this is your semester to hunt for colleges. You'll be busy."

"She knows better than that. I'll go to Elon."

"Really? Do you want to?"

He met my gaze again, his expression unreadable. "You have a lot of questions."

"I'll bet you do, too." I rolled to my side and propped my head up on my hand. "Do you think you're being fair to the other theater majors at Elon?"

"Fair?"

"Yeah. It would be hard for anyone else to compete against you in your *mother's* department. And when you get picked for something, you'll never know for sure why."

"I've never thought about it that way."

"So think. It can't hurt to go on campus visits for other schools. Either it'll prove that there is a better place for you, or it'll make you positive that Elon is best."

His grin held a trace of amusement. "Natalie says you're bossy. I have to agree."

"I'll take that as a compliment."

"That's how I intended it."

I laid down again. Silently, we watched the breeze ruffle the leaves overhead and listened to the rush of the river, completely at peace with the day.

From the bluff above us came the high-pitched voices of children and the low responses of adults. Feet thumped on the wooden steps that served as a shortcut to the river.

"Come on," I said, sitting up. "This spot is about to be over-run with little people. There are other trails to conquer."

Two hours later, we emerged from a rarely used trail into the parking lot, tired and dusty. We finished our water and tossed the bottles into a recycle bin.

When we reached his car, I said, "Stand still. It's time for a tick check."

"Go for it."

I checked his neck, collar, and hair—then scrutinized his clothes. And if I used extraordinary care during the examination, that would be because I was a conscientious person. "You look tick free. My turn."

He repeated my actions with precise movement. The touch of his fingers was fleeting, and burned into my memory forever.

"You're good, too." He looked back over the parking lot. "I enjoyed this."

The hope that had died Friday night was flickering back to life. "Micah?"

He shook his head and opened my door. "Let's go." While I slid onto the seat, he grabbed our two backpacks and carried them to the trunk.

I got the message. His feet were firmly planted on his side of the *friendly* line.

· 20 ·

The Missing Connection

While Lisa met with the cast for their Monday morning pep talk, I went on my first round of errands. Checking with Elena for news. Taking messages to counselors about absent campers. Ensuring that all props had been correctly stored.

I ended my run in the auditorium and scanned the room. Micah sat in the front row aisle seat, jotting notes and laughing with the rest of them. Natalie sat directly behind him, hands folded in her lap, head back, studying the ceiling.

He looked up, caught me staring, and smiled faintly. Natalie tapped him on the shoulder, spoke into his ear, and reclined again after he answered.

When Lisa finished speaking, Micah stepped forward. "Okay, everyone, we'll rehearse the auction scene after small groups. See you in forty minutes." As the auditorium cleared, he gestured toward the wings. "Do you have a moment?" he asked crisply.

His tone worried me. Was something wrong? "Sure."

I followed him into the wings and down the hall. When he reached the staff lounge, he waited for me to enter and closed the door behind us. "About tonight?"

"Yes?"

He crossed his arms. Dropped them again. Smiled shyly. "I'm free after the production team meeting. Can I hang out with you?"

In all the times I'd been asked on an actual date, none had ever delighted me as much as Micah's sweetly nervous question. "Definitely."

"It's your turn to decide."

"How about a baseball game?" Okay, I had a plan ready. Just in case. "My mom is umping a game in Sanford."

"Sounds good. When?"

"Seven." Impulsively, I hugged him. He smelled amazing. Fresh clothes, soap, and Micah.

His arms closed around me briefly before he eased away. "I have to get back to the auditorium."

I walked through the door ahead of him and detoured to the office to see if Elena needed anything. Before I went in, though, I watched until he disappeared into the wings.

It was early afternoon when Micah crouched beside me at the director's table. "You should check on Natalie."

"Why? What's wrong?"

"Nothing more than a feeling Norah has. The girls' ensemble is in choreography."

I found my stepsister in a practice room. Norah motioned

me over when I entered. "Natalie's anxious. She's not getting the simplest of the steps."

My stepsister stumbled a beat or two behind everyone else. She had her fists clenched against her thighs, a sure sign that she knew she was messing up.

"I'll go back to the hallway," I whispered to Norah. "Can you get her out there?"

"Yeah."

As I left, Norah was speaking. "Claire, could I borrow Natalie for a moment?"

When Natalie joined us in the hall, she sighed loudly. "What is it?" Her voice sounded tired.

"What's upsetting you?"

"Claire is doing the steps too fast. I can't keep up."

"Have you told her?"

"The other girls are getting them, and I don't want to look stupid." Her fists thumped against her thighs. "Plus it's backward."

"How?"

"When she's using her right hand, we're supposed to use our left hand, and that doesn't make sense to me. She's also using words that I don't know what they mean, but everybody else must, because no one is asking for an explanation."

Norah smiled. "Do you want me to ask Claire to face the same direction as you, so that your right hands are moving at the same time?"

"Yes."

I pulled my phone from my shorts pocket. "If I recorded the choreography, you could practice at home. Would that help?"

Natalie's fists slowed. "It might."

Norah held out her hand. "If you don't mind me using your phone, Brooke, I can do the recording. It would be less obvious, too."

Natalie nodded. "That's a good plan."

"Okay." I handed the phone to Norah and left. When I reached the next hallway, I looked back. Natalie and her counselor hadn't gone into the studio yet. They stood beside each other, heads together. Natalie listened as Norah spoke earnestly.

I went on, glad that this problem seemed solved and relieved that I wasn't the only one involved in the solution.

Micah rushed in late for the production team meeting, clutching his binder. "Okay, everyone. Since tomorrow is Independence Day, I'll keep this meeting short. Mail me your notes. See you Wednesday."

His announcement was met with a smattering of applause and whoops as the team stood and grabbed their backpacks. He waited until the room was empty to speak. "When should we leave for the game?"

"If we ride with my mom, we have to go now."

"We can take my car."

"That gives us an extra thirty minutes."

"Let me take Mom home, then I'll be over."

My mother was hovering impatiently in the utility room when Natalie and I got home from the arts center. Natalie went straight up to her room.

"You're calling it close," she said. "Keys."

I dropped them in her hand and stepped aside to let her pass. "Mom?"

"Uh-huh?" She paused, gripping the doorknob.

"When will Jeff be home?"

"He's on his way. Why?"

"I'm coming to the game tonight. Just wanted to make sure someone would be here for Natalie."

"How will you get there?"

"A friend's driving me."

"A *guy* friend?"

"Micah."

"From the theater? Natalie's Micah?"

So I wasn't the only one who recognized how important he was to her. "Yes."

"Is this a date?"

"Nope."

Her eyebrow arched skeptically.

If she only knew how much I wished it were. "No. He's driving me to the game. Nothing more."

"Uh-huh." She leaned against the doorframe, studying my face intently. "Honey, be careful there. Natalie is fixated on Micah."

"I know."

My dejection must've been clear, because Mom's lips curved sympathetically. "I'm sure the two of you don't feel the same way about him, but that doesn't change what Natalie believes. She has a prior claim, and you're poaching."

"There are different kinds of *like*."

"True, which she probably understands intellectually. But the type of *like* matters less to Natalie than its intensity. At the moment, she's intense about him. Remember how she was when Jeff and I were first engaged?"

"Yes. She didn't seem to like us much." It had been painful.

"It wasn't really that. Natalie hadn't spent much time around Jeff while he was in the military. Once he retired, she was finally able to be around him more. And just as that started to go well, you and I showed up. A new stepmom and stepsister—who got to live with her dad. It took months of reassurance before she could see that she hadn't been replaced in Jeff's eyes."

I didn't have months to reassure her. "Are you telling me to back off?"

"No. From the little I've seen of Micah, I'd say he's worth it. I'm just warning you to acknowledge the potential consequences of what you're doing."

My mother had put into words the fear I'd been carrying around for days. "Micah wants to keep it friendly. There's no poaching involved."

"Uh-huh. Then you're safe from complications, aren't you?" She pushed through the door to the carport.

I ran upstairs and into my room. After a full day in these clothes, I had to change, though the new outfit would require a delicate balancing act. It had to look nice but couldn't scream trying-to-impress. I decided on a lacy tank top, denim skirt, sandals, *cute* copper earrings—then finished with lip gloss and my hair in a knot. I'd just grabbed my purse when the doorbell rang.

Natalie managed to make it down the stairs before me. She burst onto the veranda, where Micah was leaning against a pillar. "What are you doing here?"

"I'm going to a ball game with Brooke."

"They're not much fun. Why would you want to do that?"

"I thought Micah might enjoy watching Mom ump a game," I said, crossing my fingers that Natalie would refuse what I was about to ask. "Do you want to come with us?"

"One time was enough. Will I be alone?"

"Jeff should be home soon."

She looked back toward Micah. "I sent you a text. You haven't answered yet."

"I can tell you the answer now," he said. "Yes, your dress can be loose, not fitted. And I won't forget to tell the costume designer."

Without another word, Natalie spun around and ran back into the house.

"Ready?" he said.

"Yeah."

Once we were in his Subaru, Micah keyed the destination into the GPS and pulled away. "How long has your mother been an umpire?"

"Ten years."

"I haven't seen a lot of female umpires."

"There aren't many. Do you like baseball?"

"To watch, not to play. My brother was on our high school baseball team. They made it to the state championship his senior year."

"Really? Mom's umped those games for a couple of years." I'd attended most of them, too. A thought tickled at my brain. "Which brother?"

"Jude."

"Jude Dalton is your brother." I couldn't remember a face,

but the name was familiar. "Western Alamance High School. They made it to the semifinals last year."

"Yeah." Micah's voice had tightened.

"Does he play anymore?"

"Nah. He lost interest. He likes being a star, and he's not good enough to be one in college."

Oh, wow. That was as close to snark as I'd ever heard come from Micah's mouth. What was up between him and his middle brother? I'd always wanted siblings. *Badly*. I'd hoped and waited and prayed until I'd finally accepted that it wouldn't happen. It always fascinated me when friends lucky enough to have siblings didn't get along.

I was so lost in my thoughts, I hardly noticed as Micah merged into the westbound traffic of the highway.

"Brooke." He sounded hesitant. "In a friendly relationship, is it safe to ask anything?"

I rolled my head toward Micah and frowned at his profile. That wasn't the most comforting way to start a conversation. "It's safe to ask, and it's also safe to say no if you don't want to answer."

"Sounds fair." His hands drummed a faint rhythm on the steering wheel. "Will you tell me about your father?"

I needed to have a talk with my stepsister. The story wasn't a secret, but it *was* private. I had the right to decide who got to know and who didn't. "Natalie's told you why I don't have one."

He nodded. "Does it feel strange?"

"Not in a bad way." I hesitated, uncertain about how much I was willing to say. Guess I'd just go slowly and see how it felt. "A lot of people don't have their dads around. I think it would be worse to know they're not in your life because they don't want to be."

"What's your opinion of the man?"

"I don't really have an opinion. But . . ." As always when I thought about this, a nameless void yawned inside me. "It's hard to describe my reaction toward my biological father. Mostly, it's just . . . zero. I'm not exactly happy about him. I'd have to know the guy to feel happy. But I'm not mad either. He gave me life."

Micah's brow was creased, as if he had more questions, but he wasn't asking them. Was he leaving it to me to decide whether to say more? I liked that. "When I was little, if I could have, I would've ordered a father online. The shiny deluxe model—not the version that some of my friends have." My hands curled against my thighs. "There are ways that being fatherless is good. I'll never experience the pain of losing my dad to death or abandonment. I won't have to face the disappointment of an absentee father who breaks his promises, who doesn't care enough to know me."

"Is it okay to say I'm sorry?"

"Don't be. I have an amazing mom and the best stepfather I could ever want. I know how lucky I am." I really believed that, too. Jeff was almost enough, and I'd grown used to ignoring the missing connection that could never be bridged.

I lapsed into silence and studied Micah. He drove the same way he ran the show. Controlled. Confident. Relaxed.

His lips twitched, as if he knew I was watching him. "Everything okay?"

"Yeah." I hesitated, then added, "Thanks."

His hand touched mine lightly. Comfort given and received.

I already had a long list of reasons to like Micah, and now I would add one more. I'd never noticed before how attractive *nice* was.

We pulled into the ballpark with twenty minutes to spare. Our first stop was the snack bar. After getting hamburgers and milkshakes, we moved to the picnic table farthest away from the stands.

As we were cleaning up, an older couple walked past. The woman's head twisted as she went by, obviously gawking at us.

I tossed our trash into the garbage can. "What's her problem?"

"Me." He took a distinct step away from me and slipped on his shades. "I'll bet there aren't many Asians around here, and none are hanging out with a white girl."

I stiffened. "Why does that matter?"

"It must matter to her."

I swung around. The couple had stopped to watch us. At my scowl, they hurried on. "How often does that happen? To have people acting that way because you're Chinese?"

"Not much, at least not in Elon."

"Does it bother you?"

"Not really. Calling me names might. Stuff like this isn't worth acknowledging."

But it was worth fighting. "If we're being judged, we might as well look like we're really together." I deliberately tucked my hand into the crook of his arm. "The game's about to start. Come on."

After the fourth inning, the visiting team switched pitchers. While the new guy warmed up, I faced Micah. "It's my turn to ask questions."

"Ask away."

"Tell me about your dad's farm."

"Oh, yeah. Go for the jugular." Micah polished off his water and tapped the empty bottle against his thigh. "Our farm is small. Something is always being planted or harvested, March to October. Vegetables, fruit, and flowers. Dad rotates crops, depending on what's in season."

"That sounds interesting."

"I guess it can be, to you city folk."

I laughed. "Is that what you want to be when you grow up?"

"Not at all."

He seemed so happy and relaxed that I hated to spoil the mood, but he'd asked a tough question about my bio father. I had a tough question to ask, too. "Is it hard to be a stage manager for a production like this?"

The lightness faded from his expression. "Harder than I expected." He bowed his head. "I've been the stage manager for three productions at my high school. Since I know the drama teacher and all of the actors, those productions were easy. I've worked with the school's backstage crew enough to know what they're capable of." He stared blindly before him, as if he'd retreated from the ball game to somewhere else. A place that was familiar and necessary. "I've been an assistant stage manager outside of my high school before, but always working with a crew who knew their facility well. That's not true this summer. The arts center is awesome, but it's new. The whole team is discovering what it can do together. It's . . ." He clamped his lips shut and shook his head.

He seemed down. I wanted to help him. To tell him it would all be okay. I'd been curious why he hadn't delegated more, and now I understood. He just hadn't figured out who to trust. "It must be intimidating to be running the first production in there."

"Yeah. The arts council wants the show to be great, and they're not afraid to tell us that every chance they get. Mom's used to that kind of pressure, but me?" He blew out a noisy breath. "Being paid for something changes how it feels."

"Can you ever let the stress go?"

He turned toward me, our faces only inches apart.

"I can let it go when I'm with you."

His words sank into me softly, and I smiled. I loved that he could find peace when we were together.

The noise around us increased as the next batter stepped to the plate. I looked away from Micah, like I was concentrating on the game. But I wasn't. My mind was too busy wondering whether Micah liked being personal after all.

After the home team won, happy fans drifted away. We stayed in the stands while my mom finished a conversation with the other umpire. Micah and I met her as she was coming off the field.

"Hi, honey." She held out her hand to Micah. "Hello. Nice to see you again. Did you enjoy the game?"

"Yes, ma'am."

"I like this league. There's a lot of talent . . ."

While we walked to her car, she questioned Micah like she was grilling a prospective boyfriend. He didn't seem to notice.

I looked around the park. After the brightness of the lights on the field, the parking lot was filled with shadows. Muffled voices. The roar of engines and crunch of tires as cars pulled away.

". . . Do you want to ride home with me, Brooke?"

"What?" I tuned in. Ride home with her? Mom's suggestion made sense, but I didn't want to. I was reluctant to say good-bye to Micah. I peeked at his face but couldn't read his expression. He wasn't helping me, so the decision was all mine.

Well, I'd just have to hope that he either didn't get how much I craved being with him—or didn't mind. "Micah's not familiar with the area. I should go with him to make sure he gets back okay."

His "thanks" was quiet. Neutral.

Mom mouthed *GPS*. I shrugged. She grinned as she got in her car.

Once she'd driven away, we crossed to his car on the opposite side of the lot. He put his hand on the passenger-side door, but didn't open it. Instead, he studied me, unsmiling, his eyes glittering in the light from a nearby streetlamp.

His scrutiny had me wondering if I'd guessed wrong. Would he have preferred to drive home alone? "I'm glad you came with me tonight, Micah."

"Me, too."

We stood there, watching each other silently.

"Okay, then." I inched toward the car.

"Brooke." His hand cupped my shoulder.

I stilled. He was deliberate about everything he did, and he'd initiated this. Touching me meant something to him, right?

A sigh escaped his lips. He drew me against him, one hand sliding along my shoulder to the nape of my neck, the other hand gentle at my waist.

Laughter erupted from nearby. Car doors slammed. We would soon be alone in an empty ballpark.

"We should go," I said.

"Yeah."

But we didn't move. We stayed in each other's arms as the world grew quiet around us. And in many ways, holding him felt as intimate as any kiss I'd ever shared.

· 21 ·

Regret and Apology

It wasn't until after midnight that I realized Micah and I had no plans for the Fourth of July. Was that on purpose or an oversight? Even more, should it worry me that I was becoming so attached to a guy who'd be gone soon that I didn't want to miss a single day with him?

Yes, it should.

I woke up early, wanting to call him and ask, but he didn't get to sleep in often. I texted instead.

Are you up?

He responded immediately.

Yes

    Can we hang out today?

A pause. Hmm.

> Can't. I'll be with my parents
>> Your dad's coming here?
> We're meeting in Raleigh
>> How about tonight?
> We'll watch fireworks. They start at 9
>> Skipping today then?
> Right

Disturbed by how upset I was, I walked to the window to stare into the world. It was going to be gorgeous—hot and sun-shiney. Jeff had already put our American flag out to honor the day. It was my new family's first Fourth of July together, and we probably had plans, too. So this was for the best. Really. I had to shake it off.

When I looked at my phone again, there was another text.

> What does the silence mean?
>> Disappointment

This time, he didn't respond immediately, but I would wait him out.

> I like being with my parents. This has been planned awhile
>> So you knew last night
> Don't often clear my calendar with friends

Wow. Was he being snarky or matter-of-fact? It was hard to know with Micah. Maybe we should just talk. I called.

"Hey," he said.

"I wasn't complaining."

"Kind of seemed like it."

"Micah, stop." I leaned on my dresser and glanced at its mirror. The sight of fresh-out-of-bed me didn't improve my attitude. "Why are we acting like this?"

There was a soft exhale. "You're right. I'm sorry. I should've told you last night, but I was enjoying the game and didn't want to spoil the mood."

"I enjoyed it, too. I get your decision."

"So . . . I'll see you in the morning."

"And we'll both be busy," I muttered.

"What do you want me to say?"

I had to get over myself. *Now.* "Have a nice time."

"Thanks. Bye."

Independence Day was nice at our house, too.

Jeff loved this holiday, and he hadn't spent it with Natalie in five years, so he was completely psyched about celebrating today. The two of them left in his truck and returned an hour later with bags from the dollar store and sly smiles.

He handed me a large bag. "Do you want an assignment?"

"Sure." I checked inside. Rolls of crepe paper in red, white, and blue. Patriotic dishes, napkins, and a tablecloth. "You actually trust me with the decorations?"

"I do." He grinned.

I tried not to laugh. I was not known for my decorating skills. "Hope that works out for you."

"I'm positive it will."

We gathered on the deck at six, each with our assigned contribution completed. Jeff grilled ribs, corn, and pineapple. Mom made salad and homemade ice cream. I'd decorated with sad little streamers of crepe paper, red-white-and-blue paper products, and—of course—the flag. Natalie sang the national anthem.

Afterward, Jeff and Mom snuggled on the couch. Natalie and I decided it would be best to go to a movie.

We got in the Honda, but before I backed out of the driveway, I had something to say. "Natalie?"

"What?"

"When Micah and I were driving to the game last night, he asked me about my bio father."

"Oh." Her head whipped toward me. "If this is turning into one of those lectures about being careful with secrets, let me just say in my defense that I didn't realize it was a secret until I saw the look on Micah's face. He was shocked."

Private was a better word for my story than *secret*, but it might be hard to explain those subtleties to Natalie. "Why were you even talking about it?"

"I was telling him about my custody arrangements, and he asked me if you had any with your father, and I said that Jill wanted you so badly she had you completely on her own."

Jill wanted you so badly. I loved those words. I loved what they meant. It drained the energy from my anger. "Don't do that again. It's my choice who to tell."

"I won't. But how do you just automatically know what's okay to tell and what's not?"

"That's a hard question to answer." Before I could start an explanation, she looked away, already leaving this topic behind. Time for me to do the same.

I survived the holiday.

When Mom pulled into the drop-off lane Wednesday morning, the Daltons' car was in its normal parking spot. I hurried into the auditorium. Lisa was sitting on the edge of the stage, frowning at her tablet. Behind her, the stage had already been set for today's first scene. She didn't look up when I passed her and slipped into the wings.

The door to the office was ajar. I ran in and tossed my backpack into its normal spot, then looked at the desk. Elena's in-box was full, so I thumbed through the pages to see if I could handle anything for her.

There was a sound behind me. I glanced over my shoulder. Micah stood in the doorway.

"Hey."

"Hi." Nerves slammed into me.

We stood there, eyeing each other uneasily, neither one of us yielding.

We had to get past this. It wasn't like we were dating. *Fun and friendly, remember?* "How was your day with your parents?"

"Good. How about yours?"

"Great."

"Sorry," we said in unison.

His smile drew me like a magnet. We met halfway, arms reaching for each other, locking us into an embrace full of regret and apology. I loved the way he smelled. I loved the way he felt, too—his body lean and strong against mine.

"No more surprises, Brooke." His lips brushed my hair. Intentionally?

I nodded, too enchanted by that almost-kiss to speak.

"Micah," someone called in the hallway.

He groaned. "It's time to get started, but we'll talk later." His smile sent a promise, and then he was gone.

Micah's voice came over the headset around noon. "Counselors, lunch break. It's not too hot right now, so lounge or patio. Brooke, can you meet me in the prop room in five?"

I glanced at Lisa. At her nod, I said, "Sure."

When I entered the prop room, he was already there, setting a chair in the tiny bit of free space by the door. Without acknowledging me, he pulled a handkerchief from his pocket, dusted the chair, then turned. "Sit, please."

I sat, my heart racing. What was going on?

He closed the door and stood there a moment, head bowed and hands jammed into his pockets. His breathing sounded labored.

This was disorienting. "Micah?"

His head popped up. "I've made a decision."

"About what?"

"Us." He crouched before me, our eyes at the same level. "I can't pretend any longer. We have to stop 'hanging out.'"

I gasped and shrank away. Not what I'd expected. Not what I wanted.

"Please hear me out, Brooke. I'm not giving you up. Yesterday proved to me that 'hanging out' isn't enough. I want more."

I swallowed hard. "Go on."

"The whole time I was with my parents yesterday I kept thinking about how much I wished you were there. How much I missed even one day without talking with you, seeing you smile, watching you make life better for everyone around you." He sucked in a nervous breath. "I've never done this before but . . . I'd like for us to have real dates."

Real dates? Relief struck so fast that it was dizzying. "Me, too."

He rose and held out both of his hands. I took them and let him pull me up. We didn't let go, though. We stood there, smiling at each other under the light of a bare bulb, in a musty room full of furniture and fake plants.

How do I break this to Natalie?

No. I would not allow my worries to mess up this moment.

"Hey," he said, giving my hands a light squeeze. "Is something wrong?"

I shook my head at him. At me. I wouldn't let bad thoughts intrude. For now, I would savor how amazing it was that Micah wanted me in the same way I wanted him. "I'm just thinking that you're only here for another nineteen days."

"We'll find a way to make the most of it, but no more pretending about the friendly and not-too-personal stuff."

"Agreed. Can we have our first real date tonight?"

"I hope so."

"What about tomorrow night and this weekend?"

"Tomorrow night, yes." His face fell. "Mom and I are going home for the weekend."

Why was the universe sending us obstacles before we'd even gotten started? Fortunately, I didn't care about the universe's opinion. "When do you leave?"

"She wants to go Friday night."

Disappointment had me sagging into him.

"I can talk Mom into Saturday morning."

"Could you stay?"

"I don't want to. Peter's decided to come down from D.C. for the weekend. Jude will come if he can get the day off, although I'm not telling Mom yet. I don't get to see my brothers very often. This might be the last chance for a while."

"Of course, you have to go." I released his hands. We'd gone through a lot of changes in the past ten minutes. I needed some space to process it all. "We should get back."

He reached around me for the door. "What will we do tonight?"

"Just be together."

"Sounds great."

"Micah?"

"Yeah?"

Standing on tiptoe, I touched my lips to his.

He jerked in surprise, stared at me wide-eyed for a second, then leaned forward to kiss me back. Our noses bumped, his mouth landing on my cheek before sliding to my lips.

Our first kiss.

· 22 ·

My Definition of Perfect

Micah's *I'm here* text came around seven-thirty, earlier than I expected. To distract myself, I'd been editing Jeff's website. After saving my changes, I jumped from the bed, stuffed my feet into ballet flats, and rushed out the door.

"Brooke?" Natalie called.

I halted at the stairs. "Uh-huh?"

"Are you busy?"

Yes, I was. "What do you need?"

"Check my choreography."

"Um, sure." I stared with longing down the stairs, at the front door, then turned to go into her room. As I sat on the bed, my phone buzzed. I read the text.

Ready?

Not quite

She frowned. "Who's that?"

I wanted to lie. "Micah."

"What does he want?"

"It can wait."

Her frown turned suspicious. "Does he text with you, too?"

"Some."

"Okay. Now watch." She brought up the video clip on her tablet and mimicked the dance. Her movements weren't very smooth, but they weren't totally wrong either. She had them in the right order and generally in rhythm with the music.

When that section ended, she paused the video. "How did I do?"

"You're getting better." The choreographer would have to put Natalie in the back, though, which she might prefer.

"But not good enough yet."

"You have the steps down, so all you need is more practice. You're very close." I slid off the bed and crossed to the door.

"Why are you in such a hurry?"

"I'm going for a walk."

"If I practice some more, will you watch again?"

"Of course."

She shrugged, tapped replay on the tablet, and started to dance again.

I walked sedately from her room, raced down the stairs, and hurried from the house.

Micah was reclining against his car and straightened as I approached. "Hey."

"Sorry it took so long. Natalie needed me."

"No problem. So, what's next?"

"I thought we'd have our first official date at my neighborhood park. It's not far." I pointed at a pine forest near the end of the lane. "We can cut through the trees."

It didn't take long to reach the woods. They were dim. Hushed. No sounds other than birds, insects, and our feet on the trail. I hated to break our lovely silence, but there was too much that had to be discussed. "How will this work, Micah? We can't waste a single second."

"I've been thinking about that. You can be my shadow at the theater."

"I already am."

"*Everywhere.* We'll spend breaks together . . ."

"When it makes sense."

". . . and dates every night we're both free."

As we emerged from the trees, I scanned the park. The playground and jogging trail were deserted. A couple sat on the top of a picnic table, making out. Otherwise, we had the whole place to ourselves.

I smiled up at him. "For the most efficient use of our time together, we should have rules. Mutually-agreed-upon relationship rules."

"I like efficiency. And rules."

"Which is why we're having them." I took off across the lawn, heading for the mulched path that wound through the park. "I'll go first. We're skipping the insecure stage."

"Which is?"

"Those first few weeks of the relationship when neither of you will give it your all because you're worried it won't work out."

He laced his fingers through mine and pulled me to a stop, his expression growing serious. "I'm ready to give this my all."

Wow. I just fell a little harder. "I'm ready, too."

We held hands and stared into each other's eyes, aware that we stood at the edge of something strong and sweet.

A jogger flew past us, breaking the spell.

"Second rule," Micah said. "Plenty of touching."

Yes, please. Could he tell how much I wanted that, too? I'd never thought of myself as starving for touch. Mom was a hugger, and so were many of my friends. But I eagerly approved of Micah's rule. "That works for me."

We started down the mulched path again. Ahead of us, the other couple hopped off the picnic table and left the park, disappearing down a lane.

"We should talk," I said.

"Can we get good at the touching first?" His smile was hopeful.

"Honest conversation is an essential relationship rule. You must trust me on this."

"But we had talking on the friendly plan, too."

I laughed. This was going to be so good.

Night had fallen, with only the faintest golden band visible on the horizon. We strolled along the path as it curved gently up a hill through alternating pools of shadows and streetlights. I moved in closer to him, until we were bumping hips as we walked. "Is theater what you want to do with your life?"

He shook his head. "I couldn't do it for a full-time job. It's not enough. That's why I'm taking the intensive in August. I can use sound design outside the theater."

"Are you tired of it?"

He pursed his lips as he thought.

"Micah, if you can't answer an immediate no, then it's yes."

"The answer is *sometimes*. I love the energy of a show, and I like being around talented people. But I'd also like to focus more on my schoolwork, hang out with friends, and do nothing on the weekends but watch mindless TV. Those things don't happen much."

"Have you told Lisa?"

"Dad knows but thinks it's my story to tell, and I haven't found the right time yet. It makes her happy to have one of her sons involved in the theater." He tightened his fingers around mine. "What about you?"

"I want to take care of people."

"Like medicine?"

"No, blood is gross. I'd like to do the kinds of things that I'm handling for the show. Managing the little details so that other people can focus on the big stuff. Anticipating their needs. I could be a personal assistant. Or an office manager."

"You'd be great. It takes a lot of self-confidence to watch others get the credit for what you helped to create."

"I guess you know about that, too." I loved this about him—his easy way with compliments. "So, you said today that you've 'never done this before.' Done what?"

He stopped and looked down at me, a streetlamp creating a halo of light around his head. "Dating."

"What?" I was his first girlfriend? That was unexpected—and wonderful. "You've never been on a date?"

"It's complicated. I asked a girl out once, but she, um, didn't realize it was a date. She thought we were just meeting for coffee."

"Did you make it clear?"

"Sort of, but she wasn't interested in me. She was too busy pumping me for information about . . . another guy."

Since his face was in the shadows, I couldn't see his expression, but his tone had a bite. I wanted to say *sorry*, but it somehow didn't seem like the right word. "Have you ever been kissed?"

"Only by you."

I blinked in disbelief. "What is wrong with the girls in Elon?"

He shrugged and looked away.

Admitting this had made him uncomfortable. I couldn't let that slide, because Micah was amazing. *He* wasn't the reason. "I wish I'd known."

"That I don't know how to kiss? I'm sure you could tell."

"I couldn't. Really. I assumed anything less than perfection was nerves."

"Nerves were involved."

"Well, then." We'd both committed to not wasting a second, to diving right into the secure stage. He lacked confidence, and it was time for that to change. "Come on," I said, tugging him over to the recently vacated picnic table. "Help me up."

He put his hands at my waist and lifted me onto the tabletop, as if I hardly weighed anything, which was far from the truth—jiggly thighs and big butt and all.

"Whoa," I said, bracing my hands against his arms. "You're stronger than you look."

"Is that a problem for you?"

"Not. At. All." This was even more evidence that my first impression of Micah had underestimated him. He was fast becoming the hottest guy I'd ever known. "So, let's get back to the dating thing. Since I'm the one with experience, whatever I tell you, you have to believe."

His lips twitched. "True."

I eyed him up and down, as if considering a new recruit. "The most important thing to remember is that it's best if the girl always gets her way."

"Is it, now."

"Yeah, and that'll go smoother if you learn to read my mind."

"I'll try."

"I like your attitude. And, naturally, physical contact is required."

"I believe I've already mentioned the touching. Since I'm new to this, a demo might be useful."

This was a huge responsibility—teaching someone how to become a couple, how to do the right things in the right ways. Sliding my hands up his arms, I linked them behind his neck. "We should start with holding each other. It's simple and, if done well, highly effective. And not dramatically different from hugging."

"I'm seriously hoping you're wrong about that." He moved even closer, his arms wrapping carefully around my waist. "This feels vaguely familiar and yet, it doesn't remind me of hugging."

I didn't respond, too focused on how it felt to be in his arms. Could we stay this way forever?

"Brooke?" His smiled faded. "How much touching is too much?"

"If you're paying attention, you won't get it wrong."

"I'm paying attention."

I'd known before that he was perfect, but this evening had proven that my definition of perfect had been too small. Micah was so much more. "Holding hands is also lovely. However, if I had to vote for a personal favorite, it would be kissing."

"Feel free to win me over."

I pressed my lips to his in a slow, gentle kiss. He held himself very still, as if he was afraid to breathe. When I leaned back to smile at him, he was gazing at me with longing and uncertainty.

My heart melted. He was still worried about his inexperience. Didn't he know there was no way he could get this wrong? Just knowing that he wanted me was all the expertise I needed. "Okay, it's your turn." I relaxed my hands and closed my eyes, offering him the lead.

He kissed my cheek. My jaw. His mouth brushed mine tentatively. Drew away. He kissed me again, softly, sweetly, his lips clinging as delight replaced caution. Then he buried his face in my neck and sighed.

"I think that's a good start for our first date," I murmured.

"It gets better than that?"

I laughed. "We'll save more advanced techniques for another day."

He straightened and smiled. "Which other day?"

"Tomorrow."

· 23 ·

Inevitable Questions

After Thursday's production meeting broke up, Micah waited until the staff lounge had cleared before taking me into his arms. "I have an idea."

I slid my hands around his neck. "I'm listening."

"Come with me to Elon."

Okay, brain focused now. "For the weekend?"

"Yes. We have a guest suite."

A trip home to meet the family? After we'd been dating three days?

No, wait. We agreed to go directly to the secure stage. He'd met my whole family. I'd known his mother almost as long as him. But still . . . "A whole weekend?"

"Okay, then. How about a day?"

I wanted to. We had less than eighteen days left. Missing two of them would be awful, but losing only one cut *awful* in half. And I didn't have anything planned this weekend except . . .

Boom. Reality check.

My mother was umping a two-night series in Greensboro, and my stepfather would be at the construction site. "Mom and Jeff will be gone on Saturday. I can't leave Natalie alone that long."

"Bring her with us."

Spending the day with Micah *and* Natalie wouldn't be fun for anyone. If only she had somewhere she could go instead.

And . . . she did. "Her mom lives in Durham. Could we drop her off?"

"Sure."

"My mom could get me and Natalie on her way home from the game in Greensboro. It'll be over by ten."

"Sounds great."

"Okay, don't say anything until I've cleared it with Mom and Jeff. And Natalie's mother." I glanced out into the hall. Nobody was there. "So we're on for tonight. Right?"

"Yeah, I have a surprise. Can I pick you up at seven?"

"That's fine, but I have to be home by nine. I have a project due for Jeff."

Micah's smile dimmed. "We can skip tonight, if you prefer."

"We can't skip a single moment available to us."

"Good—"

"Brooke," Natalie shouted, her footsteps slapping closer to the lounge.

I jumped away from Micah as she appeared in the doorway.

"Hi, Micah." She gestured for me to come. "Dad's here." She ran away before I could respond.

Wow. Close call. "See you at seven." I hurried to the office to get my backpack.

Micah had followed me. "Do you mind if she knows?"

"Yes."

"Why?"

"She'll freak. We have to be careful." I tried to step around him. He filled the doorway so completely that I couldn't.

"Keeping us a secret is a bad idea."

"The alternative is worse."

"Brooke . . ."

I ducked under his arm and took off down the hall at a jog. Once I reached Jeff's truck, I hopped in and spent the whole way home trying to figure out a reasonable way to tell Natalie, and coming up with nothing.

I headed downstairs a few minutes before seven and looked out the front window. Micah hadn't arrived early. Good. That would give me a minute to talk with Jeff and Mom. It was one of her rare nights off, so I found them in the den, cuddling together on the couch, a thick paperback on his lap and the cat on hers.

"I have a question, guys."

They looked up, at each other, and then at me.

"Okay, shoot," Mom said.

"A friend is driving to Elon on Saturday, and he offered to take me and Natalie with him."

Jeff's brow creased. "Why?"

"He could drop Natalie off in Durham for the day."

"Which friend?"

"Micah Dalton."

"The boy from the theater?"

"Yes, sir." I shrugged casually. "He's a nice guy."

Mom patted Jeff's hand. "I chatted with him at the game on Monday. He does seem nice."

My stepfather's only response was a noncommittal grunt.

Mom gave me a pointed look. "What exactly would *you* be doing?"

"I'd hang out with Micah."

"Uh-huh." Her arched eyebrow said that she knew things had progressed past hanging out, and her smile said she approved. "I suppose you know that I'm umping Saturday night in Greensboro."

"Yes, and I'm counting on you to pick me and Natalie up on your way home."

Jeff was nodding. "I like the sound of this. It might be a low-key way for Natalie to spend time with her mother and Luke. I'll call Mei and see if she's up to it."

Micah parked in front of my house at precisely nine o'clock.

"Tonight was wonderful. I've never spent a date baking before." I clutched the plate of warm chocolate-chip cookies to my chest. Who would've thought that baking cookies with a guy could be so much fun? We'd laughed and kissed and argued about whether it was okay to eat cookie dough. I was Team Eat Already. He was Team Food Poisoning. "It's a great idea."

"I didn't think of it. *Teen Vogue* did."

"You read *Teen Vogue*?"

"For you, yes." He cut the engine and reached for his seat belt latch.

No. Micah had these effortless, old-school manners. I loved it when he held doors for me or helped me into the car, but it was about to spoil our wonderful evening, because I could *not* let him walk me to the door. Natalie might see, and I didn't have answers for her inevitable questions. I put a hand on his arm. "You don't have to get out."

"But . . ." His expression changed from puzzled to hard. "Oh. Right."

"Micah, I know you disagree, but it's not time yet."

"When will it be?"

"I don't know."

He didn't respond. Just sat there staring straight ahead.

We couldn't end our date in silence, without touching or the assurance that we'd be better tomorrow. I kissed his cheek. He turned his head until our lips met. It was a sweet kiss, and a little sad. We drew apart and studied each other. He wanted honesty. I wanted to stay together. He thought we could have both. I hadn't figured out how to make it possible. While I hated that this had come between us, I wouldn't back down.

"Bye," I said.

"Yeah."

I slipped from the car. But instead of going inside, I headed to the workshop. It shouldn't take me long to finish Jeff's project, now that his new employee had forwarded the necessary information.

Thirty minutes later, I'd rechecked the document one last time and clicked the submit button. The final form was on its way into the North Carolina state bureaucracy. I had everything done.

This summer had gone nothing like I'd expected. I'd lost one job and found one I liked even more. I'd gained a full-time stepsister and a temporary boyfriend. I'd never been happier. Although it wasn't a perfect happiness. Not yet.

The creak of the workshop door yanked me from my thoughts.

Jeff stepped in, closing the door behind him. "I've called Mei, and Saturday is fine for a few hours."

"Great. Have you told Natalie?"

"I think it ought to come from you." He circled around behind me and looked over my shoulder. "What are you doing?"

"I've finished setting up for your new employee." There was something else I'd been working on. I hadn't planned on telling him tonight, but he'd given me the opening. "If you don't mind hearing a suggestion, I have an idea for you. You have lots of photos from your job sites. We should pick a few of the best and make a gallery."

"Tell me more."

"It would showcase the quality of your work and possibly draw traffic to the site. Make it more visually appealing."

"Could they be before-and-after photos? We could show how a piece of land looked before we started—and how well we conserved it afterward."

"Even better." My mind was already sorting through how that might look.

"I'll select a few images and let you know." He whipped out a chair and sat. "Next item of business. Tomorrow, I'll write your first paycheck. How many hours?"

I hadn't been keeping track, but it had been a lot. I would stick with my original estimate. "Ten."

"It's been more than that. I'll round up to an even one hundred dollars." He smiled. "Fair?"

"Very." I held out my hand, and we shook on the deal.

"Time for bed. You coming in?"

"Soon."

"Good night, then." He left, shutting the door with a soft click.

Three weeks ago, I'd feared that having Natalie around all the time might stall my relationship with him, but that hadn't happened. In fact, we seemed to be making even more progress. Being his "employee" had been good for us.

After turning off his computer, I locked the workshop, returned to the house, dropped the cookies off in the kitchen, and went upstairs. Natalie's door was ajar. When I knocked, it swung open.

She was sitting on her bed, her hands on her computer's keyboard, Tigger at her feet. "What do you want?"

"Can we have our evening chat?"

"I like it better when I come to your room."

"How about now?"

She closed the lid on her laptop and followed me. I landed on the edge of my bed while she hung onto the doorframe.

"I'm here now. What is it?"

"Micah and Lisa are driving to Elon on Saturday."

"And?"

"He can drop you off at your mom's, if you want."

Emotions chased themselves across her face. Surprise. Hope. And finally, worry. "What if Mama doesn't want me?"

"She does. I've already asked Jeff about it, and he called Mei. They think Saturday afternoon would be fine."

"This will be very good. Why did Micah suggest it?"

"He's a nice guy." I gave her a casual smile. "I'll ride along, too."

Her brow scrunched. "Mama didn't agree to that. She finds you annoying."

"Me? Why?"

"Because you boss me around like you're one of my parents. She thinks I have too many as it is."

Ouch. Mei would be pissed if she knew Natalie was repeating that. "Do you agree with her?"

"Not really. You are kind of bossy, but since you're a teen, I get to selectively ignore you."

I should learn to never use the word *why* with Natalie. "I won't stay in Durham. I'll go with Micah and Lisa to their house."

"Why would you do that?"

Because I can hardly stand to spend a single day away from him. "We could talk about the show."

"That won't be fun. It's the weekend." She hunched her shoulders and looked at her feet. "Will Mama let me spend the night?"

"My mom is umping a game in Greensboro that afternoon. She can come through about ten o'clock to pick us up."

"This is plenty to think about." Natalie darted from the room.

I flopped back on my bed, happy that Micah's suggestion had worked out for Natalie and me.

· 24 ·

Wonder and Awe

Natalie rode up front from Azalea Springs to Durham, talking with Micah the whole way. Lisa read a book in the backseat next to me. I had nothing to do, so I dozed.

The handoff at Mei's house was completed successfully, and thirty minutes later we were pulling off a rural highway onto a long, winding driveway. Ahead of us sprawled a red brick ranch house. The driveway curved past the front door before forking toward a detached, three-car garage.

As we parked, someone sauntered out the side door. Once he stepped into the sunlight, I could tell he was a slightly older, slightly taller version of Micah. The guy was also incredibly beautiful in a way that would require all of my self-discipline not to stare in wonder.

Lisa gave a giggle of pleasure and had hardly opened the door when he pulled her into his arms.

"Mom!" He gave her a noisy smack on the cheek.

"I didn't know you were coming," she said with an excited laugh.

The Lisa I knew had vanished, and the woman in her place was a mom who was happy to see her son. They walked around to the rear of the vehicle and opened the hatch.

Micah held the door as I slipped from the backseat.

"Your brother?" I asked.

He rolled his eyes. "Obviously."

They disappeared inside the house, with Lisa talking while her middle son carried her bag. By the time Micah and I had reached the door, Jude had returned.

"Who is this?" he asked with an assessing look.

"Brooke," Micah said with an edge in his tone, "and keep your distance."

"Hi, Brooke. I'm Jude, and I'm too polite to keep my distance."

"Hi." I smiled.

"Mom said you'd figured out how to catch a girl. This one looks surprisingly good . . ."

Really? You just said that in front of "this one"?

". . . Better than I would've expected for your second try."

Micah lunged, hands clenched. Jude dodged whatever blow was coming and took off. Micah swore at him. That made two never-before-experienced reactions from him. Not that Jude hadn't deserved it.

I preceded Micah from the utility room and halted in a large open space. It had a vaulted ceiling, a massive stone fireplace, furniture that was oversized, and a glass wall overlooking a lawn and small lake. The area behind me functioned as the kitchen, a sleek high-tech wonder of stainless steel appliances and charcoal-gray granite countertops. By the glass wall sat a trestle table with six chairs.

The kitchen smelled amazing. Trying not to be too obvious, I peeked in the oven door. A large glass casserole dish bubbled out puffs of garlic and tomato. Yum.

Micah flung his duffel bag next to a navy sectional couch and knelt to scratch an old collie behind its ears.

I joined him and waited while the dog lazily sniffed my shoes. "Where is Jude in college?"

"Virginia Tech. He goes back for his sophomore year in August."

"What's his major?"

"Don't think he's declared it yet."

"And he has a job this summer?"

"He's a counselor at a sports camp near Blacksburg." Micah rose, slid a possessive arm around my shoulders, and pulled me against his side. "Why so many questions about Jude?"

"Simple curiosity. When Peter shows up, I'll ask about him, too." I laid a hand on Micah's chest. "This can't be jealousy, because you have to know I'm all yours."

"That's a very good answer." He pressed his lips to mine.

"Excuse me." A deep, amused male voice spoke.

Micah broke the kiss. "Dad, I'd like you to meet Brooke Byers."

"Your dad?" I gasped and tried to back away, but Micah wouldn't let me go.

"Brooke, this is my dad, Charlie Dalton."

Was my face bright red? Because it felt like it was on fire. "Hi, Mr. Dalton."

"Charlie." He offered me his hand. "I can see you're already feeling welcome."

Could this get any more embarrassing? "Um, well . . ."

"Dad, give her a break. She's still recovering from Jude."

Charlie laughed. "It's okay, Brooke. When Micah brings home a girl, it's noteworthy." He strode past us and into the kitchen, checking on the dish in the oven. "We'll have lunch in another hour. Why don't you two take a walk around the farm?"

"Sure, Dad." Micah linked his fingers through mine. "Did you bring a hat?"

I shook my head.

"It's hot out there. Hats are required."

We walked around the fields, hand in hand, hats and shades on. I stayed quiet, marveling at how much Micah knew about his father's farm. He explained what was in season and what was on the way. When to harvest each crop and how much labor it took. I loved listening to him talk.

We had reached a thick line of trees when he stopped. "Am I boring you?"

"Definitely not." I looked across the fields. I was mostly uninformed about food production. As far as I knew, food appeared magically in stores, trucked in by elves. It was satisfying to learn about the real story, especially when the teacher was Micah.

He shifted so that his body blocked the sun. "What?"

"You know so much about things that are mysteries to me. It's kind of sexy."

"Yeah?" He grinned. "I've lived here my entire life. It would be odd if I didn't know things."

"Do you like farming?"

"No. Neither do my brothers." He looked toward the house, which seemed to shimmer in the heat on a ridge a good ten minutes' stroll away. "Dad's disappointed. I don't know what will happen when he's tired of doing this anymore. Or not able to." Micah's smile was shadowed with sadness. "Let's head back."

We walked in the shade of the trees for as long as it was practical, then detoured around the lake. We didn't speak for several minutes, but this silence was different, denser, as if we both sensed a shift in our relationship. Because this day had altered us. We had crossed the threshold between "What are we?" to "We *are.*"

"You seem distracted," I said.

His hands cupped my face. "I am distracted—by you. It scares me. Not just how quickly life changed, but how much I wish the inevitable end weren't so inevitable."

I waited for his kiss, confident it would come. He explored me with his lips. Softly. Sweetly. A kiss full of wonder and awe.

When I'd been with Jonas, making out could only be described as frantic. It was as if we tried to devour each other to mask how little we had in common.

Everything about Micah felt right, as if our hearts had perfectly aligned in the short time we'd been together. The intensity had taken me by surprise. Our relationship was supposed to have been for fun, not forever. Should I put the brakes on? Lighten the mood? I slipped my arms around his waist and pressed deeper into his embrace. "For a guy who had his first kiss three days ago, you're doing pretty well."

He smiled against my cheek. "YouTube has a how-to video for everything."

I smothered a laugh. "You learned how to kiss from YouTube?"

"Are you complaining?"

"Not at all."

He started to add more, but his phone buzzed. Taking a step away, he pulled the phone from his pocket and grinned at the screen. "Natalie."

"What does she want?"

"Her current interest is understudies. She's been wondering why we don't have them in this show with so many campers."

"Are you going to answer her?"

"Yeah, in a little while."

"What will you say?"

"Professionals can handle the disappointment of preparing for a role that probably won't be needed. High school students mostly can't."

He laced our fingers together and started back toward the house. We walked in silence, allowing me to take in everything about this place. The colors in the fields of ripening vegetables. The fragrance of honeysuckle climbing the wooden fence. The insects skating on the surface of the lake.

Once we were on the deck, Micah dropped my hand and reached for the door. "When Natalie and I talk, she brings you up all the time."

I shivered, not sure I wanted to hear more. "Is that good or bad?"

"It's very good. Natalie admires you a lot."

"She told you that?"

"Well, she probably used the word *awesome*. The rest was my interpretation."

I would've loved to hear Natalie say something like that to me, but she probably never would. Knowing that she had told Micah felt amazing.

He slid the door open. "Let's go. It's time to eat."

Meals lasted a long time at this house. Where my family ate efficiently and left, the Daltons made it an event.

The food was incredible. We had baked spaghetti with meatballs and a tomato sauce made from scratch. The salad greens had been harvested this morning. And Lisa had "whipped together" a blueberry cobbler that was incredible.

Micah's oldest brother had arrived while we were wandering around the farm. Peter was almost as hot as Jude and just as noisy. He was in graduate school at Georgetown University, majoring in public policy. He had a lot to say on, well, everything. Politics. Sports. D.C. nightlife (which Lisa shut down with a muttered "TMI").

Peter nodded at Micah. "You should come up for a weekend this fall. You could take the train . . ."

I ate my pasta, half-listening as the two of them made tentative plans. The conversation swirled around me, loud and overwhelming. One thing that became clear—Peter and Micah were close, and Jude was the odd man out. The twist to his lips suggested he knew. When he caught me staring at him across the table, I smiled sympathetically. In an instant, the twist changed to a sneer. Then he winked.

Beside me, Micah tensed and made a big show of reaching for my hand. "Everything okay?"

"I'm fine." I didn't know what their problem was, but I wouldn't be dragged into it. Leaning closer, I whispered in his ear, "If there's anything else you want to do to brand me, I'd appreciate the chance to weigh the options."

"Sounds like a conversation for later."

"Guaranteed."

After lunch, I offered to help with the dishes, but Lisa waved me away. "Charlie and I have this."

I looked at Micah. "Can we go somewhere and talk?"

He grabbed my hand. "My room."

His dad laughed. His brothers made silly hooting sounds. And Lisa said, "Guys, please."

All I said was "Okay."

Like me, Micah had a corner room. It was sparsely furnished and incredibly neat. The bedspread and curtains were dark green. A bookcase had two lower shelves stuffed with books and two upper shelves full of trophies and awards. I walked over to check them out. Most were for the theater, but there were also a couple of swimming trophies, a fencing medal, and a ribbon from a writing contest.

I read through them with pride. He was brilliant at so many things, but the knowledge deflated me, too. Even though Natalie had said he couldn't fit a girlfriend into his schedule, I'd begun to hope that our relationship would be different—that maybe we could survive the summer. This bookcase awakened me to reality. Next fall, he'd be busy with classes, theater, sports, and all the extra things seniors had to deal with. He wouldn't have room for anything—or anyone—else.

Micah wrapped his arms around me from behind. "What are you thinking?"

I shook off my melancholy and refocused on him. "I'm glad I'm here. You have a nice family."

He made a humming sound in his throat and kissed my temple.

"Why don't you get along with Jude?"

Micah stiffened. "For reasons."

"When you pull me into the feud, I deserve to know why."

"Jude will—"

"Stop." I turned in his arms and rested my hands against his chest. "It doesn't matter what *Jude* will. It only matters what *I* will. Okay?"

Micah gave a sharp nod.

I studied his blank expression. His unwillingness to meet my gaze. This was strange and important. "We have to discuss this. Tell me, please."

He exhaled slowly. "I told you about the girl I took out for coffee."

"Yeah. She didn't know it was a date."

"And she pumped me for information about another guy."

"Jude."

Micah winced.

So much was clearer now. "I asked you those questions about him out of simple curiosity. That's all. Because everything about *you* interests me."

He nodded.

"Did Jude ever find out about the girl?"

"They dated for a couple of months."

"Did he know how you felt?"

"Yes."

Micah needed comfort. Reassurance. Absolute confidence in *us.* I linked my hands behind his neck. "I'm sorry that happened to you, but you and I are different."

"I believe you." His arms wound around me, so tightly it was painful. But I let him, because he needed this now. *We* needed it.

"Game's starting," Peter shouted from the living room.

"What game?" I asked.

"The Nationals." Micah's arms dropped.

I reached for his hand. "Who are the Nationals playing?"

"Don't even care." He grinned.

His brothers were already sprawled in recliners, absorbed by the game. I curled next to Micah on the couch, still holding hands. The Braves and the Nationals weren't two of my favorite teams, but hey, baseball.

In the top of the third inning, Jude hunched forward, rested his arms on his knees, and gestured at me. "The runner on first will be looking for a chance to steal second."

"Um, okay." Beside me, Micah's chuckle rumbled in his chest.

His middle brother gave him a sour look and returned his gaze to me. "The batter will likely bunt."

"Thanks, Jude—"

Micah interrupted. "Brooke's mother called your semifinals game in high school."

Jude's eyes widened. "Your mother is the lady ump? The tiny one?"

"She is. I've been a baseball fan from the cradle."

Jude looked at his younger brother. "This girl is perfect."

Micah's hand tightened around mine. "I already knew that."

⋆ 25 ⋆

Waiting in the Dark

Mom arrived by eight but didn't stay long at the Daltons' house. After she spoke with Micah's parents, we were on our way. I twisted in my seat, straining to see the lights from his house flicker and die in the distance. I'd hated saying good-bye to him. We wouldn't see each other again until Monday morning—and being around him then would be frustrating, since we'd be near each other for nine hours and have no real way to be alone.

Mom didn't say anything until we reached the interstate. "Did you have a good time?"

"It was wonderful."

She chuckled. "Could I have a few more details than that?"

"His family is nice, and they're all so different." Images of the meal flashed through my brain. Everyone laughing and talking at the same time. It should've been chaos, but instead it was charming. I'd loved it. "Peter is open and happy. Jude is dark and mysterious. Charlie is just a big, friendly man. Definitely the center of the family. Lisa seems to worship him and can barely let him leave her sight. I don't know how she can live in Azalea Springs without him."

"You've mentioned everyone but Micah."

"Oh, Mom. I hardly know what to say about Micah. He's smart and interesting. A little nerdy, but he knows so much about so many things, and at the theater, he's good. Like crazy good. Kind, calm, and competent. And so talented you'll follow wherever he leads, hoping it'll rub off."

"Wow. You've got it bad."

"I *know*."

"If it's any comfort, I think he has it bad, too. I'm happy for you, honey." She sighed. "Jeff hasn't figured out yet that you're dating Micah, which is just as well. He wouldn't be able to keep it from Natalie."

"I'm hoping the issue won't come up. There are only two weeks until Micah moves home." Which was something else I couldn't let myself think about. "Thanks for not saying anything."

"I like the direction your relationship with Natalie is heading, and I think you know you're putting that at risk by hiding this from her. But I'll respect your wishes." She patted my leg. "My turn. The league supervisor called me to ask if I'm having problems with any teams." Dismay echoed in her voice.

"Is that a bad thing?"

"Someone must have filed a complaint."

"Finley?"

"He would know better than to do that. So maybe his coach. Or a fan."

Wow. My mom prided herself on how fair and objective she was, and she should because that was the reality. I might be biased, but she didn't make many bad calls. "What does it mean?"

"Nothing, really. They get regular reports from coaches, and I suspect mine are good, but it's still something that's noticed."

"I'm sorry."

Shrugging, she merged onto the off-ramp for Mei's neighborhood. My mother would stay in the car when I went to get Natalie. Although Mom and Mei were civil, they'd both been married to Jeff. That tension never went away. Now that I knew Natalie's mom didn't like me, the tension would be there for me, too.

Mei and her husband, Terry, lived in a white brick house near Duke University, in a neighborhood of old mansions with manicured lawns and massive trees. Mom pulled into their circular driveway but didn't cut the engine. I hopped out and stood at the front door, waiting in the dark for someone to respond to the doorbell.

The porch light went on as Terry answered the door. "Hello, Brooke. Come in. Natalie is reluctant to leave."

"Thanks." I trailed him into their den. Natalie had curled into a ball on a recliner, the family's schnauzer wedged against her chest. Her grandfather sat in the chair beside her, watching some unfamiliar sporting event on the TV. Her mother, brother, and grandmother weren't around.

"Ready to go?"

She wouldn't look at me. "No."

"Mom's tired and wants to get home. Can you make it easy on her and come on?"

Natalie sighed loudly and slid from the chair. After rummaging around for her shoes, she brushed past me into the foyer.

I turned to Terry and found him staring after Natalie, mouth open.

"Didn't expect that?" I asked.

"I'm shocked."

"She loves being in *Oklahoma!* She won't do anything that might jeopardize getting to her next rehearsal." I stepped around him. "Good-bye."

When I got in the car, Natalie was already buckled up in the back. I smiled at her, hoping to distract her from her grump. "Did you take any photos of Luke?"

"Why do you care?"

"Because I'd like to see them."

She smacked my shoulder with her phone.

I swiped through her photo gallery. "He's adorable."

"Yes, he is. He has lots of dark hair, which people mention all the time, although I don't see why. Bald babies can be cute, too."

"I agree with everything you said." Luke was asleep in most of the photos, but sometimes not. "Whenever you held him, his eyes were open."

"Mama says he likes me, which is predictable. We share DNA. There has to be an echo of it, connecting us. Even though he senses it, they won't bring him with them when they come to Azalea Springs. Nai Nai will stay behind to babysit Luke."

Wait. "Who's coming to Azalea Springs?"

"Mama said she wants to see one of my performances. Terry said he'd drive her down."

My mother shot me a concerned glance. Yeah, I was concerned, too. What if Mei wasn't well enough to make the trip?

"I will love it if they come." Her hand appeared beside my face. "I'd like my phone now."

We pulled into our driveway around midnight. Jeff awaited us at the door, lights blazing. Natalie dashed up the sidewalk and skidded to a stop next to him. She launched into a brain dump as they entered the house together.

I waited until the front door was shut before turning to my mother. "What do you think about Mei coming down here?"

"She probably believes that she can, but I worry that it's more than she can handle. Jeff says that she's been responding to her medications, although her days are inconsistent. I'd be concerned the stress of showing up on a bad day could set her back. How did she act tonight?"

"I never saw her. They said she'd already gone to bed."

"I'd better tell Jeff, so he can be prepared. If Mei doesn't make it to a show, it'll be disastrous for Natalie."

Disastrous for us all.

· 26 ·

A Moment to Breathe

When Mom and I got home from church, there was a stand-off in progress between father and daughter. If I'd thought it through, I could've guessed Natalie's visit with her mother might stir her up. What I hadn't realized was how much.

"Sunday brunch is something we do together," Jeff was saying as we walked in from the carport.

"You can do it alone today." She lifted her chin defiantly.

"It's not a choice, Natalie. It's your responsibility."

"It was your responsibility before I came here. You don't need my help."

"True, but I *want* it."

"Jeff, we don't—" my mom started.

His glare cut her off. Reaching into a cabinet, he brought down a stack of plates. "Set the table, Natalie." When she didn't move, he said, "Now."

Her lower lip rolled out mutinously. She huffed twice and

snatched the plates, slapping them onto the table with punishing energy.

He gave us a hard squint, and we took our seats. A platter with pancakes and bacon appeared.

"Sit, Natalie."

"I'm not hungry."

"Then you can watch the rest of us eat."

That had to be one of the most uncomfortable meals of my life, and the most unbending I'd ever seen Jeff with his daughter. He ate his food steadily, efficiently, and silently. Mom took tiny bites and slurped down three cups of coffee. I tried to open a conversation about the church service, but abandoned the effort after a sentence or two.

Natalie sat beside me, hunched over, chin to chest, radiating misery.

The instant my stepfather put down his fork, she spoke. "Can I go now?"

"Yes."

He'd hardly formed the closing consonant before she was gone, her feet pounding up the stairs.

"Jeff—" my mom started.

"Not now, Jill."

"But I think we should—"

"Watch it. I'm at my limit." He ground his teeth in frustration. "While we're on the subject of how I treat my daughter, why is it that I can never please you? You're pissed when I'm too hard on her, and you're pissed when I'm not."

"I'm a trained educator, Jeff. When I suggest that your problems with her are a matter of timing, I might know what I'm talking about."

"And I might be making mistakes with her, but I'm doing the best I can. I need you to respect that."

Mom's chair scraped against the floor. She tossed down her napkin and stalked into the utility room. The side door slammed.

"Can I say something?" I asked him.

"No, Brooke." He shot out of his chair and out of the kitchen. The side door slammed again.

Guess that left the dishes to me. It would give me time to wonder how temporary the tension between them was. And what I should do about it.

I stacked the dishes in the sink and added water and soap. A movement in the backyard caught my attention. Unease prickled over my skin at the sight of my mom gesturing at my stepfather, words pouring from her mouth while he towered over her, hands on hips. Looking away, I prayed that Natalie hadn't seen or heard them, too. The last thing she needed was yet another thing to stress over.

After I finished the dishes, I grabbed the newest Hatcher Khan mystery and headed to the hammock. Flipping open at the turned-down corner, I read.

"Jill and Dad had a fight."

I looked up from my book. I must've been deeply engrossed because I hadn't heard Natalie approach. "I know."

"Could you hear any of it?"

"No, and I wouldn't have wanted to."

"I *did* want to. It was about me. They don't agree about how strict to be. It went back and forth so much that I can't tell what they actually plan to do."

"I'm really glad I didn't hear that."

She rubbed her fingers over her knuckles as she frowned at her bare feet. "How long will they stay mad at each other?"

"Not long."

She paced around the oak trees. I closed the book and clutched it to my chest. This conversation wouldn't be ending soon. Not that I blamed her for wanting to cover the topic. It concerned me too, although not as much as it did Natalie. I'd had nine months to witness this stuff.

"Do they often argue when I'm not here?"

"Depends on how you define *often*."

"Every week?"

"More like a couple of times per month." The frequency had increased since Natalie moved in.

"Mama says that she and Dad never fought when they were married. I would think that no arguing would be a good thing."

"You argue over things you care about. If your parents weren't arguing, maybe that's because they stopped caring."

"Good point." She paused from her pacing. "Clearly, they stopped caring, since they divorced. It changed fast. They had a whispered argument one day at dinner. At the end, Dad hugged me, and his eyes were red and watery. Then he left, and he never lived with us again."

"You remember that?"

"I was seven years old. Of course, I remember. It was the worst day of my life, and I've had plenty of bad ones." She came to stand beside me, worry creasing her brow. "Dad drove away in his truck after he and Jill ended their fight."

"Yeah, I heard."

"Where do you think he went?"

"Probably driving around. It's his way of cooling down."

"Should we do anything?"

I shook my head with confidence.

"Do you really believe it'll be okay?"

"I can't be positive, but I want them to be fine so that's the story I'm sticking to."

She blinked and barked out a laugh. "We have a major commonality."

"What's that?"

"Disregarding things that we don't want to face."

I spent Sunday afternoon editing the newsletter for the camp. Once Elena had given me access to the information, I'd formatted it and added some candid photos that I'd snapped, but it was still too boring. I emailed Lisa, suggesting a "Director's Corner"—just a few sentences to let parents know how the show was doing. I'd give her until nine to respond before sending the newsletter.

There was a bang at my door. Natalie's version of a knock. She stuck her head in. "Dad wants to take us out for pizza."

"Did he say where?"

"Bella Napoli."

"That's in Fayetteville. It'll be a bit of a drive. Does this mean the two of you have forgiven each other?"

"He doesn't have to be forgiven to take us out for pizza."

"I guess that's true." Hopefully, Mom and Jeff had patched things up. Pizza wouldn't be fun if they hadn't resolved their argument.

"He says it'll be a family meeting."

I groaned. "Oh, great."

"What? I like family meetings." Natalie gestured for me to move. "How good is Bella Napoli?"

"A miracle." I closed my computer, slid off the bed, stuffed my feet into flip-flops, and chased her down the stairs.

Micah texted me while I was inside the pizza place.

Call me

I responded.

Out with family
    Later?
K

What a strange contrast to brunch, because this was one of the nicest meals my family had experienced together. The food was delicious as always. Mom and Jeff were openly affectionate and whispering things that I was pretty glad I couldn't hear. I hoped Miss Better-Ears-Than-You couldn't hear either.

Surprisingly, Natalie was the life of the party this evening. She shared the funniest observations about her visit home yesterday, and she was an excellent mimic.

This was the way a family should be. Laughing and talking. Creating inside jokes and happy memories. If I'd ever been able to picture the ideal family moment, it would look like our ordinary pizza night.

As the meal continued, though, my happiness became edged with guilt. I loved the family we were right now. I loved the

Natalie we had tonight, and I hated lying to her about Micah. But I hadn't found the right opportunity to be honest, and I was beginning to wonder if I ever would.

By the time we got home, it was after ten. I ran up to my room, locked the door, and called Micah. "Hi," I said when he answered.

"Hey." He sounded happy. "You busy?"

"Some. Jeff asked me to create a photo gallery on his website, and I'm making a plan."

"When will you be done?"

"I'm not sure."

"Can I come over?"

My heart sank. "Now?"

"Yes?"

My feelings were jumbled into a sloppy mix of confusion, regret, and dread. I couldn't handle Micah. "Not tonight. It's too late."

"I'm . . . really disappointed."

"Why?"

"Time's running out."

I slumped on the bed and took a moment to breathe through the reminder. There had been too many of them this weekend, and I'd rather put it from my mind. "Time was running out before we started."

"Fine. Later." He ended the call.

I plugged my phone into its power cord and turned off the lamp. Without bothering to change clothes, I stared out the window at the moon and hoped for sleep to overtake my churning thoughts.

· 27 ·

My Best Imitation

With only ten more days until opening night, we had our first complete run-through of the production. It was harrowing. Missed lines, missed cues, and too much giggling. I kept sneaking peeks at Lisa, wondering if she was panicked by what a total mess it was, but her expressions ranged from calm to thoughtful. Never upset.

I cornered Micah during morning group, which today doubled as intermission. "Is it always this bad during the first full try?"

"You thought that was bad?" His gaze never left the guys in his group, who were currently putting on a silly skit that the other campers were finding hilarious.

"Didn't you?"

"Just the opposite. I think it's moving along well." He frowned. "Is Mom disturbed?"

"No."

"Then don't worry." He laid his hand on my waist.

"Micah." I jerked away from him.

"Right. I'll go back to being your secret." He returned his attention to the skit.

I hesitated, remorse and yearning battling for supremacy. Then I saw Natalie in the corner, laughing with her group. The distress of her return from Mei's had fled. Today's Natalie fit in, and that's the way it had to stay.

After a quick chat with Elena, I returned to the stage, stopping when I found Micah in the wings. Instead of getting out of my way, he blocked my path. "Natalie says she's got an appointment in Lillington with your parents tonight."

"Yeah, they do. Why?"

"You said you're creating some media for your stepdad's website. Are you planning to use any video?"

"I hadn't thought of that, but I guess I could."

"Why don't I bring over my Mac? We could experiment with a few things and see what you think."

That was an idea worth considering. Micah would do a much better job of producing video with a Mac.

Oh, who was I kidding? We'd have *alone time*. "I would love that."

He glanced around. Other than us, the area was empty and quiet. Sliding a hand to my neck, he bent over me. "We haven't kissed since Saturday."

"True." I pressed closer to him, mesmerized by the look on his face.

"May I?" He touched his lips to mine in an all-too-brief kiss. "I've missed you."

"I've missed you." Something dark teased at the corner of my heart, but I ignored it. This moment was sweet, and I would claim it in peace.

Mom and Jeff picked up Natalie after camp and left for the psychologist appointment in Lillington. Micah assured them that he could give me a ride home.

It was quiet in the arts center without the campers. While Lisa wrapped up a phone call, Micah and I were in the campers' lounge. I was sorting through the snack cabinet, throwing away anything that had expired. Micah was sitting on the counter, getting in my way.

"Hey," I said, nudging his leg. "You're blocking the drawer."

He scooted over a couple of inches.

Not good enough. "What'll it cost me to get you to move?"

"Easy." He leaned forward until our lips touched. Clung. Held.

There was a rap at the door and Lisa strolled in. "Really. Guys," she said with a chuckle.

"How can we help you, Mom?"

"An arts council board member has volunteered to print the playbills. Can you drop off some samples at her shop? It closes at seven."

"Sure." He kissed a spot below my ear and whispered, "I'm getting down. You'd better move."

"Got it." I backed away and grabbed my purse.

As we reached his mom, he gave her a smile. "I'll take you

home first. Brooke and I can run the errand on our way to her house."

Micah parked in the visitors' lot near the shopping district. Since he'd only been downtown to try out the restaurants, I pointed out the other businesses as we made our way down the block.

He laced his fingers through mine. Whenever we were together, he was always touching me, as if he had no other choice. Kissing and holding hands were amazing, of course, but I also craved the little touches. The brush of his lips on my temple. The light pressure of his hand at the small of my back. I loved how affectionate Micah was with me.

We had just turned onto Main Street when I pulled him to a halt.

"What's wrong?" Micah asked.

Coming down the sidewalk, headed our way, were Kaylynn and Jonas, holding hands and eating ice cream cones.

"That's my best friend with my ex-boyfriend. I didn't know they were . . ."

"A couple." Micah's frown was wary. "You haven't talked about her since the trip to Pullen Park."

"We had an argument three weeks ago and haven't spoken much since." By now, they had spotted us. After a brief exchange, they both tossed their cones in a trash can and continued toward us.

Sadness hummed hollowly in my head. My best friend was dating my ex, and I hadn't known. It was a major enough change that I should've rated a warning. I wasn't jealous, but I was disturbed. How could we have lost each other so quickly?

Of course, she didn't know about my boyfriend either.

"Hi," she said, taking in our clasped hands.

"Kaylynn. Jonas. This is Micah."

Everybody nodded at each other. Then silence.

She looked from me to Micah. "Do you go to school around here?"

"No, I'm only here for the summer." He shifted closer to me.

He was confused, and I could do nothing to help him, not with them standing there. "So how long have you two been dating?" Oh, wow. Had I really asked that?

Jonas looked at Kaylynn. "Two weeks?"

That hurt. She and I had talked or texted a couple of times since then. She'd even mentioned having a date—but not who it was with. There had been opportunities to tell me, instead of letting me find out by accident. Why had she kept it a secret? I honestly didn't mind them as a couple. How could she not understand that?

It was time to go. I gave them my best imitation of a smile and tugged on Micah's hand. "Well, nice to see you." We walked past them.

"Where's Natalie?" she asked.

I stopped and looked over my shoulder. The question left me cold. Angry. I could smell the nastiness underneath. "Why?"

"I thought you and Natalie went everywhere together."

"Well, you would be wrong." I slipped off my shades and stared at her hard, until she flushed. This disagreement was complete crap. Our friendship should've been worth more. "My conscience is clear, Kaylynn. If yours isn't, *you* have to live with it. But don't try to unload your guilt on me." I stalked away without looking back.

Micah waited until we had handed over the samples at the print shop and were back in the car before bringing up the scene. "Will you tell me what that was about?"

"I don't know what to think."

"Did it bother you to see Jonas?"

"What?" I shook my head firmly. "No." I sorted through several ways to explain, but none seemed to work. Maybe because my emotions were so tangled over this. "I don't care that they're dating. I split up with him months ago, and we've hung out at the same events since. It hasn't been a problem."

"What was the guilt thing about?"

My throat thickened. "Kaylynn and Natalie don't get along. It's best to keep them apart."

"Translated, Kaylynn can't take Natalie's quirks, and since you and Natalie are a package deal, your friend doesn't call anymore."

"That sounds really bad."

"Because it is." He lifted my hand and kissed it. "She's wrong. You're not. Done."

True, but being right didn't fill the void.

He released my hand, backed out of the lot, and drove to my house.

"We only have two hours before my family gets back," I said, leading him inside the house.

"That should be enough." At the top of the stairs, he halted on the threshold to my room, took it all in, then walked over to my shelf of baseball collectibles. "Nice. Not what I expected but better."

"What did you expect?"

"Something frillier."

Hands on hips, I gaped at him. "Where did you get that? There is nothing frilly about me."

"I still wouldn't have guessed a collection of bobbleheads."

"Don't forget the foul ball that I caught myself." Grinning, I went to my desk and opened my laptop. "Come here. I'll show you what I've prepared."

As I played a rough slideshow of the images I'd found on Jeff's computer, Micah's expression didn't change nor did he speak. When I came to the end, I elbowed him. "Do you have any opinions?"

"When have I ever not had opinions?" He pulled his Mac from its case. "I like the flow you have with the before-and-after shots. You've got a nice mix. And having captions is good. I'd also suggest adding voiceover."

"Whose voice?"

"Yours. Sound is my thing. I'll make it work."

It bothered me to hear my own voice on recordings, but Micah wouldn't have suggested it if I sounded bad. I flipped open my notes for the gallery, oddly nervous. Jeff wasn't big on surprises. I could make the video both ways and see which presented better. "If I don't like it, we'll skip the voice track."

"Sounds like a plan."

"Alright, let's do it."

An hour later, we'd reached a stopping point with the first pass of a video. It lasted less than a minute, but it was solid.

I stood and stretched. "That went by fast. Thanks."

"You're welcome. We're a good team." He pulled me onto his lap and kissed me.

I froze. Jonas had never allowed me to sit on his lap. He said I weighed too much, which had been a jerk thing to tell me. I would never claim to be thin, but I liked the way my body looked. I'd once read in a romance novel the words *lush curves*. Secretly, it was how I thought of myself.

"Anything wrong?" Micah asked, studying my face.

"No." I always felt exactly right in Micah's eyes. He wanted my lush curves on his lap. "We're perfect."

He kissed me again, then settled me more securely in his arms. I snuggled against him.

My phone buzzed. A text from my mom. I drew the phone over.

Should be home in 20

Why was Mom warning me? Had she assumed—correctly—that Micah and I were together? I looked at him apologetically and wiggled off his lap. "You have to leave. They'll be home soon."

With a curt nod, he shoved his computer into its case, the lingering tension of our disagreement hovering between us.

"Micah, please."

"I'm dealing with it, but I'm worried that your luck will run out." He left my room and thudded down the stairs.

I caught up with him as he was opening the front door.

"Wait."

He paused, then closed the door and set his case on the floor. Turning, he reached for me. I stepped into his arms eagerly, sighing with relief when he drew me to him.

"It's time for some honest conversation, Brooke."

I didn't have to ask the topic. "I know you don't like the secrecy. I don't either. But I'm afraid of what might happen when she finds out. The world is black-and-white to Natalie, and we've created a shade of gray she'll never understand."

"She's stronger than that."

"I can't take the chance."

"Okay." He eased away and reached for his case. "But I won't lie for you." He opened the door again and disappeared into the night.

When Natalie wandered into my room around eleven, I'd finished my share of edits on the video and forwarded the file to Micah.

"How did you like the psychologist?"

Natalie shrugged. "I don't know what I think yet. I'll go again before I decide." She took a deep sniff. "Has Micah been in here? It smells like him."

My throat went dry. *Busted.* "Yes. He helped me with a project."

"Like what?"

"I'm creating a photo gallery for Jeff's website." I kept my expression neutral.

She eyed me warily. "You do a lot of stuff together."

Had the moment arrived? Could I slide the real story in now? "We're . . . friends."

"Huh. What kind of friends?" She was staring at my chin as her fingers rubbed her knuckles.

"We're, um, friendly friends." And there, I'd done it. Deliberately deceived her.

Her fingers slowed. Crisis delayed.

She looked away. "We haven't had many late-night chats recently."

If she'd missed our conversations enough to say something, she must really enjoy them, which made me happy because I did, too. "We've both been busy."

"I haven't been. What are you doing?"

"Working all day at the arts center, and helping Jeff with his business at night."

"His website doesn't need that much effort."

"I've also been submitting government forms and filling out paperwork."

She went to the window and looked out. "Can we talk now?"

"Sure." I closed my laptop. "What?"

"The show will be over soon. What will I do after that?"

"Good question." I spun the desk chair around. I'd better think this through. Neither Mom nor Jeff had talked about a vacation since Natalie arrived. It could be an oversight—but probably not. "We'd planned to take you to the beach in August."

"Which one?"

"At the Outer Banks."

"Dad and I went there last summer, but it might be alright to go again."

"There are other options, especially if we drive over and come back on the same day." Which I could handle, if our parents could spare me a car.

"We should do that. I prefer to sleep in my own bed." She walked to the doorway. "I like having something to look forward to."

"Yeah. Me, too."

⋄ 28 ⋄

Shielding Her Face

By Wednesday, the show still looked pretty bumpy to me, but Micah assured me it would be spectacular. I believed him.

He spent most of his time in the booth now. I stayed at Lisa's side, although my job was winding down. I didn't have to hunt down missing cast members. They knew their cues. Our deck crew, led by Elena, was handling the scene changes. We were off-book this week, so no prompting lines. I'd volunteered to be the house manager on show nights, but that didn't kick in for another week.

After watching every scene and hearing every song at least a dozen times, I was fighting boredom. It fascinated me, though, to observe Lisa and Micah. They never lost enthusiasm as they coached, praised, and urged the cast on to success.

We were focused on Act One this morning. Laurey and Ado Annie were having a girl-to-girl dialogue downstage. Behind them, the scene change was visible and noisy, practically drowning out the actors. Lisa twisted in her seat and scowled at the booth.

Micah's sigh was loud over the headset. "Tell her I'm on it."

"Don't worry, Lisa," I said to her. "He's noticed."

She jotted a note on a legal pad. "It needs to be faster. Try to cut five seconds."

"I heard that, too," came over the headset.

I hid a smile. The Daltons were cute.

At the end of Act One, the cast returned to the auditorium and fidgeted through Lisa's review of her notes. I joined Micah in the booth and scooted my chair over until it bumped his, but I didn't touch him. We were completely visible in here.

"That's a lot of suppressed energy out there," I said.

He pulled off his glasses and rubbed his temple. "I know." He sounded odd.

"Are you okay?"

"Yeah." He met my gaze, his face solemn. "The band director is meeting with Mom tonight. She wants me there."

It took a moment for the impact to sink in. If his expression was any clue, there would be no date for us. The disappointment stunned me. "Wow."

"It's my job. I can't miss it."

"I understand," I said, upset and struggling to hide it.

"Thanks." He frowned at his binder.

Lisa's voice drifted in through the speakers. ". . . That's all I have. Anyone else?"

Silence.

He grabbed the mic. "Lunch break. The counselors will be outside in thirty, so head there after you eat." He clicked it off.

"Did the counselors know that?"

Shaking his head, he picked up a pencil and wrote a note. "Can you tell them to make a schedule? One at a time is fine."

"Sure." I stood and stared at his bent head uncertainly. "I packed us a lunch-for-two today."

His hand stilled, then he threw down the pencil, stood abruptly, and placed his hands on my hips. Seconds later, I found myself backed into an equipment closet, his body blocking me from view.

"You're distracting me, and I like it." He lowered his head until our lips touched. I'd just closed my eyes when he deepened the kiss—and boom, the world shattered and bright lights sparkled behind my lids and all that mattered was him.

The door to the booth rattled. With a groan, he wrenched away.

"Hello, Micah," the light designer said as she walked in. She blinked when she saw me. "Brooke." An understanding smile stole across her face. "Don't let me interrupt. Go back to whatever you were doing." She chuckled and plopped down in front of the light board.

Close call. That could've been anyone coming in.

I was too happy to care.

"Find the counselors," Micah murmured. "I'll meet you in the staff lounge in twenty minutes. For our lunch-for-two."

Even though we couldn't have a date Wednesday night, we talked on the phone for thirty minutes until Natalie came in for her late-night chat.

Thursday's date lasted barely an hour. I drove over to the

Daltons' house so that Micah and I could watch a movie, but he fell asleep midway through, his head on my lap. I turned off the TV and sat in the dark, smoothing his hair and listening to him breathe. He'd been so stressed lately, I wouldn't wake him. Carefully, I eased away and slipped from the house.

Micah arrived Friday morning looking better rested, although his greeting held an edge. There would be no stolen moments for us today; we were too busy. That worried me, because I wanted to explain.

Although he wouldn't be taking over official control of the show until Monday, today he and Lisa would be in "transition"—a word that seemed to mean more to the two of them than anyone else. As the morning progressed, I couldn't see any difference in their interactions.

We'd finished a complete run-through by midafternoon, and the cast went on break. Some parents had banded together and brought in a snack extravaganza. I watched from the doorway to the campers' lounge, trying to choose between my jiggly thighs or the nachos.

"Brooke." Micah spoke over the headset. "Meet me in the wings, stage left."

"On my way."

I practically ran—as fast as safety allowed. Micah stood by himself, headset off. When he opened his arms, I flew into them.

He kissed my forehead. "Hey."

"Hi." I smiled at him, my palms pressed to his chest. "How are things?"

"Going great. Why did you abandon me last night?"

"You needed the sleep."

"You should've let me make that decision. We wasted another night."

I didn't respond. He was right and I was right—and it was too late anyway. Break would be over soon. I wouldn't waste *now* on arguing. Time for a diversion. "This set is amazing. The show's going to be good."

He was slow to speak, probably irritated at my obvious attempt to change the subject. "I think so, too."

"Nervous?"

"No, things always go wrong. Part of the thrill is fixing the problems in the moment. I'd be nervous if everything was going smoothly." He leaned in and gave me a light kiss.

"What are you doing?" Natalie screeched from the opposite side of the stage.

We sprang apart.

"You're kissing!"

Horror gripped me. The moment I'd hoped would never come had arrived. One moment of letting down my guard was all it had taken. "Natalie—"

"Like you're girlfriend and boyfriend."

"We are," Micah said as he gripped my waist possessively.

I shrugged him off. *What the hell?*

Her gaze transferred to him, eyes wild. "How long?"

"Since last week," I answered, my voice soft with guilt.

She turned her back on us and muttered, "How could you?" Then she repeated it, over and over, faster and faster, till the words slurred. Behind her, more campers had trickled into the auditorium, some watching the three of us with interest.

"Natalie? Let me explain."

"Don't need to. I get it." She took off into the wings.

When I started to follow, Micah caught my arm. "Wait, Brooke."

"No. I have to rescue her."

"How?"

"By taking her home."

"That seems drastic. Just give her some time to calm down."

I pulled my wrist from his grasp. He had never understood how bad this would be. He didn't see friendship or mentorship or whatever kind of *-ship* they had in the same way she did. "I don't think she'll be able to do that here."

Lisa walked up. "What's going on?"

"Natalie isn't feeling well. I'm taking her home."

Lisa lowered her voice. "A meltdown?"

"Yes."

She frowned. "I was planning to rehearse the girls' ensemble again before we bring in the band tomorrow."

"You'll have to do it without Natalie and me. Now, I'm sorry, but I have to go." I ran through the curtains and into the shadows of backstage, hunting for Natalie, but she wasn't in any of her typical hiding places. In the lounge, I grabbed a bottle of water and my purse, then headed through the side exit. I knew I would find Natalie pacing in the garden.

She didn't look my way, but she must've known I was there, because she diverged from her current path to head for a tree. She circled it, fists thumping, mumbling to herself.

"Natalie, if you need your meds, I have them with me."

"Stop. Talking."

I clamped my lips together. At least she hadn't asked me to leave. I held out a bottle of water with one hand and her pill with the other. She looped past me three more times before ripping both from my hands.

"When you're ready to go home, I'll be by the car." I crossed to the parking lot and leaned against the trunk of the car—easily visible to my stepsister—to wait. It took fifteen minutes before the edgy pacing slowed.

Spinning abruptly, she stomped toward me. Her hands were empty of both the pill and the water. "We can go now."

A movement from the lobby drew my eye. A brooding Micah stood in the window, arms crossed. I slid behind the wheel without any indication that I'd noticed.

The drive home was made in silence. She was out of the car before I'd put it in park, but I was determined not to let this wound fester. I ran behind her, catching up by the time we reached her room.

She slammed the door shut in my face. I counted to twenty, then knocked.

"What?"

I opened it. "What do you want to say to me?"

She was lying on her bed, staring at the ceiling. "Don't you think it's bold to confront me when you're to blame?"

"I didn't intend for you to find out this way—"

"Failed at that, too. Who knew?"

"The other campers didn't. Jeff didn't."

"Did Lisa?"

"Yes."

"Jill?"

"Yes, but she thought I should tell you."

"What about Micah?"

"Him, too. He thought you should know."

"So you're saying you're the only one determined to deceive me?"

"Yes."

She opened her mouth and panted. "If I hadn't surprised you today, I still wouldn't know."

I inched farther into the room. She gave no reaction. Good. As long as I could keep her talking, I might be able to keep her from losing it. "I was trying to avoid the reaction you're having now."

"Clearly, that was a legitimate concern." She rolled off her bed, away from me, and crossed to the window. For several long, painful seconds, she stared out, her fingers plucking at her knuckles. "Do you have suggestions for how I'm supposed to recover?"

"No."

"In summary, my mentor is dating my stepsister. You knew I would hate that, so you kept it quiet and involved other people in the conspiracy. And you hoped I would never find out because you had no plan for how I would get over the betrayal." She collapsed onto the floor and drew her legs to her chest. When she spoke again, her voice sounded like a lost child's. "I knew him first. We were connected first."

"You still are." I started across the room but halted when she shrank away from me. "My relationship with Micah doesn't change yours."

"Yes, it does." She bowed her head and her hair slipped forward, shielding her face. "I've noticed the changes, Brooke, which says a lot because I don't notice social stuff. He's had less time to talk to me. He takes too long to respond to texts and knows things before I tell him."

"He's busy with the show, and I *am* the director's assistant. Of course, we talk. That was true before we started . . . getting closer."

"Do you ever talk about me?"

"Some."

"Do you tell him private things about our family?"

Had I? I frantically combed through my thoughts, but nothing came to mind. "I can't remember."

"Then you probably have, because you would remember if you had specifically decided not to. I guess I get why he's been different lately. He's changed you. You've changed him."

"Change can be good."

"Shut up with the justifications." Her head lifted. "I can't trust you anymore. I know that people can't always tell the truth, but it ought to be for a good reason, and yours wasn't."

"I thought it was."

Her voice had softened. Saddened. "It was all a lie."

"No, it wasn't. He refused to lie to you, and I didn't either."

"You let me believe things that weren't true. Call it what you want, but that's deceitful. You've become more important to him. He's taken parts of *you* away from me." She slammed her fists against her legs. "I don't get this. You say I'm your sister. Is this how sisters treat each other? Because if it is, I don't want to be one."

My eyes stung with tears, and I tried to blink them away. "I was trying to protect you."

"Sure, Brooke. Believe that if it makes you feel better. Except let's think about how it worked out. I'm worse off. Honor is important to Micah, so he's worse off, too. But you? You'll be fine." Her phone hummed. She pulled it from her pocket, glanced at the text, and tossed the phone onto the carpet. "That's from Micah. He wants to know if I'm okay."

"Are you going to respond?"

"No. He'll text you, and you can tell him."

On cue, my phone buzzed with the Micah tone.

I'll drive over after dinner

I stared at the screen, wracked with shudders.

"What does it say, Brooke?"

Why had he sent the message now? "He's coming over to see me."

"I get a text. You get him. It did change things. Go away, Brooke."

"Natalie—"

"I want to be alone. I think better without people around."

I left and trudged into my room. Behind me, the lock on her door clicked.

I dived into my bed face-first, shaking and dizzy. Thanks to the pill, she hadn't melted down. But I hadn't been prepared for the dejected, logical, betrayed Natalie, and that was somehow worse.

· 29 ·

The Innocent Person

Micah's text arrived around eight.

I'm here
   On my way

When I walked out the door, Micah was waiting on the steps to the veranda, leaning against the banister. I stopped on the step above him. Our eyes were at the same level.

He enfolded me in his arms. "How are you doing?"

I leaned into him, and breathed in the rightness that he always brought. "It's been a rough evening."

"Sorry. What about Natalie?"

"She's confused and sad."

"Will she be okay?"

I started to say that her meds were working—and stopped.

This was what Natalie meant about privacy. I hadn't liked it when she'd violated mine. I couldn't do the same to her. "Eventually."

"I'll talk to her tonight."

Was she standing at a window, reliving that horrible moment all over again? I hoped not, but if she was, I couldn't let her see us like that. I pushed him away.

He held on for a surprised second before letting his arms drop. "What's going on?"

I skipped down the steps and into the yard, out of the light cast by the house. Out of earshot of anyone who might be listening from a window.

From the beginning, I'd known that Natalie would hate the thought of us together. She now believed that two of the people she relied on most had deliberately fooled her. My relationship with Micah could only succeed if it had remained a secret from her. We lost the gamble.

I had to fix this. My irritating, opinionated, cranky stepsister had crept into my heart. I wanted her life to be the best that we could make it. Knowing I'd made it worse was killing me.

I'd been selfish. I'd reached for something I shouldn't have and set this disaster into motion. The failure was all on me.

"Brooke?" Micah stood by my side. "Tell me what's wrong."

Dread twisted in my gut. There was only one option available to us, and I could hardly bear telling him. I gestured between us. "*We* are wrong. We have to . . . change."

"How?"

I was such a coward. I couldn't get the words out, so I just shook my head.

He exhaled softly. "Whatever is happening here, we'll survive it. Natalie will get used to the idea."

"I don't know if she can. She thinks we've abandoned her for each other."

"She'll never understand how relationships really work if you shield her from every negative emotion. You can't be held hostage to her feelings."

Yes, I can. "How would you feel if your sibling had stolen someone you cared about?"

His jaw clenched. "I can tell you exactly how that feels."

Damn, I'd forgotten. He did know.

Micah was the innocent person in this mess. I hated how much my decision would hurt him, but I couldn't let that affect what I had to do. There'd been too many blows for my stepsister this summer, and this might be the one to make her crack. "I have to do what's right for Natalie."

"Which is . . . ?"

"We have to end."

"What?" He shook his head as if he hadn't heard me correctly. "You're breaking up with me?"

Grief swelled inside me, clogging my throat. I had to answer him, but it was so hard to force the word past my lips. "Yes."

His eyes widened with horror. "You can't mean this."

I didn't *want* to mean it, but Natalie had to come first. "I'm sorry, Micah." My response came out in a hoarse whisper.

"No, Brooke. This is insane. Natalie won't learn about the world if you protect her from everything that's bad. She needs a sister, not a servant." He stepped closer.

I stepped back.

"Don't do this."

"I have to. She can't take any more. Her happiness is important to me."

"And mine isn't?"

I hesitated, not sure how to respond. Of course it was, but how could I compare them? "Micah—"

"Shit. I got my answer."

"She's my sister. She has to win."

"There is a third choice. You can have us both."

He hadn't seen her a few minutes ago. *Both* wasn't possible. "No, I can't."

"Aahhhh. I don't believe this." He turned his back on me, his hands clawing through his hair. "Please, Brooke. You're more than a girl I'm dating for the summer." He spun to face me and pleaded with bleak eyes. "You're my last thought before falling asleep and my first thought in the morning. You're the person I tell my dreams to, even the private things I don't tell anyone else. I can't imagine me without you."

My legs were trembling. For almost two weeks, I'd had this smart, talented, humble, beautiful boy look at me like I was a gift. Treat me like I was necessary for his happiness. I couldn't imagine me without him either. "For my whole life, I've felt out of sync with the people I l—" I stopped. Not ready to use *love.* "With the people I care about. I've wondered if I would ever find someone who felt the same way about me that I felt about him. Then I met you. Now I know how equal feels."

"Then don't give up on us. We'll find another solution."

I shook my head. "We would've ended in nine days anyway."

"Not for me. Do you think I could've walked away from you?" He searched my face, anger twisting his lips. "Wait. Have you never thought about what came next? Were you just going to stick with your original plan—to dump me after the show? To say, 'Thanks, that was fun, good-bye'?"

"I didn't have a plan. I haven't let myself think too much about the future."

"So, I'm just a temporary boyfriend who will conveniently disappear in a week."

"*No*. You're so much more, but Natalie wins. Why can't you understand that? She will always win."

"A game can have more than one winner."

"Not this game."

He stood before me, his face in the shadows, breathing hard as he battled to accept the end. Minutes ticked past. The breeze picked up. Thunder rumbled in the distance. And still we stood here, watching each other in agonizing silence.

"Okay." His shoulders slumped in defeat. "I guess there's nothing else to say." He took one of my hands in his, then the other, and closed the gap between us. "I can't bear this." His lips touched mine. Lingered. Drew away.

He would be breaking my heart, if it weren't already broken. "Micah."

"No. Don't." He released our hands and stumbled back a step. "Well, then. I'll just . . ." Whipping around, he jogged to his car. Seconds later, it roared away.

I closed my eyes, not wanting to see him drive out of my life. Micah had been mine for ten amazing days, and now I'd lost him.

It hurt to breathe. Sinking to the grass, I laid on my side and cried.

· 30 ·

A Force Too Intense

Natalie hadn't come out of her room last night, not for dinner or anything else. She let Jeff in once, but even that didn't last long. She must not have said much to him, because he left looking puzzled but with no accusatory look, toward me.

It was ten on Saturday morning before Natalie wandered into the kitchen, looking for breakfast. I was sitting at the table, saving a change to Jeff's website. Micah had emailed the video around two a.m. I'd stared at the subject line of the message for five minutes before reading it. The video was uploaded now.

Natalie leaned against the island and reached for the fruit bowl. "Will we get to take a car to the arts center today?"

I frowned. She seemed quiet and somber, but I couldn't sense any anger. "No, somebody will have to drop us off."

She peeled her banana and took a bite. "What did Micah say last night when he came over?"

"We broke up."

"Huh. He didn't tell me that."

"You've talked to him?"

"We texted last night."

"When?"

"At ten-thirty."

Two hours after he'd left here. Wow. "Did he mention me at all?"

"No. He wanted to know how I was doing. Nothing else." She took another bite of banana. "I didn't expect you to break up."

"I didn't either."

"This is more logical for you both. I'm not sure what the point of that relationship was. You're better off this way. Less complications."

"Natalie, stop." I snapped the lid down on my laptop and stood.

"Are you crying?"

"Yes."

"Why?"

"It killed me to give him up."

"Huh. What about Micah?"

I gave a bitter laugh. "He resisted. Strongly."

"Then why . . . ?" She frowned. "Clearly, my meltdown had something to do with it, but what were the other reasons?"

Micah's voice rang in my head. *Natalie won't learn about the world if you protect her . . .* I checked the clock. We had two hours before we had to arrive for the rehearsal with the band. Enough time for her to recover from a bad reaction to the truth. "There were no other reasons."

She tossed the banana peel in the trash can, then turned to me, her expression blank. "I won't thank you, since I don't know what I think. But I'm not glad either."

Her reaction was milder than I expected. "Okay."

"What will it be like for the two of you backstage?"

"We're mature. We'll work it out."

We rode in complete silence to the theater. Jeff dropped us off and pulled away. The Daltons were walking in from the parking lot.

"Hey," Natalie called.

They stopped.

She marched up to him and said in her not-quiet voice, "Brooke dumped you."

Lisa gaped at him, then me, and back again at him.

"She certainly did." His gaze met mine for a hard few seconds before returning to Natalie.

I stood, frozen in place, unprepared for how cold he was.

"Why didn't you tell me when I texted you last night?"

"I expected you to find out from her."

"Correct assumption, in this instance." She gestured toward me. "Will you be okay if she's around?"

I glared at Natalie. "*She* is standing right here."

He shrugged. "We're mature enough to make it work. Excuse me." He stepped around her and jogged toward the lobby doors.

Natalie gave a satisfied nod. "He said almost the same thing you did." She ran after him.

I watched him, forgetting for a moment that I wasn't alone.

"Wow," Lisa said and followed her son.

When I entered the rear of the auditorium, Micah and Lisa stood at center stage, having an animated discussion. I had to press my lips to hold in a moan. We'd made it past the first awkward moment. It had been even more painful than I would've guessed, but it should've made things easier. It hadn't.

They didn't see me. I shifted uneasily on my feet. Although I couldn't hear the words, it felt wrong to be here.

The movement must have drawn his attention, because he scanned the shadows and found me. He looked at his mom, muttered, "My decision," then stalked behind the curtains.

Lisa remained in her spot, arms crossed. "Did you hear any of that?"

"No."

Her voice lowered. "We were talking about whether you should stay."

The sentence jolted me. Why had I never considered that possibility? The thought of leaving left me shaken. "He wants to fire me?"

"I suggested it, but he disagreed. He thinks you're too critical to the production."

My eyes widened in surprise. Not just that she'd admitted this, but that Micah had defended me. "I'm . . . grateful. I love being part of the show."

"I don't know what went on between the two of you, but I can see how much you've wounded him. Be careful."

At intermission—also known as snack time—the cast went to the campers' lounge and tore into the feast provided by parents. I didn't feel like company, so I headed for the staff lounge. The door to the business office was slightly ajar, and the lights were out. I peeked inside.

Micah was bent over the desk, braced on his fists, chin tucked to his chest, eyes closed.

A force too intense to resist drew me into the room. "Hi."

He shuddered and opened his eyes. "What?" Softly. No anger.

This was awful timing, but I needed to explain. Or thank him. Or . . . something. "Can we talk?"

"About the show?"

"About us."

"There is no us."

"Yes, there is. Just a different us." I laid a hand on his shoulder. "Micah—"

"Don't touch me," he ground out. "Now, please go."

I hesitated, hating what I was about to suggest, but knowing it had to be said. "I'll quit. Elena will be able to find someone else to be the house manager for the shows."

"Right, Brooke. Quit when it gets tough. Of course, Elena needs the hassle of finding someone else at this late date." He shrank away, clutching his binder. "And forget about Natalie. The stress won't get to her anymore. She doesn't need you either." He pushed through the door as he switched on his headset. "Hey, guys, I want everyone back in ten . . ."

"Jill," Natalie said as my mother was pulling away from the arts center, "I guess you knew that Brooke and Micah were dating."

"Yes, I did." Mom glanced at me and mouthed: *Were?*

I gave a curt nod and put on my shades so that Mom couldn't see my shiny eyes. Not a topic I could speak about right now.

"Why were you willing to be part of the conspiracy?"

"It wasn't a conspiracy, Natalie. It was Brooke's business, and I didn't have the right to violate her confidence."

"So if I tell you something, you won't violate mine?"

"You can count on me to keep your secrets"—Mom's gaze met Natalie's in the rearview mirror—"unless I think your safety is compromised."

"You sound like an adult."

"Why, thank you."

They smiled at each other. The conversation turned to plans for the rest of the weekend. I rested my head against the window and tuned everything out.

After dinner, Mom announced, "Brooke and I will clear the table tonight."

Natalie took off for the backyard. Jeff shot us a concerned glance before heading out the door.

Mom didn't make a move to clear the table. Instead, she gestured for me to follow her. We went out to the veranda, to rock on the glider. My go-to place as a kid when I was upset. I curled next to Mom and laid my head on her shoulder.

She smoothed my hair. "This has devastated you."

Sniff. "Yeah."

"Will you tell me what happened?"

I paused long enough to figure out whether my vocal cords could last through the answer. "Natalie didn't like us dating, and I didn't like being the person who'd broken her trust."

"Did she ask you to dump him? Because that wouldn't sit right with me."

"She didn't. It was completely my decision."

"How did he take it?"

"Badly." I'd sent away someone who adored me, someone I adored back. It was the best choice, and the worst thing I'd ever done. "He doesn't think we should cater to her."

"That's none of his business."

"I know." Which didn't make it easier. He was just as gone.

"He's right, though. We do cater to her, and it's not healthy for her or us."

Of course it wasn't, but that didn't change the reality. "I knew she would fall apart when she found out, and I went after him anyway."

"Oh, honey." Mom slipped an arm around my shoulders and pulled me closer to her side. "If you wanted him for the right reasons, then it wasn't wrong."

"What are the right reasons?"

"That he's such a great guy; you couldn't resist his brilliance. That however rough the path ahead might be, what you could be together made it worth trying."

The truth of her words deepened the ache in my heart. I had to close my eyes against the pain.

"You never felt this way about Jonas. He was practice. Micah is . . ."

"Everything."

We rocked silently. The wind whirled around us in gusts, whipping at my hair. Rain had hardly begun to plop on the roof when there was a boom and a torrent.

"Brooke, don't beat yourself up because you went after something glorious."

"I knew that Micah would get hurt."

"Did he know that you were worried about Natalie?"

"Yes."

"Micah's a big boy. He could've said no." She kissed my brow. "I'm glad you're trying to think things through. To care about how you've affected others. But this outcome isn't all on you. A lot of people made a lot of choices. You own your share, and let Micah and Natalie own theirs."

Hearing his name had become more than I could take. I slipped from her arms and stood. "I'm scared this might mess with Natalie so much that she'll screw things up in a performance—or even quit."

"She won't, Brooke. She loves that show. She won't sacrifice it because she's mad at you."

"She could be so upset that she can't control—"

"If we would teach her better coping skills instead of heading off every possible problem that comes along, we might believe that she *can* control her reaction." Mom rose, too. "It made sense to be lax when she first came. It doesn't make sense anymore."

"We can't strengthen the rules yet."

"Maybe not, but we have to start sometime."

"What does Jeff think?"

"He'd spoil her rotten for the rest of her life, if he could. He says it's too soon to toughen things."

"I agree with Jeff."

"Traitor." Her smile was strained. "After the show, we have to sit down as a family and work this out. Natalie has the right to learn how to navigate the bad parts of life."

· 31 ·

The Not Knowing

I brought a paperback mystery with me on Monday and hid in the back row of the auditorium, out of range of the booth. As the story drew me in, the rehearsal retreated into the background.

Midmorning, during a break, someone appeared at my side. I read to the end of the paragraph and looked up.

It was Lisa. "I need you to pick up the playbills."

She'd warned me about being abrupt, so I'd known it going into this job, but it had gotten worse since Saturday. "I don't have a car."

"Ask Micah for his keys."

I drank in his name like I was parched. "Okay."

"No. Wait. Bad idea." She glanced at her watch, shook her head, and said, "Go on. I told her that someone would be there soon, and I don't have the time to come up with a different plan."

He was in the booth with his back to the door, talking to the light and sound designers. They froze when they saw me.

He glanced over his shoulder. "Yes?" The word was clipped.

"I need the keys to your car."

He stared for several seconds, filling the booth with an uncomfortable silence. After digging the keys from his pocket, he lobbed them onto a nearby table.

Reaction rippled through the room—from his team and me. The possibility of touching me disgusted him that much?

A fresh wave of grief—barely restrained since Friday— overwhelmed me. Ducking my head, I took three steps to the table, snatched the keys, and darted from the room without making eye contact again.

After I got the box of playbills, I left them in Micah's car and walked around the downtown shopping district, looking in windows, greeting people I knew. I stopped at the jewelry store and looked in. Della was with a customer, but she gave me a tiny nod of acknowledgment. I nodded back.

It was lunchtime before I got back to the arts center. After parking the car in the Daltons' favorite spot, I walked inside, took the box to the office, and went into the staff lounge. Lisa was there with some other members of the production team, but no stage manager.

I went to the booth. He was the only one there. "Micah?"

He didn't look up. "What?"

"The keys."

"You can leave them on the table."

I set them down and hesitated, unable to make my legs move. I'd never been this hurt with Jonas. Instead, I'd been relieved.

"Go, Brooke."

I stared at the top of his head, willing him to look at me. Why couldn't I leave him alone? I'd broken up with him. I was the one who'd ended things. Why was I the one who couldn't let go, who couldn't resist even the smallest sight of him? "Do you want me to avoid you?"

It took him a long time to answer. "No."

"I will, if that's what you need."

"I said no." His head lifted slightly, but he didn't meet my gaze. "Now, please. *Go.*"

After dinner, my stepfather handed me a second check, this time for seventy-five dollars, the correct amount this week. I thanked him, ran upstairs, and got out the scrapbook. Flipping to the back, I updated the balance.

~~5870~~

5795

Progress was gradual, but at least it was going in the right direction.

There was a sharp *rap, rap, rap* at the door. That was strange. I slid the scrapbook behind the pillows and said, "Come in."

Jeff stood on the threshold. "You've been working on my website."

He sounded mild enough, but his arms were crossed. "Yes, sir."

"I was clear about which changes you were allowed to make. A video was not on the list."

"It was supposed to be a surprise."

"It was—and not a good one."

"So what's wrong with it?"

His eyes narrowed at the defensiveness in my tone. "For starters, the voiceover is amateurish."

Maybe I wasn't professional voice talent, but *amateurish* was an exaggeration. "I'll take it down."

"No need to. I already have. But that's not the worst problem with the video. You also used images I didn't authorize."

Deep breath. Remain politely calm. "I added a couple of extras. Why does that matter?"

"I'm planning to bid on one of those sites. I didn't want that to be known, and now it's out there."

Ohmigod. The shot that didn't have an *after* photo. It had been such a beautiful piece of land, I couldn't resist including it. I looked at him, panic twisting my stomach into knots. How bad was it? "What will happen?"

"I don't know." His voice was growing louder. "Why couldn't you just stick to the agreement, Brooke?"

My cheeks heated. "I thought I was doing a good thing."

"You weren't." He dropped his head back and sucked in some tense breaths. "When did you upload the clip?"

"Saturday morning."

He swore. "Did you load it anywhere else? YouTube?"

"No, sir." The word came out hoarse. "Micah might have it on his Mac."

"*Micah?*" Jeff's gaze snapped to mine. "Why would he have it?"

"He came over to help."

"Where were your mother and I?"

"In Lillington with Natalie."

"You had a boy in this room while we were gone?"

"You make it sound like—"

"So you did. We have rules, Brooke."

"I know, but—"

"What precisely were you doing?"

This conversation was already humiliating me, and Jeff's implication shot it into the sickening zone. "None of your business. You're not . . ." I bit off the sentence, but it was too late. *You're not my father* shimmered in the air between us.

Jeff jerked as if slapped. "I see. Thank you for the clarification."

My throat clogged with tears. I hadn't meant that. It was the humiliation talking. But those horrible words were out there. I wanted to be so much more to him. Instead, I'd pushed him away and put that excruciating look in his eyes. How did I fix this?

"Jeff." My mom stood in the doorway. Her voice was quiet and soothing. "This discussion needs to end."

"She said . . ." He shuddered, then started over. "She said that the boy was alone with her when we weren't home. Without our permission."

"I heard. Natalie heard. It's possible the whole neighborhood heard."

He clamped his lips and faced her. They stared at each other in silent communication before he gave a sharp nod and edged past her. Heavy footsteps thudded down the stairs.

"Brooke." Mom came into my room and shut the door. "May I stay?"

At my nod, she wiggled onto the end of the bed and crossed

her legs, settling in for whatever I needed next. She had the look on her face that always stole my breath, the expression that whispered *I love you unconditionally no matter what you say.*

Her silence encouraged me to search through my mind, choosing only the best thoughts. I tossed the noise and the doubts into the corners and concentrated on the elusive truth, even if it hurt to look. "I've been trying too hard."

"Why do you try too hard?"

"To make a difference."

"Honey, you make a difference every time you walk in a room. It's as effortless as your smile." She reached for my hands. "Close your eyes."

I did, squeezing them tight.

"Whenever I ask a question, tell me the first thing that comes into your head. No filtering. Just gut reaction. Okay?"

Nodding, I focused on her voice and the gentleness of her hands.

"What do *you* want?"

"I want what Natalie has." *Wait.* Where had those words come from?

"What does Natalie have?"

"Micah."

"What else?"

"A dad." My eyes blinked open. Had I really spoken those disloyal words out loud? *To my mother?*

She didn't look upset. More like . . . happy? "You could have one if you asked."

"Jeff doesn't act interested."

"He's trying to respect your wishes. You just told him he's not your father."

"I don't know why I said that. I adore Jeff."

"Well, honey, I couldn't tell. I'm sure he couldn't either, because if he did, Jeff would be all in."

"How was I supposed to know?" I tugged my hands away from hers and pressed them to my burning face. "He's affectionate with you and Natalie. He avoids contact with me like I'm contagious."

"Of course he does. Jeff spent half of his life steeped in regulations, rules, and protocol. You are a minor. No honorable man would touch you unless you invited him. You haven't given him any indication that you'd welcome his affection."

"It would be welcome." *Completely, desperately welcome.* "How do I let him know?"

"Decide what you're comfortable with, and then be honest with him."

Could it really be as simple as saying *I'm ready for more than fist-bumps*? "I just tell him what I want?"

"Yes. That's all you have to do. He's been in a daddy-daughter relationship for fifteen years. You've never been in one. If you ask, he'll meet you halfway." She leaned closer and kissed my forehead. Then she slipped from the bed and out the door, shutting it behind her.

I put the scrapbook away and stood, too restless to sit any longer. But what should I do? Jeff had been hurt by my comments, and I felt the same way about his. Yet, if my mother was right, on the other side of the misunderstanding lay a better relationship. We could be two apologies away from something that I'd dreamed of for as long as I'd known what a daddy was. It was tempting to run out to his workshop and ask *now*.

But I wouldn't. I should wait until we both calmed down. If

the conversation went the way I hoped, I'd want the memory to be lovely—with the hard feelings kept at a distance.

My thoughts had continued to race all evening, so I'd come out to the hammock a few minutes ago, to rock and watch the fireflies, hoping the distraction would help. And it had. I'd nearly made up my mind to go back inside when the workshop door squeaked open. Jeff's heavy footsteps shushed through the grass toward me. I clutched my hands against my waist and stared at the night sky. Had the time come?

"Brooke, I'm here to apologize for getting angry with you."

I nodded and said around the thickness in my throat, "I'm sorry about the photo."

He took a deep breath. "I've been negligent about telling you what a great job you're doing for my business. But no more surprises, please."

"Okay."

"I also want to apologize for implying that you've done anything inappropriate. I trust you." His voice throbbed with hurt. "But I thought your safety *was* my business. Is that how you feel about me? That I'm not—"

"No, Jeff. *No*." I pushed out of the hammock. Here was our chance to make things right. The moment demanded honesty. Respect. Courage. "You've been my stepfather for nine months, and I still don't get how we should act around each other. We're so careful and formal. Is it because I'll be gone in another year? Is a relationship not worth the trouble?"

He was already shaking his head. "You're worth the trouble to me, Brooke. I'll be your stepdad forever. Just tell me how."

I hadn't realized what a huge burden the not knowing had been, because now it had eased and I could breathe freely. And since blurting out my thoughts unfiltered was working for me, I'd keep it going. "I wish we were closer."

He smiled, a big, happy smile. "It's what I want, too, but you'll have to be patient with me. I'm kind of inexperienced with this stepfather gig."

"You're a great dad to Natalie."

"Because she taught me how to be the best father for her from the day she was born. You were already grown up when I entered your life. I won't get everything right, but I'll give it my all."

He'd just handed me the perfect opening. What if I asked for too much? He wasn't likely to refuse me, but even the tiniest possibility that he might was terrifying. Maybe we should start small. "We could do more than fist-bumps."

"I would like that, if you'll set the boundaries."

"Hugs would be a good start."

"Then come here." He opened his arms.

I launched myself into his embrace, trying not to cry as he held me. I was surrounded by the strength and scent of him. And like Natalie had said, it smelled like love.

· 32 ·

Unadorned Facts

Dress rehearsal had gone well. We had a small crowd, but they were laughing in the correct places and applauding often. The cast ate it up. They'd never performed better.

There were a few mistakes. A dancer who came onstage without a skirt. No butter churn for Aunt Eller in the opening. A scene change that took eight seconds too long. But after Lisa and Micah finished going over their notes, we all cheered.

Natalie was so hyped. The whole way home, she talked my ear off. When we entered the quiet house through the kitchen door, her monologue continued.

I opened the fridge and pulled out a bottle of water. "Want one?"

"Sure."

I tossed it to her.

She didn't even attempt to catch. Just watched it clatter to the floor, bent over, and picked it up. "Is Jill at a ball game?"

"Yes."

"What about Dad?"

"He's at the town hall, at a planning board meeting."

She walked away and stomped up the stairs without another word.

I took my bottle of water to my room, turned on my lamp, and laid against the pillows on my bed. I wasn't sleepy, but I didn't want to move. Or think. Or feel.

"Are you sad, Brooke?"

Although I'd rather divert her, that technique wouldn't work with Natalie. She needed unadorned facts, baldly delivered. "I'm crushed."

"How long will it take you to get over it?"

"Not sure." *Never?*

"Dad says it's hard to get over things until all of the apologies have been said."

"Jeff's right, and that option isn't available to me."

She was leaning against the doorframe, staring at the ceiling, asking me about emotions. Had she ever done that before?

It might hurt to continue with this topic, but I would try. "Do you still talk with Micah?"

"Yes. Why would you think we stopped?"

"I didn't know."

She crossed to the window and stared into the moonlit yard. "We mostly talk on breaks now. He hasn't mentioned you since you dumped him. He's sad, too."

"Really?" Since our breakup, I'd seen him angry, tired, impatient—but sad? "How do you know?"

"He said so."

"He told you he was sad?"

"No, he told his mom while I was eavesdropping. I wouldn't have figured that out on my own." Her fingers wiggled but no knuckle pinching. "He said he hurt so much that he could hardly think."

"Please don't tell me anything else. I can't take it." I flicked off my lamp and squirmed in the bed until I was lying flat. Why did I prefer baring my soul with the lights off? "Micah was your mentor before he and I started dating. And during. And now afterward."

"I know all that. What's your point?"

"Your friendship with him hasn't been changed by whatever relationship I had with him. When we were together, yours was good. Now that we're apart, yours is still good."

"You don't get it, Brooke. You think this mess is about Micah, and while that's partially true, the biggest part of the problem is *you*. Since I moved to Azalea Springs, everything about me involves you. Everything." She crossed to the end of the bed and looked at me with full eye contact. "You do a lot of things *for* me—and everything else, I have to share *with* you."

"Like what?"

"My dad. This house. I even had to share the musical with you, too. I'd like to have something that is purely mine."

"You can't own people, but you can have relationships that you don't have to share." How could I make her understand this? Where were the right words? "You don't share your dad with me. At all. He's my stepdad, which is different. I adore Jeff. I know he cares about me, but he'll never love me the way he loves you."

She rolled her eyes. "Maybe."

"Definitely."

"All right, then. I'll just say it. I had to share *you*."

"Me?" I held still, hardly daring to breathe.

"Yes. When you were dating Micah, you weren't the same. I noticed. You had less time for me. When you did have time, you didn't pay attention. I minded that."

"I'm sorry, especially the part about not paying attention, but you haven't got the reason entirely right. I was busy and tired and excited. Yes, Micah soaked up a lot of my hours, but so did the show. And my job. And having a full-time stepsister when I'd been an only child for seventeen years."

"We've been stepsisters for nine whole months."

"But not full-time. Two weekends a month and a few days over Christmas didn't prepare me to be around you every hour of every day. That's huge. There have been a lot of things that changed for me this summer. It's not fair to blame only the dating."

"Okay, those sound like plausible excuses. I'll have to think about them." Her face scrunched. "When exactly did you start dating?"

"We began hanging out on July first. Purely friendly. It didn't switch to actual dates until two weeks ago today."

She wrinkled her nose. "I was having a hard time around then with the choreography. I was thinking about dropping out."

"Why?"

"I wasn't that good, I couldn't seem to get better, and it was hard to keep it together. I was afraid I might spoil the show. Since I only had one line to sing, I knew someone else could've taken over easily."

"One person can't ruin a performance. A show is bigger than that."

She gave me a pitying look. "You've never been in a production before. You don't know how it can get backstage. I'd reached the point where I figured I should quit to save everyone the trouble."

I wished she'd told me this sooner. I hated that she'd been carrying it around, all bottled up inside for so long. "There are thirty other people in that show who could screw up."

"If they do, it will be an accident. If I do, it will be predictable." She bowed her head and her hair tumbled forward, hiding her face. "I often sit in fear, because I know I'll do something bad, and everyone will blame me for destroying the show. They'll be right, too."

"That's the thing about live theater. Mistakes are part of the fun. The audience would be disappointed if there weren't any mistakes, because then we get to see you recover. We get to see you be clever and save the day. You go from being talented to being heroes."

"Sometimes you can be so incredibly naïve. Maybe there are some people like that in the audience, but not many. Not the parents of cast members. Not the cast members themselves. If I'd known two weeks ago that you and Micah were dating, it would've thrown me over the edge."

I closed my eyes and let her statement sink in. The breakup had hurt. I couldn't foresee a time when it wouldn't, but I'd been right to fear her reaction.

"You've really messed up Micah. He used to be awesome, but he's not anymore. Now he's merely above average."

My eyes popped open. "How do you know?"

"I observe things. He's lost his energy. I said something to him about it, and he told me to back off."

"Wow. That was rude."

"It's a legitimate response." She left my room and disappeared down the stairs. Seconds later, the front door slammed.

Our conversation forced me to think about feelings I'd hoped had been buried. But I guess not. I missed being part of Micah's life. I was tired of tiptoeing around the theater, scared to see him and just as scared not to. Even though I'd wounded him, I'd wounded me more.

· 33 ·

Extreme Composure

O ur opening night performance had been a huge success. The audience had been happy. The screwups had been small, even funny. And no one had been injured. That was a pretty good record.

Only two evening performances and one matinee left.

I was in the lobby on Friday night by six-forty. We wouldn't open the house until seven, and already we had a big crowd.

Over the headset, Micah muttered a curse word, then said, "Major problem. Angelica's stuck in traffic on I-95."

I gasped. One of the principals wasn't here yet?

"When's her ETA?" Elena asked.

"She estimates that she can arrive in an hour, but I'm not sure I'm willing to trust that."

"Should we delay?"

"No."

"We can't pretend her role doesn't exist. Gertie is memorable."

There was a long pause. "We'll find someone in the ensemble and hand her a script."

I had a solution for Micah that I didn't want to say over the headset. I waved over an usher. "I'm going backstage for a moment. I won't be gone long." Without waiting for a response, I slipped into the auditorium and ran for the wings.

Micah and Elena were huddled together, both dressed completely in black, nearly blending with the walls. They were peering at a script, speaking in low voices.

"Hi," I called.

They turned.

"Natalie can do it, and she won't need a script."

Elena frowned at me. "What do you mean?"

"I think Natalie could replace any character in the musical. She practically has the show memorized."

"You're right. She does." Micah checked his watch and gave a sharp nod. "Okay, find her."

Just like that. He made the decision, then put it behind him. "Micah?"

He glanced at me, a question in his look.

"Thank you."

"Sure." His mouth relaxed into a smile. "Go."

I knew exactly where my stepsister was. When I walked into the campers' lounge, it was buzzing. Gertie's absence had been noted.

"Natalie?" I called. "We need you."

The room fell silent as she crossed to the door. "Why?"

"Come on. I'll tell you on the way." I charged down the hall in the direction of the changing rooms.

She caught up. "Am I in trouble?"

"Exactly the opposite. Do you know Gertie's lines?"

"Yes."

"Her blocking?"

"Mostly."

"Angelica can't make it tonight. Could you take her place?"

"Yes."

I spoke into the headset. "Natalie's agreed."

"Divert to the staff lounge." Micah's voice.

Laurey, Curly, and Aunt Eller were with him. He gestured us over. "These three will help you get into the right places."

Natalie said, "It won't be necessary."

"Yes, it will. Let them help you," he said firmly. "I'd worry too much otherwise, so do this for me. Curly, come here. Stand next to tonight's Gertie."

Once they were in place, Elena studied them, hands on hips. "You're taller than Angelica, but not enough to be a problem. Will it bother you if Channing touches you to push you into place?"

Natalie shook her head. "As long as it's not my bare skin, like on my arms."

"If you wear Gertie's costume, it has long sleeves."

"Then I'll be good. Do I still get to sing my line?"

"No," Micah said. "Someone should replace you."

"Tesla. She knows it."

Micah gestured with approval, and Elena was on the headset, getting someone to take the message to Tesla.

Things happened fast after that. Curly disappeared with Micah. Laurey and Aunt Eller went with Natalie to help with the costume change. I returned to the lobby, frantically texting Jeff and Mom, asking them to get here as soon as possible. Then I opened the house while the ushers braced for the crowd.

"Brooke?"

I looked up. Kaylynn was here with Jonas. "Hi," I said, handing her a playbill. "I hope you enjoy the show."

They went into the auditorium, pausing just inside the door. I turned to the next patron. A few seconds later, there was a touch on my arm.

It was Kaylynn again. "Your boyfriend, Micah, is in this show."

"Yes, he's running it." I controlled a wince. "And he's not my boyfriend anymore. We split up."

"I'm sorry." She lowered her voice. "I'm sorry about a lot of things. We should talk, and get past this."

"I agree."

"Okay, I'll call." She hurried to Jonas, took his hand, and went to look for their seats.

It would take some time to process that, but not now. I had an audience to get into the auditorium, and a musical to watch.

By the time the overture started, Natalie was dressed in her new costume and waiting with extreme composure for her cue.

Natalie's big sister? That was a different story.

The applause for Friday night's performance was enthusiastic. The audience had been told of the substitution, and I'd bet that none of them could tell.

Angelica was almost right about her estimated time. She got to the theater about thirty minutes after the performance started. She sobbed and begged to take over during the second act—which got a big no from Micah.

Jeff and Mom made it in time to see Natalie's first entrance. They sobbed, too.

I could understand why. When her first cue came, she sauntered right onto stage, swaying her hips, flinging her hair, latching onto Curly like she would never let go.

It wasn't a flawless performance. The principals had to nudge her into place a couple of times, and her braying laugh wasn't as obnoxious as the other Gertie's was. But for an unrehearsed, last-minute replacement, Natalie did an amazing job.

The cast went out for ice cream after the performance. Natalie went with them, but I passed, preferring to sit in my bedroom and stare at the wall. I had to recover from worrying about how well she'd do, and I couldn't bear the thought of running into Micah.

A car pulled into the driveway. Natalie's footsteps smacked up the front steps. Once the door shut behind her, the car drove away.

My door opened a minute later. "What did you think?" she asked.

"You were great."

"Some people said I did a better job than Angelica."

"I think you did. Except the laugh. Angelica's laugh is more annoying."

"She's welcome to being better at that. I couldn't bring myself to sound ridiculous." My stepsister sat on the end of the bed. "Channing is nice. He makes a good Curly."

Okay, interesting. "I agree."

"Channing asked if I'd be at your high school next year. He said their productions could use me."

I smiled without saying anything.

"Did I say that wrong? Because it was supposed to invite you to respond."

"Can you be more precise with the question?"

"Will I attend your high school in the fall?"

"I don't know." I really didn't know, but since no one had mentioned when she'd be returning home, her staying here was becoming more probable.

"I don't want to, but it wouldn't be horrible either."

"Nice to know."

She flopped backward so that she was half-lying across the end of my bed. "This will sound bad, but I'm saying it anyway. It was good for me that you broke up with Micah."

I clenched my hands under the covers. "That does sound bad."

"It made me feel important that you did it." She rolled her head to look in my direction. "Tonight made me feel important, too. That's when I realized it's what I actually needed. Not you breaking up with Micah specifically, but me being so important that you were willing to."

"Thanks for telling me."

"Whatever." She looked at the ceiling. "I don't feel the same way about you as I feel about Luke. I don't know if that's because he's a boy. Or a baby. Or because we share DNA. Well, it's probably that. Blood has to make a difference." Her head moved restlessly back and forth on the bed. "The only reason you and I are siblings is because our parents married. Would we stop being siblings if they divorced?"

"I think so, yes."

"Sisterhood should be our choice." She sat up and frowned at the floor. "I would choose to keep you."

This was the closest Natalie would ever get to saying something loving to me, and I would likely never hear it again. I memorized the words, the expression on her face, and the way it resonated into my bones. "I would choose to keep you, too."

· 34 ·

A Hopeful Sign

Saturday's performance wasn't quite as good as Friday's, but we got through it, and everybody was happy. We only had one matinee performance to go. Tonight, we had the cast party.

No party had ever scared me as much as this one did. I would've skipped it if it hadn't meant so much to Natalie. This production had been a triumph for her, a game changer in her life with us. If I wasn't there, it would come back to bite me. Natalie didn't forget details.

I had to survive being in the same place with Micah for an evening without embarrassing myself. He would be in Azalea Springs for two more days. I hated that we . . .

No, I had to let it go.

The cast party was being held in the fellowship hall of a cast member's church. From the size of the crowd, it looked as if Natalie and I were among the last to arrive.

People jammed the space. It took about two seconds for my

gaze to meet Micah's. He stared back boldly, his face settling into stern lines. How could I have ever thought of him as ordinary? He might not be tall or ripped or gorgeous in the classic sense, but it was hard to imagine him being in a room and not being the center of attention.

He was surrounded by a small fan club, yet his unwavering focus remained on me. I turned away first, walking to where some tables had been set up for food. I slid a jug of lemonade in with the other drinks and hunted for a spot to set the macaroons.

"Three shows down," a voice said behind me. "One to go."

I looked up. "Hi, Lisa. It went well tonight."

"That's what the others have been saying. Tomorrow will be good, too."

"The edge will be gone."

"Knowing it's the last performance always adds an extra kick." She took a sip from her bottle of root beer. "How are you doing?"

I knew what she was really asking, and I might as well be honest. I wouldn't see her again after tomorrow. "I didn't want this, Lisa. I miss him."

"Have you told him that?"

"I can't find him alone. He won't let me get near him."

"Well, if it helps any, he misses you, too. Okay, it's time for my final pep talk." She turned, then said over her shoulder, "If you ever need a reference, let me know. You've done a fabulous job."

Wow, I hadn't expected that, but I would happily accept the offer.

Lisa had reached the front of the hall and was standing on

a low dais, banging a spoon against a metal tray. "Can I have everybody's attention?"

The noise decreased. "We've been rocking this show. Give me a moment of complete silence." She waited until they did. "I love guest directing jobs. It gives me a chance to discover talented teens—some who don't even know they're talented yet. I'm reminded how amazing it is when everyone comes together to create something remarkable. I love how a different cast and crew can take a well-known script, inhabit its world, and make the show their own. I leave Azalea Springs a better director than when I arrived. So that's it, everyone. I'll join you to strike the set tomorrow. Find me before you leave the theater. I would like to thank each of you." She scanned the group. "Would anyone else like the opportunity to speak to the company?"

"I would." The actor who played Will Parker ran to the front and launched into a monologue that was as funny as it was vain, the same way he was at the high school whenever he could find a captive audience.

Wait. A captive audience?

Excitement buzzed in my head. Maybe I should go up there. Micah would have to listen. Right?

What would I say? My brain had turned to mush. It held no coherent thoughts except *I wish I had him back* and *He leaves Monday*.

It would be humiliating if he walked away while I was speaking. But would he?

Probably. I'd really hurt him.

What about Natalie? Would she freak? I looked across the room at her. She was talking with Channing, acting relaxed, but was that enough to prevent something bad?

I had the car. If she melted down, I could take her home.

"So, guys," Will Parker was saying. "It's been cool. See you this fall."

My chance was slipping away.

Reaching into my pocket, I pulled out my phone and texted my stepsister.

I'm going to talk in front of everybody and make Micah listen to me

"Anyone else?" Lisa prompted.

It was quiet. Some looked around eagerly, wondering if there was another ego in the house. Others looked down, hoping she wouldn't go crazy and call on them.

"I will."

The crowd turned to me, surprise rippling through the room. I'd been mostly invisible to the cast until a week ago. As I wove through them, they parted, forming an aisle. Micah half-sat on a table, hands gripping the edge, scowling at the floor.

I sucked in a shaky breath. I preferred being behind the scenes. Standing there in front of everyone, with all of those eyes staring at me, was scary. But if it was the only way to get Micah to listen, it would be worth it. I grasped my hands together and let my thoughts flow. "The theater has always been something I attended, not something I did. This production was the first time I've ever been involved. So, at tech rehearsals, when the show seemed like a complete mess, I didn't see how it could possibly come together . . ."

My audience laughed.

". . . But then something magical happened."

With fluid movements, Micah straightened and slipped around the back of the crowd. His destination, the exit.

"Micah, don't leave yet."

He paused, his body in profile. Everyone shifted, angling to see what he would do.

"Please stay until I'm finished."

He hooked his hands into his pockets and faced me. "Why?" The word was soft. Hurt.

"Because you're the magic."

There was a respectful moment of silence, then the company turned to him, applauding and cheering. He inclined his head, watching me steadily.

"I'd like to say . . ." I hesitated.

He radiated intensity, the air between us electric.

"When I joined the show, I didn't know what I was doing. You really made me feel like part of the team. Even when I made mistakes, you would patiently show me how to be better. I've learned so much and . . ." I paused and looked at Lisa, who smiled with encouragement. My gaze swept the audience until it landed again on Micah. "I'm grateful. For *everything*."

He drew his hands from his pockets and walked toward me, his steps deliberate and purposeful. He stopped two inches away and said, for my ears only, "Why are you doing this?"

"I miss you, and I'm sorry, and I want you back."

His eyes narrowed. "I'm only here for two more days."

"I'll take whatever I can get."

An eternity passed—or maybe just an instant—before he reached for my hand, his fingers closing securely around mine. "Let's go."

Noise broke out around us, but I didn't care. I was with Micah. I might be getting a second chance. Nothing else mattered.

We ran from the hall. He led me over to a walled brick courtyard and into its farthest corner, plunging us into shadows that the moon struggled to pierce.

"Hey."

"Hi."

"I can't believe you did that."

Me neither. "Does this mean we're good?"

"I want it to." He released my hand and took a step back. "Just give me a moment to take this in."

So much had to be discussed. Natalie. His departure. What kind of us there could be after tomorrow. "I need to finish my apology."

"I'm listening." He leaned against the wall, arms crossed. His tension felt wary, instead of angry. A hopeful sign.

"I'm sorry that I hurt you and that we've lost so much time."

"I sense a *but* in there."

"Yeah." The truth was a risk, but lies and secrets were what had brought us to this point. I owed it to us to go with honesty. No omissions. "I don't regret my choices."

"Dumping me was the right thing to do?"

"No, choosing Natalie was. She told me that she thought about quitting a couple of weeks ago. If she'd known about us, it would've thrown her over the edge."

He looked at his feet and swallowed hard. "If we get back together, is this what I'll have to look forward to? Waking up each morning, hoping that today isn't the day you sacrifice me again?" Pain and fear colored his voice.

I moved closer to him and rested my hands on his arms. "From tonight on, only you and I are in this relationship. Only we decide where to go next."

He gave a tiny shake of his head as he raised his gaze to mine. He wasn't convinced.

"You're still Natalie's mentor or friend or whatever it is you want to call it. She knows that her relationship with you isn't threatened by what we have. If that's not enough for her, then my family will have to help her learn. But I won't let it affect us."

"I want to believe you."

"Then please give me a chance. I'll earn your trust all over again."

He closed his eyes, breathing slowly. Carefully. I wanted so badly to hold him. To fill him with my confidence. But he had to do this himself. It was his turn to choose.

When his eyes opened again, they shone with decision. *Which one?*

The tension eased from his face. His arms slipped around my waist to pull me against him. "I want to be with you."

"Really?" I held myself still, almost afraid to believe him.

He smiled. "Yes."

The pain faded away, replaced by relief and joy. I locked my hands behind his neck, stood on tiptoe, and planted an *I'm so grateful* kiss on his lips. He took over, changing the kiss to *I've missed you.*

From the fellowship hall, a door squeaked and a group of cast members burst out, their loud voices fading into the direction of the parking lot. The party was breaking up. Our last show was only a few hours away.

"It's late, Micah." Nope, that was not a whiny tone in my voice.

"I know." His lips brushed my temple.

"What about . . . ?" We spoke in unison.

He laughed. "Tomorrow, after the show, you're mine."

"I'm yours now."

"Yeah, but tomorrow, I'll have a plan."

I nodded, too happy to speak. This evening had turned out so much better than I could've imagined.

"Okay," he said, "let's find Natalie."

· 35 ·

Chaos to Quiet

Natalie and I left the cast party around midnight. It was hard to say good-bye to Micah, but we'd agreed to go running together early in the morning. Tame and wonderful.

As soon as I got home, I went to my room and got ready for bed.

A shadow appeared in the door. "This has been a decent summer."

Okay, late-night chat. "It has?"

"Yes. It's not as tedious as I expected. This house feels like a place I don't mind being in, and you and Jill are fine that I'm here."

"Can't understand why you ever thought we weren't."

"Nai Nai. She says I'm a lot of trouble and that Jeff's new family would lose their patience fast, because I'm nothing to you."

"Your grandmother is not a nice person." I sat on the end of my bed. Neither Natalie nor I had won the grandma sweep-stakes. "I'm sorry. I shouldn't say that out loud, but it's true."

Natalie leaned against the doorframe and stared at the ceiling. Her fingers tapped lightly against her thighs as she struggled with whatever it was that she wanted to say. "Are you and Micah a couple again?"

"Yes."

"How will that work?"

"I don't know." Confusion clouded her face. Well, I was confused, too. "We'll spend as much time together as we can before he goes home on Monday. We haven't talked about what will happen after that."

"You can see him every night on Skype."

"Not the same."

"So what if it's minus touching. Is that such a big deal?"

"Oh, yeah."

"I'll try to tolerate how this turned out, but don't tell me any details. I don't want to know." She darted from the room, her footsteps thumping down the stairs.

I wiggled under the covers and smiled at the world. Natalie might not be the best friend/sister I'd imagined, but we were getting close, and that was good enough.

As I drove Natalie over to the arts center on Sunday, she couldn't stop talking about her mom.

"She'll be here today, right?"

"I hope so."

"She said she would last night."

"That's good, then."

Natalie sighed. "But she hasn't texted today, and neither has Terry. What do you think that means?"

I wouldn't tell her a lie, and I couldn't tell her the truth. "If she called you last night, then she really wants to come."

"I agree. Can you hold on to my phone while I'm backstage? Just in case they call?"

"Sure."

Two hours passed, and there was no sign of them. No texts. Micah had given the fifteen-minute warning. We had a nearly full audience, with a heavier volume of little kids than previously. This could be a wild performance.

"Brooke?"

I turned. Mei and Terry had walked in.

"Thank you for coming," I said, trying to filter out the squeal of joy. "Natalie will be so happy you're here."

Her mother frowned. "I told Natalie I would come."

Okay, not responding to that. Mei's irritation could be a reaction to how annoying she found me. I exchanged glances with Terry. He winked.

"Did you bring Luke?"

"No," Terry said. "He's at home with his grandparents."

Mei had always been thin but was even more so now. There were dark circles under her eyes and a grayish tint to her skin. When she placed her fingertips against her lips, her hand shook from a faint tremor. She looked physically ill, but she'd come here today anyway, and I was glad.

I pointed to the right side of the auditorium. "Why don't you sit over there? You'll have a clearer view of Natalie during her solo."

Terry said, "Thanks."

They walked down the aisle, Mei clinging to her husband's arm. For a moment, I debated whether or not to tell Natalie. She could become so agitated that she wouldn't calm down. Really, though, she ought to know. She might do badly if she thought Mei hadn't made it.

The ushers were in good shape. I headed to the green room to tell her. Micah was standing in the wings as I was walking by. I tried to slip past him.

"Hey." He stepped into the spot I'd intended to be.

"Hi."

He muted his mic. "Anything I can help you with?"

"Maybe. But not in public."

His smile wrapped around my heart. "That can be arranged."

I sighed in anticipation. "I have to speak with Natalie first."

"Can you meet me in the booth during intermission?"

"I'll be there."

"Good." Looking around, he clicked the unmute button and spoke into his headset. "Ten minutes everyone."

The entire cast showed up for strike except Natalie. She left to hang out for another hour with Mei and Terry.

It didn't take long before everything was done and people had gone. Only a few crew members remained. We went from chaos to quiet in a matter of minutes.

There was nothing but an empty stage now. I strolled into the center of it and looked out at the silent theater. Micah joined me. No headset. No binder. Just my guy, dressed in all black. Looking hot.

"Hey." He slipped an arm around me.

"I can't believe the difference." I leaned into him. "Is this the way it always feels after a show ends?"

"Sort of anticlimactic—mixed with a sense of victory and sadness?" His hand tightened against my waist. "Yeah."

"When do you get started on your next production?"

"I have to let go of this one first," he said with a laugh. "Not until October. Or maybe nothing this fall. I might be too busy being a senior."

"Really? Branching out?"

"Catching my breath." He turned me in his arms and kissed me. "Stage kiss."

"I like it." But my smile faded as a wave of regret sloshed over me, stealing the moment.

"Is something wrong?"

"No. It's just . . ." I stared at my hands, pressed to his chest. I felt shy about explaining, but I would. No more secrets. "I missed you so much last week, and I almost lost you. If I hadn't spoken up at the cast party, you would've gone home and—"

"You did speak up and made me listen. And now we're back together. Let the rest go." He kissed my forehead and tightened his arms.

I yielded to the embrace, loving the strength of him and the sweetness of having things right between us again. "How much time do I get you today?"

"How about an all-night date?"

"All night? Really?"

"Yeah."

A delicious excitement filled me. "What will we do?"

"A picnic in the park. A midnight movie. Breakfast at a Waffle House. Watching the sunrise together."

"That sounds like four dates."

"It is. They were listed in this dating guide I found online, and I'd been planning them separately before. I was hoping—"

I kissed him, silencing the words, silencing the pain of our days apart. "Whatever you want," I whispered.

"And your parents?"

"I'll text my mom. She won't question it."

"So one last suggestion. Can we ask Natalie if she wants to go on the picnic with us?"

I smiled at him, surprised and touched and in love. "Perfect."

Our all-night date had been wonderful. Every. Single. Moment. But now it was over. He pulled to the curb in front of my house as the sun streaked the eastern sky with pinks and purples.

In three hours, Micah would be driving home to Elon.

My body felt flushed and stretched. Saying good-bye had been a guarantee before we'd even met, but the actual moment was pure misery.

He shifted on his seat to face me and reached for my hand. "It'll be okay."

"Sure about that?"

"Yeah. A ninety-minute drive isn't that far."

"It is when you don't have a car."

"But I do, and I know where you live. Since it's too late to talk me out of wanting to be with you, we have to make a plan."

Okay, yeah. I liked plans. "We can trade off on Friday-night football games." I would figure out a way to schedule Mom's car when it was my turn.

"You can stay over sometimes and experience the fun of helping Dad harvest on Saturday mornings."

Actually, it did sound like fun. "When you're here, we'll play miniature golf."

His eyebrow arched. "I'm not much into miniature golf."

"You haven't played it with me before."

His smile was slow and sexy. "Sounds like that might be worth trying."

"Definitely."

His expression grew pensive. "We should talk or text whenever we want."

"As long as we're honest about how much time we need for school and friends and our families." I'd throw something else out there, just in case. "Would it be distracting if I came to Elon while you're running a show?"

"It would be distracting if you didn't." He raised my hand to his lips.

I loved it when he did that. "Did you learn hand-kissing from YouTube, too?"

"No, I figured that out all by myself." He leaned closer and cupped my face in his hands. Our kisses started soft and sweet, then lingered. Deepened.

He pulled back with a sigh. "Are you free Labor Day weekend?"

"Yes. Why?"

"Save the whole weekend for me. I'll be here."

· 36 ·

Every Part of Me

I hadn't seen Micah since he moved back to Elon two weeks ago, and now he was in New York City at his theater intensive. We talked at night, but he'd been so hyper-excited about what he was learning that I hadn't done much more than listen and say "wow."

I'd been busy too, finishing the final details with Jeff's new employee. Kilo had been on the job for one week, and already I could see what a positive difference it had made on my stepdad.

After checking the latest changes on their website, I clicked the update button in WordPress. That was it. No more tasks for Jeff.

I'd been putting together some ideas for my own business. Pretty much what I'd been doing this summer. Website updates. Managing email lists and newsletters. Once I had reliable transportation, I might branch out to running errands for local businesses. I was almost ready to launch my website.

The door to the workshop creaked open. My stepfather stood on the threshold. "What's up?"

"Just finished the new and improved gallery."

"We'll be adding more to it." He grinned. "We won the bid."

"Oh, that's great." I shot out of the chair and gave him a hug. "When do you start?"

"It'll be September before it gets going, but we'll start prepping soon. I have another proposal for you."

"What?"

"It's about a car."

"A car for me?" *A car for me?*

He chuckled. "Yes. Now that I've landed this new contract, Jill and I will buy a second truck. If you want, we could sell the Honda to you for a dollar."

"That would work." A Honda wasn't what I'd planned, but it would be a good solution for now. *Oh, please, I should just go ahead and smile so big my lips fly off my face.* "How soon will you look for a truck?"

"Not this week. We won't be here."

"Where will we be?"

"Steven is loaning us his family's beach house. We're going down there on Friday."

"Oh, wow. That's . . . great." I kept a big smile pasted onto my face, to hide how torn I was. Normally, I would love a weekend at the beach. My family hadn't gone anywhere this summer, and this would qualify as the only "vacation" we'd have. But Micah was supposed to come home to North Carolina this weekend. I wanted to drive to Elon, or talk him into doing the reverse.

With school only two weeks away, we were running out of

time to simply be together, and now we'd have to wait a little longer.

The house that Steven loaned us might be small by beach standards and a one-block walk to the ocean, but it was beautiful. Four bedrooms, three baths, and decks everywhere on the ocean side of the house.

We'd arrived around noon and had lunch, staying inside during the hottest part of the day. Midafternoon, Jeff called up the stairs and asked me to come down. When I got to the great room, he was standing next to Natalie.

"Are you certain?" he asked.

"Yes, Dad. I already said so."

"Okay . . ." He stopped when he spotted me.

"What's going on?" I asked.

Mom sat on the couch and pointed at the chairs opposite her. "Sit. Before we hit the beach, we're having a family meeting."

Natalie rolled her eyes and flopped into a recliner, facing toward the windows.

I perched on the edge of a chair and watched my parents warily. They were pressed together, side by side, gesturing back and forth.

My stepsister looked over her shoulder, exhaling with attitude. "Flip a coin or something. Just one of you start speaking."

Jeff gave her a *Watch it!* look. "You'll be living with us this fall."

She slumped deeper into her chair and stared at the ceiling, foot wiggling.

A wiggling foot was a new reaction. Was that good or bad? I was going with good, because that's what I wanted it to mean.

"Your mother isn't ready for you to return full-time," he said.

Natalie nodded. "I knew that. She isn't her old self yet."

"She wants you to visit on the weekends. Are you okay with this arrangement?"

"Yes. I mostly like living in Azalea Springs. I can tolerate a semester."

Mom's gaze went from my stepsister to me. "Jeff and I think that it's time to talk about how the two of you should treat us."

Natalie lowered her chin until she could meet Mom's gaze. "Just so I'm clear. You're talking about my relationship with you and Brooke's relationship with Dad."

"Yes."

"If we're going to have a meaningful conversation about behavior, I'd like to establish that I'm too old for obedience and punishment and concepts like that."

Jeff clamped his lips against a laugh. Mom patted his thigh and focused on Natalie. "I don't want to be a guest parent that you put up with until your dad comes home. I want to be a full parent to you. If you need something, you can go to either me or your father. You have to respect my wishes and act at our home the same way you act at your other home."

"Uh, Jill, you don't really want that." Out came Natalie's sly-ish smile. "I act better with you."

Jeff lost it, snorting beer up his nose.

Mom shook her head, ignoring her husband. "Any questions?"

"No. Just so you know, though, I won't be mentioning this

conversation to Mama. She would prefer that you remain a guest parent."

Jeff laughed harder.

Mom patted his thigh again. "Wise decision, Natalie." My mom elbowed her husband. "Your turn."

He sobered instantly, set his beer down, and took a deep breath. "Brooke."

My smile faltered. I didn't need this speech. "I respect Jeff's wishes. Why would you think otherwise?"

"That's not what this is about." Jeff rubbed a hand over the back of his head, then hitched forward. "Are you ready to be my daughter, Brooke?"

I've been ready. "Yes."

"What I mean is . . ." He blew out a breath. Clasped his hands together. Unclasped them. Looked at my mom, then back at me. "I'd like to file adoption papers. What do you think?"

My heartbeat jumped into overdrive. Had I heard that right? "You want to adopt me?"

"Yes, Brooke. I do."

A dad—to love me.

I looked at Natalie, who was staring in my general direction, wiggling her foot. "Are you okay if Jeff adopts me?" *Please say yes.*

"More than okay. It means we could be full sisters now." She wrinkled her nose. "Well, technically half-sisters."

A sister—to be my best friend.

For so many years, I'd been waiting for this to happen. I didn't have to go online to order the shiny-deluxe-model father. He had simply arrived. And Natalie wasn't the sister I had expected, which was a good thing because she was so much better than anything my imagination could've created. I looked at Jeff and willed the tears stinging my eyes not to spill over. "I would love for you to adopt me."

He stood and held out his arms. When I stepped into them, he cradled me so tenderly. My first hug with my real father. I could hardly breathe. "Thanks. Dad."

"While I'm okay with the idea of the adoption," Natalie said, hopping to her feet, "I'm saturated with all of the emotion in here. Anything else? Because I'd like to go walking on the beach."

The doorbell rang.

"Oh, wait. Never mind." She sat again.

Mom waved her hand at me. "Why don't you answer that, Brooke?"

"Why?"

Mom shrugged.

Okay. I crossed the room and into the front foyer. Peering through the peephole, I saw . . . *Micah?* I yanked open the door.

"Hey." He pulled off his shades.

I dived into him with a force that made him stagger, but it only took a millisecond before his arms had closed about me.

"I'm glad to see you, too," he said.

"Why are you here? When did you get back from New York?"

"Your parents invited me. I got back from New York this morning."

"And you drove straight down?"

"I did take a long enough break to eat lunch with my parents." He cupped my head with a gentle hand, his expression softening. "Are you crying?"

I nodded. Clearly, that was the right explanation for my wet eyes.

"Why?"

"It was already the best day of my life, and now it's even better." Words were no longer enough. I slid my arms around his neck and urged him down for a kiss. Or kisses. They multiplied. And lengthened.

He drew back and smiled in his lazy, sexy way. "I guess you don't mind your surprise."

"I love my surprise." I smiled, feeling happy in every part of me. "It's perfect that you're here."